It seemed almost as if Ryder were… courting her again.

Except for two things.

First, the constant presence of two pint-size chaperones.

Second, the fact the Ryder hadn't so much as made a move to hold Sara's hand. Not since that night when he'd kissed her. When, against her better judgment, Sara had kissed him back.

Not that she was complaining, of course. She'd made it perfectly clear that night that she had no intention of getting involved with Ryder again, and she'd meant it. She could hardly object if he abided by the rules she herself had laid down.

But it bothered her that she couldn't quite figure out what Ryder's angle was—what he hoped to accomplish by spending so much time with her and the twins.

Almost as if they were some kind of…family.

Dear Reader,

What better cure for a hectic holiday season than settling in with romantic stories from Special Edition? And this month, we've got just what you've been searching for.

THE JONES GANG is back, with bestselling author Christine Rimmer's latest title, *Honeymoon Hotline*. Nevada Jones is November's THAT SPECIAL WOMAN!, and this adviser to the lovelorn is about to discover love firsthand!

Andrea Edwards's latest miniseries, GREAT EXPECTATIONS, continues this month with *One Big Happy Family*. If Big Sky Country is your kind of place, you won't want to miss *Montana Lovers*, the next book in Jackie Merritt's newest series, MADE IN MONTANA.

And the passion doesn't end there—for her first title in Special Edition, Helen R. Myers has a tantalizing tale of reunited lovers in *After That Night*…. Rounding out the month are a spellbinding amnesia story from Ann Howard White, *Making Memories*, and a second chance for two lovers in Kayla Daniels's heartwarming *Marriage Minded*.

I hope you enjoy all that we have in store for you this November. Happy Thanksgiving Day—all of us at Silhouette would like to wish you a happy holiday season!

Sincerely,

Tara Gavin
Senior Editor

Please address questions and book requests to:
Silhouette Reader Service
U.S.: 3010 Walden Ave., P.O. Box 1325, Buffalo, NY 14269
Canadian: P.O. Box 609, Fort Erie, Ont. L2A 5X3

KAYLA DANIELS

MARRIAGE MINDED

Published by Silhouette Books
America's Publisher of Contemporary Romance

To my grandma, Mildred Blom,
who served me my first cup of coffee,
made a Minnesota Twins fan out of me
and taught me how to bake the best banana cake
in the whole world.

ISBN 0-373-24068-6

MARRIAGE MINDED

This edition published by arrangement with Harlequin Books S.A.

Printed in U.S.A.

Books by Kayla Daniels

Silhouette Special Edition

Spitting Image #474
Father Knows Best #578
Hot Prospect #654
Rebel to the Rescue #707
From Father to Son #790
Heiress Apparent #814
Miracle Child #911
Marriage Minded #1068

KAYLA DANIELS

is a former computer programmer who enjoys travel, ballroom dancing and playing with her nieces and nephews. She grew up in southern California and has lived in Alaska, Norway, Minnesota, Alabama and Louisiana. Currently she makes her home in Grass Valley, California.

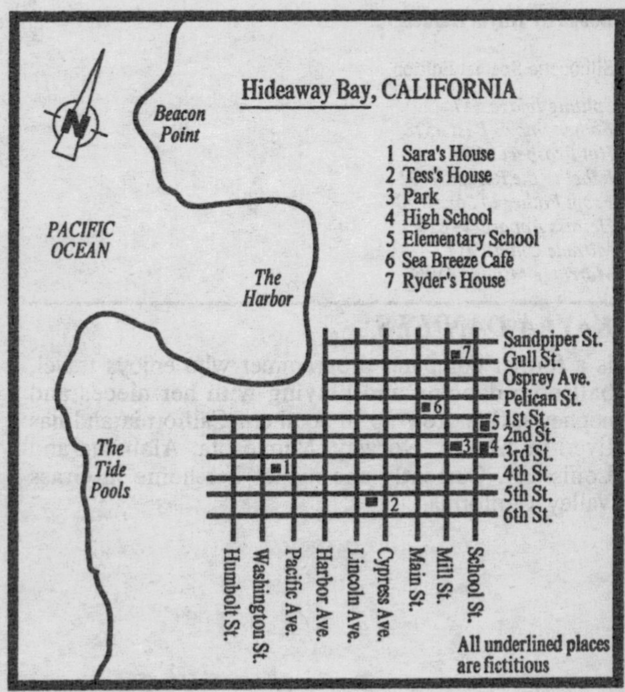
Hideaway Bay, CALIFORNIA
N
Beacon Point
PACIFIC OCEAN
The Harbor
The Tide Pools
1 Sara's House
2 Tess's House
3 Park
4 High School
5 Elementary School
6 Sea Breeze Café
7 Ryder's House
Sandpiper St.
Gull St.
Osprey Ave.
Pelican St.
1st St.
2nd St.
3rd St.
4th St.
5th St.
6th St.
Humbolt St.
Washington St.
Pacific Ave.
Harbor Ave.
Lincoln Ave.
Cypress Ave.
Main St.
Mill St.
School St.
All underlined places are fictitious

Chapter One

Ryder Sloan felt like a third-rate spy in a B movie as he lurked across the street from the old Monahan house.

Chilly tendrils of September fog swirled around him, slithering through the folds of his trench coat to pluck at him with icy fingers. From out of the mist drifted the eerie, warning groan of a foghorn at the entrance to the fishing-boat harbor a mile away.

He had to admit the scene had all the right ingredients for a spine-tingling thriller—the weather, the sound effects, even the trench coat. Perfect atmosphere. Oh, yeah. The only wrong note in it was Ryder himself.

As he strode up and down the sidewalk, trying to summon the nerve to cross the street, he caught the occasional flick of a lace curtain in the windows of the houses he passed. The uncomfortable sensation of being watched made the hair on the back of his neck prickle.

And the gut-wrenching roller-coaster ride taking place in the pit of his stomach only enhanced his misery.

"Old buddy, you'd make a terrible spy," he muttered.

During the past decade he'd dodged bombs and bullets, witnessed famine and disease, journeyed across typhoon-whipped seas and over rugged mountain passes where even one misstep on the narrow dirt track could send him plunging down the steep rocky slopes to certain death.

Yet right now, the prospect of coming face-to-face with Sara Monahan for the first time in ten years terrified him in a way none of those physical dangers had.

And the short trip across the street and up the front steps to knock on her door seemed far more daunting than the long, hazardous trek over the Khyber Pass.

Ryder withdrew his hands from his coat pockets, blew a stream of warm air between them and briskly rubbed his palms together. "Quit being such a coward," he chided himself impatiently. "You haven't come all this way just to pace back and forth and gawk at the outside of her house."

Then why have *you come?* asked that maddening little demon inside his skull.

"Shut up," Ryder growled into his closed fists. He hadn't quite figured out the answer to that one yet.

From down by the harbor soared the cry of a gull, distant, plaintive and haunting. Just like the memories that had beckoned ever more insistently from halfway around the globe, calling Ryder back to the northern California coastal town where he'd grown up.

He'd fought the lure of those memories, told himself there was nothing to be gained by raking up unfinished business that was better left buried.

But, in the end, he'd been drawn back to his hometown by a force that was as irresistible, as inevitable as the tug of a magnet toward the North Pole.

Until last night, Ryder Sloan hadn't set foot in Hideaway Bay for over ten years. Not since he was twenty-one. Not since the night he'd fled from his past, from his fears and guilts and failures . . . and from the only woman he'd ever loved.

A faint click from across the street froze Ryder in his tracks. The sound of a dead bolt being unlocked. To Ryder's panicked ears, it echoed as loud as a gunshot.

He shivered, but not from the cold.

The front door of the turreted Victorian house swung open.

Ryder's heart began to pound like a sledgehammer.

Sara.

"Come on, you two slowpokes. Get a move on! They can't start second grade without you."

Resting one slim-fingered hand on the polished walnut banister, Sara Monahan peered up the curving, narrow staircase of the hundred-year-old home she'd grown up in. Upstairs she could hear the twins squabbling over whose pencil box was whose. The ruckus was music to her ears.

They'd been so subdued, so withdrawn in the aftermath of last spring's terrible accident. For the first several months, Sara's own grief had been pushed onto the back burner by her overwhelming concern for the twins' emotional recovery. Now, she rejoiced in the sounds of the quarrel raging overhead.

"Give it back, Nicholas. It's mine!"

"Isn't either. Yours is the one with the dumb giraffe on it."

"Nuh-*uh! You* picked that one. Mine has the whale on it. Now give it back!"

"Attaway, Noelle," Sara cheered under her breath. In reaction to her parents' deaths, Noelle had turned inward, withdrawing into herself so that the previously sunny, outgoing seven-year-old had become almost painfully shy.

Equally heartbreaking to witness had been her complete apathy regarding the world that continued to go on around her. For months after the accident, Noelle had been either unable or unwilling to express a preference about even the simplest matter—what she wanted Sara to fix for dinner, or whether she'd rather go to the beach or see a movie.

It was an enormous relief to Sara, therefore, to see some signs of spunk returning, along with this blessedly normal display of sibling rivalry.

An ominous *thunk!* from upstairs made her wince. Then, complete silence. Even more ominous.

"Noelle... Nicholas..." she called in a warning tone. She didn't know whether to be relieved or suspicious when the two golden-haired twins flew down the staircase in a flurry of bouncing backpacks, both racing to get to the bottom first.

"I won!" Nicholas crowed, dropping his backpack with a thud. "Didn't I, Aunt Sara?"

Noelle's lower lip pushed out, quivering. Her backpack drooped off her shoulder and slid slowly to the floor.

"I'd call it a tie," Sara replied diplomatically. "And you're not supposed to run up and down the stairs, remember?"

Nicholas cocked his head to one side and regarded her with puzzled blue eyes. "But you *told* us to hurry up, 'member?"

Sara rustled his silky blond hair with exasperation. "What have I got here, a budding lawyer on my hands? You can hurry and still be careful. Now, go get your lunches out of the kitchen, or we'll be late. Scoot!" She swatted him fondly on the bottom to send him on his way.

Then she knelt next to Noelle and tugged up her niece's sagging knee socks. "All set for the first day of school, sweetheart?"

Of the two children, Noelle was the one Sara was most apprehensive about today. Her niece had only recently begun to emerge from her shell, and Sara worried that an unfamiliar mob of new schoolmates and teachers would send her scurrying back into it.

Noelle scuffed a toe of her shiny black Mary Janes on the hardwood floor. "Guess so."

Sara's heart went out to the poor child. She tucked a dangling curtain of butterscotch hair behind Noelle's ear. "It's okay to be scared, honey. Everyone's a little bit scared the first day of school."

Noelle peeked at her. "Even you?"

"Me?" Sara clapped a hand over her heart. "Why, I was so scared my first day of second grade, Grandma had to pry my fingers off the banister." She gripped the railing and pantomimed a terrible struggle. "I was hanging on for dear life, let me tell you! Poor Grandma thought she was going to have to saw right through the banister and carry me to school that way!"

Noelle giggled.

Sara took her niece's hand. "But you know what? Once I got to school, I had the best time in my whole life! I made three new friends, and the teacher let me be line leader after recess."

Noelle stared at the floor. "All *my* friends live in Chicago," she said in a small voice.

"Oh, honey..." Sorrow and sympathy gripped Sara's heart in an agonizing stranglehold. Poor Noelle and Nicholas had lost not only their parents, but their playmates, their school, and the only home they'd ever known. They'd been uprooted and dragged two thousand miles across the country to live with an aunt they'd previously only seen once a year at Christmas.

The twins had lost so much—everything, really, that was important in their young lives. Sara knew she could never replace their parents, could never hope to make up for the terrible losses they'd suffered.

But by God, no matter what sacrifices she had to make, no matter how tough her instant parenthood turned out to be at times, she intended to make sure that the twins grew up feeling loved and secure and happy.

"Noelle, what about Alex and Jenny? You and Nicholas played a lot with them this summer...." Sara's best friend Tess Carpenter and her two children had been a godsend. Sara didn't know what she would have done without Tess's support and down-to-earth advice on everything from childhood earaches to which cartoon heroes were the current rage among the peanut-butter-and-jelly set.

"Alex and Jenny will be at school today, and they're your friends, aren't they?" Sara smoothed Noelle's hair back from her pale, unhappy face.

Noelle shrugged. "I guess so."

"Sure they are! So, you already have two friends at your new school, and I bet by the end of the day, you'll have lots more."

Nicholas must have overheard the tail end of their conversation as he bounced back into the entry hall from the kitchen. "I'll be your friend, Noelle," he said solemnly, handing her a brown paper sack. "Here. I brought your lunch."

Sara could have kissed him. However, one thing she'd discovered about seven-year-old boys during the last few months was their inclination to screw up their faces, wipe off kisses and say "Yuck!" whenever their doting aunts indulged in such mushy stuff.

Sara settled for a grateful squeeze of his shoulder instead. "Okay, time to go. Got your lunches? Backpacks?"

She must be getting the hang of this parenting thing, Sara decided as she helped the twins into their jackets. Even bona fide parents couldn't possibly suffer from the first-day-of-school jitters as badly as she was.

Every time she thought of the devastating trauma Noelle and Nicholas had already endured, she could hardly bear the idea of sending her precious niece and nephew off to cope with yet another frightening ordeal all by themselves.

They'd been so brave, through all the nightmares and all the tears. It had been so tough on them, adjusting to a whole new life, learning to accept the kind of tragedy that even adults would have a difficult time coping with.

And now, their hard-hearted aunt was forcing them into yet another unfamiliar situation, one where she wouldn't even be there to protect them. For about the dozenth time that morning, Sara had to resist the urge to bundle them into her arms, smother them with kisses and promise they didn't ever have to go to school or anyplace else out there in the big, bad world if they didn't want to.

But deep down inside, she knew she had no choice but to drive them over to the grade school, hand them over to a strange teacher they'd only met once before, and then watch their sad, scared, brave little faces as she waved goodbye.

It was for the twins' own good. Sara had to let them go through this first day of school on their own. Even if it killed her.

She grabbed her purse from the antique hall tree beside the front door. "All set?" she asked with forced cheerfulness as she unlocked the dead bolt. "Last one in the car's a rotten egg."

The twins scrambled out the front door, across the porch and down the steps, backpacks bouncing against their shoulders as they raced around the side of the house to the old carriage barn which now served as a garage.

This time, Sara's smile was genuine as she turned to lock the door behind her. As she hurried down the front steps, she caught sight of a shadow across the street in front of the Ingersolls' house. With a jolt, she realized the dark blur was a man, his tall, trench-coated figure nearly obscured by the thick fog.

Sara's smile flickered uncertainly, faded, then died.

No. It wasn't possible.

It just couldn't be him.

When the two children spilled out the front door, Ryder exhaled a muffled gasp, as if someone had just landed a sucker punch to his gut.

For a few seconds he just stood there, blinking, his mind reeling as it tried to process this unexpected information.

Sara had kids. Two of them.

When Ryder had looked up her number in the phone book last night, not really expecting it to be there, he'd been surprised to find her listed under her maiden name. Ever since then, he'd just assumed . . . well, that was stupid. A husband certainly wasn't a prerequisite for children. Anyway, maybe she was divorced and had gone back to using her maiden name.

Now, a startling possibility exploded inside Ryder's dazed brain. Inside his pockets, his nails dug into his palms with a convulsive clench of his fists. Could one of those children be . . . ?

No. A quick calculation dashed that idea. Ryder had had only a brief glimpse of the kids as they tore around the side of the house, but both looked to be about six or seven, certainly no older than eight.

Not quite old enough to have been the product of that one fateful, bittersweet night.

Surprisingly, a thorn of disappointment pricked Ryder's chest.

But then a more primitive, possessive emotion poured through him, blotting out everything but his fierce jealousy that Sara had borne another man's children.

Ryder knew his jealousy was completely unreasonable. After the unforgivable way he'd hurt Sara, he'd certainly had no right to expect her to carry a torch for him all these years, to remain faithful to the man who'd abandoned her.

Still, the vision of her creamy, smooth belly growing ripe and round with another man's babies was pure torture.

For a few agonizing moments, Ryder was so consumed by disturbing thoughts, he didn't even notice that Sara herself was standing right across the street, staring at him through the mist.

She must be hallucinating.

She'd thought about him so many times over the years, no matter how hard she'd tried not to, and now her poor conflicted brain was conjuring up his image right in front of her disbelieving eyes.

Sara's heart was thumping so wildly, her blood was racing so fast, she couldn't hear anything but the pounding in her ears.

Dear God in heaven, that *couldn't* be Ryder!

Despite the fog, despite the concealing beard he wore, despite the ten long years that had passed since the last time she'd laid eyes on him, something about the way the man was standing reminded her so strongly of Ryder. Something about his half wary, half defiant stance, or the tense hunch of his shoulders, or the way he was staring directly across the street at her...

How many times as a teenager had she discovered him loitering out on the sidewalk like this, pretending he was just passing by, hoping to avoid the poorly concealed looks of disapproval he figured he'd get from her parents if he just knocked on the front door and asked for her?

The man started across the street toward her. Whether it was the deceptive effect of the fog or Sara's own distorted perceptions, he seemed to be moving in slow motion, as if the thick, damp air were viscous enough to hinder his progress.

Or as if he were dragging his feet because he was reluctant to complete the short journey across the street.

Sara swallowed, her mouth so dry she nearly choked.

His jet black hair was shorter than he'd worn it as a rebellious youth. And, of course, the beard was new. Behind it, Sara could still discern the lean, hard contours of his face, arranged in that lazy, half-lidded, seemingly indifferent expression he used to hide his feelings from the world.

Then he got close enough for her to see his eyes—those blazing, laser blue eyes that could sear right through a person, right into the depths of her soul.

All at once Sara was cold, so cold, colder than she'd ever been in her life.

"Ryder." In a half gasp, half whisper, his name emerged from her lips on a white puff of air that dissipated and vanished in the space of a heartbeat.

He stopped about five feet away. "Hello, Sara."

And with those two words, the achingly familiar timbre of his voice catapulted her back in time, to her last few months of high school, when she'd been so blissfully, so confidently, so head-over-heels in love with Ryder Sloan.

Memories rushed back in an unstoppable flood—the warm, delicious tingle of his hand touching hers . . . the heart-stopping excitement of their first kiss . . . the sweet, awkward stutter in his voice when he'd told her he loved her.

The passion, the tenderness, the glory of the night they'd finally made love.

The night before Ryder had disappeared from her life forever.

Except that forever, it seemed, had come to an end.

"What—" Sara had to pause to collect enough moisture in her mouth to speak. "What are you doing here?"

Brilliant, you ninny, scorned a little voice in her head. *Of all the scathing, disdainful greetings you've rehearsed over the years on the off chance of ever coming face-to-face with Ryder again,* that's *the best you can come up with?*

Ryder himself was having trouble summoning the proper words to mark this momentous occasion. How was he supposed to answer her? That he'd been in Tanzania, filming a documentary on the Serengeti Plain, when he'd had a sudden urge to visit his hometown?

Maybe he should explain how he'd been having a drink in a local watering hole one night, when in had walked a tourist who'd stunned him with her resemblance to Sara—the same flowing, strawberry blond hair...gorgeous, jade green eyes... long, fabulous legs.

Should he confess that suddenly, the need to see Sara again, to discover if she was still as sweet, as loving, as beautiful as Ryder remembered, had simply overpowered him?

She was still beautiful, all right. But she wasn't exactly regarding him lovingly.

"I came back to make some arrangements about my father's house," Ryder said, lying through his teeth. "It's been empty for ten years now and I thought it was time to do something about it." He rasped his hand over the beard he'd grown while on location and hadn't gotten around to shaving off yet. "And I—I wanted to see you."

"Yes, well, now you've seen me. You can go back to wherever it is you've been hanging out for the past decade." Now that Sara's shell-shocked brain had sputtered into life again, she'd managed to collect a few of her scattered wits. And realized she didn't *want* those memories flooding back. She didn't *want* to know the reason Ryder had left her without so much as a farewell note.

And she *certainly* didn't want to risk stirring up any old emotional embers that might still be smoldering, despite her best efforts to extinguish them.

Ryder's brow furrowed with surprise and uncertainty. "I know I've got some explaining to do..."

"Save your explanations." Sara hiked her purse strap onto her shoulder. "I'll wait and read about them in your memoirs."

"Sara—"

"I don't have time for any nostalgic trips down memory lane, Ryder," she informed him with a toss of her head. "I've got two kids waiting in the car who are late for school." Perhaps she only imagined it, but for a second, a grimace of some turbulent emotion seemed to cloud Ryder's rugged features.

Sara ignored it. "So, if you'll excuse me..."

"Sara." When he grasped her arm, a tremor jolted her entire body. Maybe it was the shock of his abrupt, urgent movement. Maybe it was outrage that he would attempt to physically detain her. Or maybe it was something that Sara didn't care to identify.

"Quit manhandling me," she said, yanking herself out of his clutches. "I'm not some starry-eyed, moonstruck adolescent anymore that you can control with your macho posturing."

To her amazement, after a brief flash of almost comical surprise hoisted his brows, Ryder burst out laughing. The sound seemed to vibrate along Sara's nerve endings and resonate deep inside her. She didn't care for the sensation one bit.

"It wasn't like that between us at all," Ryder said when he finished chuckling, "and you know it."

"I know that whatever it was we once had between us, you and I certainly had different ideas about what it meant."

The shock of discovering that Ryder had left town echoed through Sara's memory, bringing back all the confusion, all the disillusionment and heartache of that terrible time in her life.

Why? Why? Why? she'd been so desperate to know. Here at last was her chance to find out. Only now, she didn't want to listen.

"I've got to go," she said, whirling abruptly and heading toward the garage.

She hadn't gone two steps before Ryder grabbed her arm again. "Sara, wait."

Her lips sewed a tight seam of impatience. "I told you, I'm in a hurry."

Ryder glanced toward the garage, toward the two eager faces who were observing their encounter with lively interest through the back window of the car. Guilt stirred inside him. Sara had built a new life for herself while he was gone. She had kids now, probably a career, a lover or even a husband for all Ryder knew.

He had no right to barge back into her life this way, bringing chaos to the settled, peaceful rhythm of her days.

But he simply couldn't stop himself.

He squeezed her arm. "We have some unfinished business between us, you and I," he said in a low voice.

Sara jerked up her chin in that haughty gesture she'd always resorted to when she was feeling unsure of herself. "Any business between us was finished long ago."

But Ryder caught a fleeting glimpse of something in her eyes that told him she was lying. Maybe it was too late to recapture the magic, the passion of what they'd once shared. But they were a long way from being finished with each other.

Sara was breathing hard, almost as hard as Ryder was. They were standing so close, he could feel the warmth pulsing from her body as her chest rose and fell. He inhaled that same mysterious, feminine fragrance that had always clung to her skin, reminding him of a field of spring wildflowers.

So much about her was exactly the way he'd remembered, and so much was different. He drank in the changes like a man dying of thirst in the desert.

The clear, emerald eyes that had always telegraphed her emotions as visibly as the lighthouse on Beacon Point were shuttered now with suspicion. She still had the same high, aristocratic slant to her cheekbones, the same regal tilt of her head that had always made Ryder think of a princess.

The long, silky curtain of strawberry blond hair that had haunted his dreams was trimmed to her shoulders now, but Ryder still had that same reckless urge to run his fingers through it, as a pirate might sift through a treasure chest of gold and rubies.

She was even more beautiful than she'd been at eighteen. Even more desirable.

And, judging by the chilly reception he'd received, even more out of reach than she'd been when Ryder was the town bad boy from the wrong side of the tracks, and Sara was the cherished only daughter of Hideaway Bay's most prominent family.

At that moment, they both realized that Ryder was stroking her arm, and had been for some time.

Annoyance flared inside Sara. Annoyance at Ryder. At herself.

She glanced pointedly at his hand, and arched one disdainful eyebrow—a neat trick she'd mastered as a teenager after months of practice in front of a mirror.

Ryder let go of her arm. He rubbed his shaggy jaw. "Sara, is there some time, some place where we could talk?"

"We've got nothing to talk about. Now, if you'll excuse me..." She pivoted on her heel and marched briskly toward the car, hoping Ryder couldn't tell how wobbly her knees were.

She could feel him watching her, every step of the way.

But by the time Sara had backed the car out of the garage, Ryder had vanished.

She was halfway to the elementary school before she stopped trembling.

Chapter Two

Sara tugged the quilt up to Noelle's chin, then brushed a good-night kiss against the sleeping child's soft cheek. Noelle smacked her lips, made a small purring noise, then burrowed even deeper under the covers.

In the dim glow of the Snoopy night-light, Sara gazed fondly down at her adorable niece. As she did every night at this time, she sent up a silent prayer of thanks that Noelle and Nicholas had been spared from the tragic fire that had claimed their parents' lives.

Crossing to the other twin bed, Sara knelt beside Nicholas. His drooping eyelids were half shut, his blond head nodding like a sunflower in the breeze. Sara settled him back against the pillows and smoothed his silky hair away from his forehead.

"Did you have fun at school today?" she asked, whispering so as not to waken Noelle. She already knew the answer to her question. Nicholas had been chattering nonstop with excitement ever since she'd picked up the twins after school.

He nodded drowsily. "I got to play tetherball at recess, an' I got a gold star on my spelling test."

Sara smiled. She'd already heard Nicholas's long list of exploits several times over, each time with a renewed sense of relief. So she wasn't an evil monster after all for sending the twins off to school!

Noelle, as usual, had been more subdued in her response to the first day of second grade. But third-grader Jenny Carpenter had come over and played with Noelle at recess, and by lunchtime Noelle had found yet another new friend to trade sandwiches with.

Sara crossed her fingers. At last, it seemed, the twins were taking the first tentative steps toward regaining some semblance of a normal childhood. In the months since the accident, Sara's primary concern had been making the twins feel safe and loved, assuring them that the three of them were a family now, promising that she would never abandon them.

At times, they'd clung to her emotionally, psychologically, even physically, with a desperation that was heartbreaking.

Hopefully, the familiar day-to-day routine and orderly structure provided by school would strengthen the comforting sense of security and stability that was so critical for them to redevelop, after the very foundations of their universe had been shattered by unspeakable tragedy.

Sara's heart contracted with a painful throb as she gazed down at Nicholas. He looked so much like Brad! With their strong resemblance to their parents, Noelle and Nicholas were living, breathing reminders of Sara's brother and his wife.

At times, Sara was so focused on the twins' emotional needs, it didn't dawn on her that she, too, had suffered a terrible loss.

And at times, like now, the pain caught up with her, the grief so intense she could barely breathe.

On impulse, she caught Nicholas up into her arms. She sat on the edge of the bed, rocking him back and forth, hugging him fiercely, as if somehow that could bring Brad and Diana back.

Nicholas didn't struggle—probably because he was half asleep, Sara thought with a crooked smile. A tear plopped down onto the top of his head.

She laid him gently back against the pillows, tucked him in and watched for a minute while his eyes drifted shut so that his lashes dusted his freckled cheeks.

"Now's my chance," she whispered. She bent down and kissed his forehead, knowing that Nicholas awake would have squirmed at such a tender gesture.

Sara hovered in the doorway for a moment, studying their sleeping forms by the light that spilled in from the hallway. Then she walked slowly downstairs, leaving the hall light on and the door to their bedroom ajar as usual, so they wouldn't wake up scared and disoriented in the middle of the night.

In the kitchen, she picked up a mug of coffee she'd been drinking that afternoon, and absently took a sip of it. She grimaced. Cold and bitter. Just the way she'd felt this morning, when Ryder Sloan had turned up on her doorstep.

With a sigh, Sara set the mug into the microwave oven and pushed the proper buttons to heat up the coffee. All day long, she'd been trying to force thoughts of Ryder out of her mind. She'd had plenty of other things to worry about—how the children were coping at school, the sorry state of her new client's haphazard bookkeeping records, her struggle to install another client's computerized accounting system by the deadline she'd promised.

Now, it was evening. Things had quieted down. The kids were in bed, Sara's work was finished for the day. There was nothing to distract her attention except the hum of the microwave and the series of electronic peeps that informed her the coffee was heated.

She removed the mug, selected a book from the shelves in the library, and settled herself onto the comfortable, overstuffed sofa in the living room. Kicking off her shoes, she curled her feet beneath her and arranged one of her mother's knitted afghans over her legs. After adjusting the stained-glass Tiffany lamp on the end table, she took a sip of coffee and tried to read.

Thirty seconds later, she flung the book across the room.

"Oh, hell," she muttered.

It was no good. Ryder's devilishly handsome, infuriating face had danced across the pages in front of her eyes. In the otherwise silent living room, the monotonous *tick...tock* of the grandfather clock seemed to echo Sara's own maddening questions—why?...why?...why?...why?

Why did you leave me, Ryder?

Why did you tell me you loved me?

Why didn't you drop me so much as a postcard in ten long years to let me know what had happened to you?

And, the most important question of all right now...

Why have you come back?

Sara jumped to her feet and moved restlessly around the room. The nineteenth-century ceilings were quite high by today's standards, but suddenly she felt boxed in, suffocated.

We have some unfinished business between us, you and I. Ryder's words this morning barged into her mind like pushy, unwanted houseguests.

Of all the unbelievable nerve! To pop up out of the blue like that, expecting Sara to welcome him with open arms. And exactly what *business* did he hope to finish, anyway?

She'd been a child back then. Eighteen. Naive in her trust, in her feelings, in her vision of the future.

Well, she wasn't eighteen anymore. And if Ryder thought he could waltz back into her life and win her over again with his brooding good looks, his snake-oil sincerity, his—

A soft rap at the front door startled Sara like a sudden barrage of pounding fists. She whirled around with a gasp, her hand flying to her throat.

Ryder. It had to be him, of course. Now, she realized she'd been half expecting him all evening.

For a few panicked moments, she considered not answering the door, ducking into a back room where he couldn't see her silhouette through the front lace curtains, waiting for him to give up and go away.

No. She wasn't going to cower inside her own home like a frightened rabbit cornered by a fox. She wasn't going to let Ryder reduce her to such pathetic, undignified behavior.

Sara pushed back her hair, hoisted her chin, and grasped the doorknob. Her heart hammered as if trying to escape from her rib cage. After a moment's hesitation, she swung open the door.

The golden aura of the porch light illuminated the face she'd expected to see, but with a disorienting difference. Ryder had shaved since this morning, so that the man on Sara's doorstep appeared younger, bore a much stronger resemblance to the youth she remembered. The same angular jaw...the same lean, hungry cast to his chiseled features...the same oddly sensual slant of his frown...

"You." Sara cleared her throat. "I should have expected as much."

Tension simmered in his eyes. He didn't smile. "At least you didn't slam the door in my face." He held out a bottle of wine like a peace offering. "May I come in?"

Sara gnawed her lower lip. She'd made her feelings crystal clear this morning, but it looked as if Ryder were ready for round two. Indeed, his eyes reflected the grim determination of a man who was prepared to pound on her door and holler her name all night long, if necessary.

Terrific. Wouldn't *that* give the neighbors something to gossip about over their morning coffee! By noon, all four thousand souls in Hideaway Bay would be speculating about Sara's private life.

"Come in," she said, grudgingly opening the door a hair wider. "But keep it short." As Ryder moved past her, Sara caught a faint whiff of after-shave that reminded her of the ocean and made her slightly dizzy. Probably because she was allergic to it.

She didn't offer to take his coat as they passed the hall tree. Ryder wouldn't be staying long. She did notice that it was an expensive British raincoat, however. Whatever he'd been doing for the past decade, he'd obviously prospered.

Too bad. How much more satisfying it would have been if Ryder Sloan had turned out to be a penniless good-for-nothing!

Ryder halted in the middle of the living room and made a 360 degree scan of his surroundings. "This place looks exactly as I remember it."

Cozy furnishings. Antique family heirlooms that were actually used instead of displayed like museum pieces.

Framed seascapes and scenes of Hideaway Bay painted by a century of local artists.

To Ryder, the Monahan house had always embodied the love and warmth, the stability and security of a loving family life. Tradition. Dignity. Respect. All the qualities his own home life had lacked.

Growing up as the son of the town drunk and a mother who'd abandoned him, Ryder had seen the Monahan house as a symbol of everything that was unattainable to him. Like Sara.

"Your mom and dad," he said, glancing at the framed black-and-white wedding photo perched on one of the end tables. "Are they still...living here with you?" Ryder had spent the day trying to scout out up-to-date information on Sara's life, but hadn't been too successful. Recalling him as a troublemaker, even the local gossips had been rather closemouthed toward him.

Sara picked up a book that had fallen to the floor. "They moved to Florida about three years ago, when the board of directors voted to sell the bank to a statewide chain." She set the book on the fireplace mantel. "Dad wasn't in favor of selling, so he decided to retire, rather than accept a position with the new organization."

Ryder let out a low whistle. "I can't imagine the bank without a Monahan at the head of it. Your great-grandfather founded it, didn't he?"

"Great-*great*-grandfather. Over a hundred years ago."

Ryder peered at her curiously. "I always figured you'd take over yourself someday."

Sara shrugged, punched up an embroidered sofa pillow. "I did work there for a while, after college. But I wasn't much interested in staying on with the new bank, either."

"So what do you do now?" Ryder's gaze dropped for a quick check of her ring finger. Bare. No telltale white mark.

Sara intercepted the glance. Her lips pressed into an irritated line. "I work as a freelance accountant, doing the books for a number of local businesses."

"Wow, that's great! I always knew you'd be successful someday." All at once, Ryder's inquisition ran into quicksand. It was easy asking questions about Sara's family, about her job. But he couldn't figure out a tactful way to ask the questions that intrigued him most.

Who fathered your children? Is he still around? Is there another man in your life?

Ryder could just picture Sara's reaction if he actually voiced any of that. She would throw him out on his ear in two seconds flat.

"I brought some wine," he said lamely, holding up the bottle of chardonnay he'd forgotten about. "Would you like to have some?" Geez, he felt as awkward as a teenager on his first date! Sweaty palms and everything.

Sara's eyes narrowed as if she were about to decline. Then, to Ryder's relief, something changed her mind. "All right."

Not exactly enthusiastic, but at least she hadn't told him to state his business and get out.

Ryder watched her walk into the dining room, fascinated by every little move she made. When she flipped on the switch for the chandelier, light scattered through her hair as if someone had tossed a fistful of gold coins. She knelt in front of the oak sideboard with the grace and fluidity of a dancer. When she frowned at the wineglasses, holding them up to the light to check for dust, tiny pleats gathered between her eyebrows.

Ryder catalogued every detail, committing it to memory, like a miser counting his hoard. For so long, he'd had the exact same collection of memories to flip through over and over. He wasn't about to waste this chance to store up a whole bunch of new ones.

God, he couldn't believe he was actually seeing Sara again, hearing the melodic lilt of her voice, able to reach out and touch her if he wanted to!

On second thought, touching her might not be such a smart move right now. Not if he didn't want to get his face slapped.

Sara handed him the glasses, careful to avoid any contact between his fingers and hers. Ryder arched his eyebrows. "Wine opener?"

"In the kitchen."

He followed her there, trying not to ogle the seductive sway of her backside, the curving perfection of her hips, the long, shapely line of her legs. The coltish teenager Ryder remembered had definitely filled out in all the right places.

The sudden rush of heat to his loins startled him. After all, he hadn't come here to seduce her. He'd come here to...to talk. To make a start at setting things right between them, so that the guilty conscience that had plagued him for ten years would give him some peace.

So why this sudden urge to push his hands up beneath her mint green sweater, to plunder her mouth with his, to rekindle the passion, the madness of that one incredible night they'd spent together?

Ryder pressed the chilled bottle of wine to the side of his face. Down, boy.

"Mind if I take off my coat?" he asked.

Sara looked as if she minded very much, but that impeccable Monahan breeding won out. "I'll hang it up for you." Once again, she was able to take his coat without so much as the tip of her little finger touching him.

Ryder located a corkscrew in one of the cabinets and poured the wine while she was gone, taking the opportunity to study the kitchen. The old white-and-chrome gas stove, the copper pots dangling from their wrought iron rack, the homey smell of coffee were all still there, familiar and reassuring. What was new was the children's artwork splashed across the front of the refrigerator, held in place with cheery little magnets shaped like vegetables.

He bent down to examine the printed signatures. Noelle. Nicholas. A wistful smile touched Ryder's lips. Twins, he guessed. Not too hard to figure out when *their* birthday was.

He heard the approaching tap of Sara's footsteps, but had time for one quick inventory of the dinner dishes still stacked in the sink. Three sets. If Sara had a man in her life, he didn't join them for dinner every night, it seemed.

Ryder was back beside the kitchen table, holding both glasses of wine when Sara returned. "Here you go," he said.

This time, when he handed her a glass, he deliberately brushed his fingers against hers.

Sara jerked her hand back as if she'd been scalded, nearly spilling the wine. She glared at Ryder over the top of the glass as she took a small sip. "Look, let's stop playing games, shall we?" Her eyes glinted like angry chips of emerald.

Ryder lowered his glass. "I haven't come here to play games, Sara."

"No?" Her head angled upward in a challenge. "Then why *have* you come back?"

What could he tell her, when he didn't know the answer to that himself? To satisfy his curiosity? To tie up some emotional loose ends? To beg Sara's forgiveness?

"I had a break in my work schedule. I make documentary films for a living, and right now I'm between projects, so I decided it was a good time to come back and finally take care of selling my father's house. As long as I was in town, I figured . . . well, I know I owe you an apology, Sara. Even though there's no excuse for the shabby way I treated you." There! He'd managed to dress up the lie with enough truthful accessories to almost convince himself.

Sara regarded him thoughtfully as she took another sip. "Nice speech," she said finally. "I guess it ought to be, considering you've had ten years to work on it."

Ryder swallowed some more wine. The chardonnay hit the back of his throat, cold and tart. "I don't blame you for being angry," he said.

"Angry?" Sara set down the glass so hard, it was a miracle the stem didn't snap. "I'm not angry, Ryder. Why should I be? So I got my heart broken by a bad case of puppy love. Happens to everyone, right? Besides, it was a long time ago."

The steel edge to her voice, the crimson flush staining her cheeks, the lines of tension bracketing her mouth proclaimed her true emotions. And at that moment, Ryder comprehended that he'd hurt Sara even worse than he'd ever dreamed.

He set down his glass and stepped toward her. She took a matching step backward. "It was more than puppy love, and you know it," he said in a low voice.

"*You* were the one who took it so lightly," she retorted, shoving a loose tendril of hair from her face in an impatient gesture. "*You* were the one who led me on, who made me believe you really cared for—"

"I *did* care for you," Ryder almost shouted. Immediately he lowered his voice, assuming the children were asleep upstairs. He backhanded a sheen of sweat from his forehead. "I never led you on, Sara. I never said anything to you I didn't mean."

Sara expelled an exasperated puff of air from her lips. "No, you just snuck off like a thief in the night after you finally got what you wanted from me."

Ryder moved toward her. She moved backward again. "You think that's all I wanted?" he asked, astonished and wounded to the core. "Another notch on my bedpost?"

Sara inched up her chin. "What was I supposed to think, when you disappeared without so much as a goodbye, right after the first time we made love?"

Ryder dug his nails into his palms as he stepped toward her. And once again, she stepped back, so that the two of them appeared to be dancing a crazy tango around her kitchen. "I didn't want to hurt you," he said through gritted teeth.

"Oh, really?" Sara let out a sarcastic laugh. "It never occurred to you that it might have been painful to have all my hopes and dreams for the future crushed in one fell blow?"

"Of course it did."

"To have my happiness destroyed, to lose the one person I felt closer to than anyone else in the universe?"

"Sara, if there'd been any other way—"

"You want to know what hurt the most, Ryder?"

He could hardly bear the remnants of long-ago anguish scrawled across her beautiful face. "Tell me."

"What hurt the most was that we were *friends*. Long before we became lovers, that's what we were. *Friends*."

Her voice caught in her throat, sending a dagger of guilt through Ryder's heart. "People get dumped by their lovers every day—I knew that even back then. But what really *destroyed* me, Ryder—" she pounded her fist to her heart "—was that you were my best *friend.*"

"Sara—"

"I didn't just lose a boyfriend. That would have been hard enough. I lost my *best* friend." Impatiently, she dashed a tear from her eye. "And I just couldn't believe he would betray me like that."

God, how he ached to wrap his arms around her, to smooth his hands over her hair and tell her again and again how sorry he was!

But he held himself back on a tightly straining leash. Sara would never let him comfort her now. He had no right to, anyway. Not after the way he'd hurt her.

Ryder was startled to discover how much he'd meant to her. He'd been crazy about *her,* of course. But somehow, his miserable upbringing, his insecurities and battered self-esteem had never allowed him to believe that Sara could truly return his feelings.

He'd been a nothing, a nobody, a poorly paid garage mechanic with dirt under his fingernails who'd barely managed to finish high school. While Sara had been the crown princess of town royalty—smart, pretty, popular.

She didn't know what it was like to have your mother run off with a visiting artist when you were five, and to grow up amid the whispers, the snickers, the rib nudging every time you walked down the street.

She didn't know what it was like to be forced to steal food because by Monday morning your pop had spent every last dime of Friday's paycheck on booze.

She didn't know what it was like to be looked down upon, shoved around, jeered and taunted and pushed to the end of your rope, until it seemed like fighting back with your fists was the only way to gain any respect.

She didn't know how much Ryder had loved her.

And it was too late to tell her now.

"Maybe it was a mistake to come here," he muttered, more to himself than to Sara.

Sara's eyes glittered. "That's the first thing you've said that I agree with." She stepped up to him, cheeks blazing like autumn leaves. "Make no mistake about *this,* Ryder. I want you out of my house and out of my life forever. You can just go back to wherever it is you came from—" she began to jab her finger into his breastbone for emphasis "—and leave . . . me . . . alone."

With that last jab, something broke loose inside of Ryder, so that all the guilt and restlessness and loneliness that never gave him a moment's peace came crashing together, colliding in one giant explosion. Without the slightest regard for the consequences, he seized Sara in his arms and kissed her.

Caught off guard, she seemed on the verge of responding for a second. Her lips were sweet and warm and familiar, the soft curves of her body melding easily with his. Ryder felt like a man who'd crawled out of the desert on his hands and knees to find the oasis he'd thought was a mirage was real after all.

She felt so soft, so good, so right in his arms. She'd been the first woman Ryder had ever loved, and the last. He'd spent ten years wandering the globe, but never during his travels had he ever come anywhere close to recapturing the feelings that Sara had stirred inside him.

For the first time since arriving in Hideaway Bay last night, Ryder felt as if he'd finally come home.

Then, all at once, Sara's body went rigid. She wedged her hands between them and pushed furiously against Ryder's chest.

"Let go of me!" The words tore from her throat as she wrenched her mouth from his.

He released her immediately, reluctantly.

Her eyes were wild, her cheeks scarlet. Her expression destroyed any comforting illusions that Sara Monahan was still the same innocent, trusting young girl Ryder had once known so well. It struck him that, in some ways, he didn't know the grown-up woman she'd become at all.

"Get out of my house," she said, chest heaving as she wiped the moisture of his kiss off her lips with the back of her wrist.

Ryder made a superhuman effort to slow his ragged breathing. "I'm sorry. I shouldn't have grabbed you that way."

Sara speared her arm in the direction of the front door. "Leave, Ryder. Now."

He saw his last chance to set things right slipping away. "We can't just leave things like this."

"Out, or I'm calling your old friends, the cops."

He'd blown it. He'd said all the wrong things, made all the wrong moves. Especially kissing her. Boy, had *that* been a mistake! Like giving a tiny taste of a drug to an addict. It had stirred him, excited him, made him crave more.

Digging in his heels and refusing to budge would just make matters worse. Besides, it was Sara's house. She had every right to kick him out if she wanted to.

She met Ryder's apologetic look with an icy, implacable stare as he edged past her to leave the kitchen. He was about to lift his coat from its hook in the entry hall, when a terrified cry from overhead came tumbling down the staircase.

"Mommy! Mommy, help me!"

He caught only the briefest glimpse of Sara's startled, white face before she whirled around and raced up the stairs.

Without a moment's hesitation, Ryder lunged for the banister and followed her flying footsteps, taking the stairs two at a time.

Chapter Three

Light spilled into the twins' bedroom when Sara pushed open the door from the hallway. Nicholas had continued to cry out during her headlong rush upstairs, and each frightened wail had felt like a knife thrust to her heart.

She found her nephew huddled upright in bed, cowering against the headboard, covers pulled up to his chin as if they could provide some protection against the terrors of the night.

Sara lowered herself to the bed and wrapped her arms around him. "Shh, it's okay, baby...everything's going to be all right...I'm here now."

"I w-want my mommy!" Nicholas sobbed against her chest, his small, thin body quaking with each sob.

"I know, sweetie. I know." Sara cradled his face against her and kissed the top of his head. She felt like bursting into tears herself. "Shh...Aunt Sara's here."

She rocked back and forth, trying to soothe him, murmuring meaningless words into his soft, sweet-smelling hair.

Miraculously, Noelle continued to slumber peacefully in the other bed. More often than not, Nicholas's nightmares resulted in Sara's having to comfort both children at once.

Tonight, it seemed, she only had to worry about Nicholas. "You just had a bad dream, sweetie." She stroked his cheek. "Want to tell me what it was about?"

Nicholas buried his face into her side and shook his head wildly. But eventually he looked up at her and rubbed his tear-filled eyes. "It was a f-fire," he explained, hiccuping on a sob. "Everything was so bright, but I couldn't see anything, and then it got all smoky an' I could hardly breathe, an' I tried calling my mommy and daddy, but they din't answer."

Sara brushed sticky tears from his cheeks with her fingertips, unable to speak around the lump in her throat. From what she'd been able to learn about the real-life fire, Nicholas's dream was essentially a replay of what he'd gone through that night. He'd had the same nightmare dozens of times, but each time he recounted it, Sara's own horror and grief welled up afresh.

When she was able to speak, she said, "Your mommy and daddy loved you very much, Nicholas. And so do I."

Nicholas sniffled. "But what if there's a fire *here,* Aunt Sara?"

"Well, then, we've all practiced just what to do, remember?"

"If the door's closed, don't open it if it's hot. Drop to the floor and crawl to the window. Use the rope ladder to climb to the ground," he recited dutifully.

"And where do you go as soon as you get outside?"

"Run to the sidewalk out front, so we can all meet there."

Sara hugged him. "We'll probably never have a fire here, Nicholas. But you and Noelle know all the right things to do if there is."

When the twins had first come to live with her, it had seemed heartless—brutal, even—to drill them on how to escape in case of fire. But in addition to possibly saving their lives someday, Sara had hoped that teaching them what to do would give them some sense of control and security.

Nicholas's recurring nightmares were troubling, if understandable. But for tonight, at least, the crisis seemed to have passed.

He yawned hugely, snuggling closer against Sara.

"Think you can go back to sleep now?"

"Mmm-hmm."

A half smile quirked her lips as she laid him back against the pillow. All the terror had seeped from his limbs, leaving him as limp as a sleepy rag doll. By the time Sara had finished rearranging the tangled bedcovers over him, Nicholas was sound asleep.

Sara touched her lips to his forehead, bent over to check on the still-sleeping Noelle, and nearly screamed when she turned around and saw the tall, backlit silhouette of a man looming in the bedroom doorway.

She managed to swallow the scream, though her hands were trembling as she pulled the door partway shut behind her. With a curt tilt of her head, she motioned Ryder to follow her downstairs.

"I thought I told you to leave," she said crossly when they were back in the living room and safely out of earshot of the slumbering children.

Ryder spread his hands. "I didn't know—when I heard him cry out—I thought maybe I could be of some help," he finished lamely. After the scene he'd just witnessed upstairs, his mind was a chaotic jumble of emotions.

It was one thing to accept intellectually that Sara was a mother. It was another matter entirely to watch how she cradled her child to her breast, curving her body around him like a protective maternal shield. To hear the soft, comforting murmur of her voice. To feel the love and tenderness that radiated from every word, every touch, swirling outward to encompass those two children upstairs.

Ryder had hovered silently in the open doorway, knowing his presence was unwanted and unnecessary, yet unable to tear himself away from this new, unfamiliar vision of Sara.

Though the words that she and her child spoke to each other had been inaudible from where he stood, something in the curve of her posture, a certain tilt of her head, a special, secret undertone in her voice had revealed an unexpected side of her that had rocked Ryder to the core of his being.

He'd never known the special bond of a mother's love himself. It was awe-inspiring and strangely moving to witness it, even from the outside looking in.

"Is he all right? Your little boy, I mean."

Confusion wrinkled her forehead. "Nicholas? Yes, he's fine. A nightmare, that's all."

Ryder considered his next verbal step carefully. This might be his last chance to coax out some more answers about Sara's personal history. "How old are they? The twins, I mean." He settled himself against the arm of the sofa, hoping Sara would subconsciously accept this signal that he had no intention of leaving just yet. "They *are* twins, right?"

"Hmm? Oh, yes." Sara combed her hair back with her hands, the same gesture Ryder's fingers had been itching to perform all evening. She seemed distracted—worried, perhaps, about her son's nightmare?

"They're seven. Seven years old." Her eyes darted back and forth as if she were watching some private showing on the movie screen of her mind.

Prying answers out of her was about as easy as prying open the clams Ryder used to dig up on the beach when he was a kid. "I'll bet you a nickel they were born on Christmas Day," he teased, risking a grin.

The barest hint of a smile danced around Sara's lips. "You'd lose," she said. "They arrived a day late. But the names were already picked out...it didn't seem right to call them anything but Noelle and Nicholas."

Ryder extracted a nickel from his pants pocket and thumb-flipped it in a high arc.

Sara snatched it out of the air. But her amused smile faded. "How did you know their names, anyway?" Her feathery eyebrows formed a puzzled V.

Ryder jerked his thumb toward the kitchen. "They signed the finger paintings on the fridge."

"Oh." Sara's brow smoothed. "The finger painting." She rolled her eyes. "I was wiping red and blue smears off the kitchen appliances for a week—not to mention the floor, the walls, even the ceiling."

Ryder chuckled. "I guess kids can be quite a handful." He crossed one foot over the other and added with what he hoped sounded like offhand casualness, "Especially when you're raising them all by yourself."

Well, that *was about as smooth as a street full of potholes,* Ryder's internal voice taunted. *Where's some of that famous subtlety your films are so frequently praised for?*

Sara glanced at him sharply, not fooled for a second by his clumsy conversational probing. "Yes," she said neutrally, refusing to rise to the bait.

Ryder held his breath, afraid she would suddenly remember that she'd been in the process of kicking him out of the house a little while ago. But once again her attention wandered off, as if she were wrestling with some internal dilemma that had nothing to do with Ryder.

He watched her float aimlessly around the living room, moving various knickknacks a quarter inch from their previous positions, adjusting pictures on the walls that were already hanging perfectly straight. Her slim, restless hands fluttered like birds.

As she hovered near the Tiffany table lamp, light from the stained-glass panels showered her with multicolored jewels. She looked gorgeous. Radiant. Troubled.

Ryder wished he had the right to ask her what she was thinking about.

Should I tell him or not? Sara asked herself for the tenth time in the last few minutes. The answer kept seesawing back and forth between yes and no.

She didn't know why it hadn't dawned on her until now that Ryder was bound to draw the obvious if erroneous conclusion about the twins. She'd been so stunned to see him again after all these years, so distracted by the disturbing feelings he'd aroused, it never occurred to her that someone in town hadn't told him the whole story already.

But tonight, some turn of phrase he'd used, or perhaps the nature of his not-so-subtle questioning, had clicked in Sara's mind, alerting her to the fact that Ryder assumed Noelle and Nicholas were her own children.

How tempting it would be not to correct him, to let him go on believing that she'd found someone else after he'd left town! Otherwise, he might think she'd been carrying a torch for him all these years.

But Ryder was bound to learn the truth from someone eventually. Better to hear the actual facts from Sara herself, rather than some inaccurate version distorted by gossip.

Besides, Sara couldn't bring herself to deceive him deliberately. That would just be sinking to his level.

She leaned back against the mantel and folded her arms. "Ryder, there's something I need to tell you."

He turned his handsome face toward her, unable to hide the eagerness behind his sober, attentive expression. Well, if he thought she was about to break down blubbering, swoon into his big strong arms and melodramatically confess her undying love for him, he was in for a serious disappointment.

"It's about the twins," she said, still reluctant to reward him with even the slightest tidbit of information about her personal life. "Noelle and Nicholas... they're not mine."

They *were* hers, of course, and always would be from now on. But not in the way Ryder had assumed.

He frowned uncertainly. "You mean, they're adopted?"

"No." Sara took a deep breath. Her heart was pounding, her mouth dry. The worst part was coming up. "They're my brother Brad's children."

"Brad's kids?" Understanding lit up the rugged angles of Ryder's face, followed by something that looked like relief. "Oh, I see. You're just baby-sitting them while he's on vacation or something, is that it?"

"No." Sara hugged her arms as if to steady herself. "They live with me now." She felt tears prickling the insides of her eyelids. Dear God, she still couldn't believe it, still couldn't believe her beloved older brother was gone....

Ryder cocked his head to one side, baffled, awaiting her explanation.

If she could just get through this next part, the rest would be easy. But it still felt so strange, so awful to say the words, even though she'd had plenty of practice over the last six months.

Sara forced out the words through clamped jaws. "Brad and his wife Diana died in a fire last March."

Horror leaped across Ryder's face, propelling him off the arm of the sofa. "My God!" The color drained from his face, giving him the sickly expression of a man who'd just had a fist driven into his solar plexus. "Oh, Sara."

He came toward her, obviously bent on comforting her. Sara stiffened her spine, kept her arms firmly crossed in front of her. Ryder got the message and halted several feet away.

"Sara, I'm so sorry." His features were pinched, haggard, shell-shocked.

She nodded once in acknowledgement, her lips pressed together, unable to speak with her throat closed up.

Ryder's eyes scanned her face as if he were worried she might collapse. "What happened?" Quickly he held up his palm. "You don't have to talk about it if you don't want to."

Sara's chin trembled. She gritted her teeth even more tightly together and said, "I'm okay."

"Why don't you sit down?" He motioned toward the sofa.

Her legs did feel a little wobbly right now. When Ryder solicitously took her elbow, Sara even managed to be grateful for the support. She sank onto the sofa, letting her head drop back, and stared at the ceiling while she kneaded her temples with her fingertips.

"God, it's still so difficult, even after all this time," she said in a thin, tired voice.

Ryder sat beside her and took her hand in his. "Six months isn't that long, not when you've lost someone you love."

Sara thought distantly that she should extract her hand from his, but the movement would require far too much effort in her present drained condition. Besides, his hand felt rather nice.

"I remember after my mother left, how tough it was. How much I missed her." Ryder's fingers tightened. "Even years later, sometimes the pain would come back, just as intense and overpowering as it was when she first went away."

Sara sat up straight and looked at him in surprise. "I never heard you talk about your mother before. Even when you and I were . . . close. You never even mentioned her."

Ryder shrugged and glanced down at their joined hands. "I was ashamed, I guess. Ashamed that my mother abandoned Pop and me. Afraid that maybe I did something that made her want to run away."

Sara squeezed his hand. "Oh, Ryder. Surely you realize now that you weren't to blame for—for what your mother did."

He blew a stream of air through his lips. "Yeah. I guess."

"And you certainly had no reason to be ashamed."

"That's easy for you to say. Other kids didn't poke fun at you. Their parents didn't forbid them from playing with you, like you had some contagious disease they might catch." His eyes, when he met Sara's gaze again, were filled with the ghosts of past humiliation. Hurt. Anger.

Sara had never realized before how deep those wounds had run. How deep they still were. "People can be cruel," she said softly. "There's no excuse for the shabby way you were treated growing up. Just like there's absolutely no reason for you be ashamed of what your mother did."

Ryder's eyes bored into hers like twin blue laser beams, nearly incandescent beneath the black slash of his eyebrows. He lifted his hand to touch her cheek. "I've missed talking to you," he said, his voice gentled with wonder. "I don't think I realized exactly how much, until just this minute."

Sara felt herself being drawn into those eyes, mesmerized, lulled into a dreamy state....

Like a cobra being hypnotized by a snake charmer.

Quickly she looked away. She'd made the mistake of falling under Ryder's spell once before. She wasn't about to let it happen again.

"Tell me about Brad." Ryder's voice was sympathetic, soothing, unsettling.

Sara drew a deep breath and studied a silver-framed photo on the mantel. It had been taken at Brad's wedding, and included Sara and her parents, as well as a beaming Brad and radiant Diana.

"Brad and his wife lived in Chicago," she began, recalling the first time Brad had brought his new girlfriend Diana back to Hideaway Bay to meet his family. "Brad was an architect—they both were, actually, though Diana worked full-time taking care of the twins after they were born."

Ryder had begun to stroke the back of Sara's hand with his thumb. She wished he wouldn't do that.

"They'd recently bought a big old fixer-upper of a house, that they were going to live in while Brad restored it." The last time Sara had spoken to him on the phone, he'd been so excited, so enthusiastic, so full of plans. "Then, last March, an old gas heater that needed replacing exploded during the night and started a fire."

"Oh, no." Ryder stopped stroking her hand and gripped it tightly instead.

Sara stared straight ahead. The room shimmered through unshed tears. "The neighbors managed to rescue Noelle and Nicholas, thank God, but it was too late by the time they found Brad and Diana."

"Oh, Sara..."

When Ryder draped his arm around her trembling shoulders, Sara didn't resist. She'd had to be strong for so long, it seemed—for her parents, for her niece and nephew. It was such a relief to have someone *she* could lean on for a change, someone with big, strong shoulders...a broad chest that felt as solid and sturdy as the old rock jetty protecting the harbor...and comforting hands as reassuring and familiar as the house she'd grown up in.

She buried her face in the crook of his neck and let Ryder hold her until the shaking stopped. His warmth seeped into her, banishing the chill in her soul. His breath rustled her hair, like the caress of a tropical breeze. She listened to the steady, soothing rhythm of his heartbeat through the wool sweater he wore, savoring the pleasant scratch of the yarn against her cheek.

Lord, but his skin smelled good! Like the sea that had been the lifeblood of this town and a constant, dependable presence in Sara's life for as far back as she could remember.

Then she remembered that Ryder was neither constant *nor* dependable.

She would *not* allow herself to rely on him again.

She disentangled herself from his embrace, averting her face in case he tried to kiss her. Even when she scooted as far away from him as she could without falling off the couch, it wasn't nearly far enough.

The room seemed crowded with old memories, with the intensity of the emotions they'd just shared, with the unspoken, haunting presence of the passion that had once bound them as close together as two people could be.

Sara sprang up from the sofa, all at once feeling too suffocated, too jittery, too restless to sit still. Ryder's gaze followed her around the room like a blinding white spotlight around a stage. His unwavering scrutiny only heightened her discomfort, made her want to run away and hide in some nice, safe dark corner.

"Your folks," he said finally, cautious concern edging his voice. "How are they doing?"

Sara shut her eyes, trying to blot out the sight of her mother's hysterical tears and her father's bleak, zombie-like expression. "They were devastated, of course, when Brad and Diana died. They're handling their grief as well as anyone could expect, I think."

"I'm glad to hear that."

Sara sighed. "My mother's health has been declining over the last few years—that's one of the reasons they decided to move to Florida."

Ryder frowned in sympathy. "I'm sure this terrible blow didn't help any."

"No. Dad's got his hands full taking care of her now. I think they would have liked to take Noelle and Nicholas themselves, but it just wasn't possible."

"What about Diana's relatives?"

"She was an only child. Her parents died years ago."

"It's lucky for all concerned that you could take the children."

"I'd do anything for those kids," Sara said fiercely. "I couldn't love them any more if they were my very own."

Ryder didn't doubt her for a second. He'd witnessed firsthand her tender compassion for Nicholas, had heard the unmistakable sound of love echoing through every word she'd murmured to him.

Ryder himself remembered what it had felt like to be the lucky object of Sara's love, of her loyalty and devotion.

For a moment, he was envious of those two kids upstairs.

"Our lives sure haven't turned out the way we once expected, have they?" he mused, startled to hear himself speaking the words out loud.

Sara's eyes narrowed, as if she suspected him of laying some kind of verbal trap for her. Ryder hated the way she was so on guard, so suspicious around him. He also knew he had no one to blame for that but himself.

"How did you expect *your* life to turn out, Ryder?" she finally responded, lobbing the ball back into his court.

He stood up from the couch and wandered over to where Sara was perched against the closed keyboard of the old upright piano. He took up a similar position at the opposite end. "I guess I worried that I'd end up like my pop. All alone. A drunk. Working some dead-end job on someone else's fishing boat."

Sympathy relaxed the rigid lines of Sara's posture. "You're not your father, Ryder. You never were."

"When Pop finally drank himself to death when I was eighteen, I was almost relieved." Ryder shook his head, jammed his fingers through his hair. "God, what a terrible thing to say."

Just like in the old days, Sara came rushing to his defense. "Your father made your life hell, Ryder. The bitterness, the drinking, the beatings..."

Ryder's head shot up in astonishment. "How did you—?"

A sad, rueful smile tipped her lips. "No one's as clumsy as you claimed to be. All those black eyes, the bruises..."

"God, I can't believe anybody knew." He exhaled a gust of air. "I could never bring myself to hit him back, you know? Not even when I got big enough to whip him if I'd wanted to."

"It's only natural that you'd feel some relief when you didn't have to deal with that any more."

"Maybe." Ryder massaged the nape of his neck, which felt like one big knot of tension. "The thing is, whenever I looked at Pop, it seemed like I was looking at my own future—at a living, breathing image of what I was destined to become someday." He dropped his hand and sighed. "That's why part of me was relieved when he died. Because I no longer had to face the reminder of my own dismal future every day."

"Oh, Ryder." Sara bit her lip. "There was no law of genetics, no—no cosmic conspiracy forcing you to follow in your father's footsteps."

Ryder fisted his hands. "I was scared, Sara. Scared that if I stayed in this town, I'd wind up working as a garage mechanic the rest of my life, or hauling salmon onto some fishing boat, or feeding logs to a saw blade at the lumber mill over in Eureka."

"There's nothing wrong with those jobs," Sara said with a touch of indignation. "They're all decent, honest work."

"Of course they are, but they weren't right for *me*." Ryder pounded his fist to his chest. "I wanted more. Something else. And I was afraid if I stayed in Hideaway Bay where everyone knew my background, where people thought I was nothing but trouble, I'd get pigeonholed into some go-nowhere job—trapped in the kind of life I'd sworn to escape from."

Sara had gone white as chalk. Her skin stretched taut across her high cheekbones, giving her a tense, pinched appearance that made her eyes look enormous. "I guess that life you were so eager to escape from included me," she said in a strained voice. "That's why you left."

"No! I mean, not the way you—Sara, wait!"

She marched across the living room, her head held high. "I think it's time for you to go, Ryder."

He dodged in front of her and grasped her shoulders to bring her to a halt. "Sara, I didn't leave to escape from you." Ryder gave her a little shake. "Believe me, you were the only *good* thing about my life."

"*Believe* you?" she echoed, gingerly removing his hands as if they were a pair of mackerel that had sat out in the sun too long. "Why should I believe you, Ryder? I did once before, and look where it got me."

The skeptical slant to her mouth warned him any further argument was pointless now. But it grated on him, that she considered him a liar. "I never said anything to you that wasn't the truth."

Sara rolled her eyes and stepped around him. "I'm not interested in dredging up our youthful fling for a play-by-play analysis, Ryder." She crossed the entry hall to the front door, and stood there holding it open for him. "As far as I'm concerned, our relationship is history. A closed chapter. A done deal." She blinked at him. "Do I make myself clear?"

What was all too clear to Ryder was that any vague ideas he might have entertained about starting something up with Sara again were not only foolish, but downright impossible. Ten years ago, he'd made a choice. Now, he saw that the price of that choice was Sara's trust.

And without trust, any meaningful relationship between them was out of the question. Sara had been the best friend Ryder had ever had. Obviously, the most he could hope for now was to salvage a few scraps of that friendship.

If she would even allow him *that* much.

"I'll be in touch," he said.

Sara tilted up her chin. "Don't bother."

Maybe the fact that she kept rebuffing him was all for the best, anyway. Emotional entanglements were something Ryder made it his policy to avoid, because the nomadic life-style he'd chosen required him to travel light. Starting something heavy with Sara would be an unforgivable mistake.

The last thing he wanted was to hurt her again.

But the queasy, unsatisfied feeling that roiled in the pit of his stomach like a bad case of indigestion informed Ryder he hadn't yet accomplished whatever his purpose had been in coming back to Hideaway Bay and seeking out Sara.

He unhooked his coat from the hall tree. "Good night," he said, taking his leave reluctantly, knowing that for *him,* at least, it wouldn't be a good night at all.

His only reply was the soft but resolute *click* of the door closing in his face.

On the other side of that door, Sara pressed her forehead against the wood, and let the exhausting aftermath of today's astonishing events wash over her.

After a minute or two, she shoved her hair back from her face with a sigh. She began to drift aimlessly, restlessly through the house, rubbing her hands up and down the sleeves of her sweater, even though the thermostat was set at seventy degrees.

In the kitchen, she spotted the partially finished wine that Ryder had brought, sitting on the counter next to the sink.

After a moment's thoughtful pause, she upended the bottle and carefully, deliberately, poured its contents down the drain.

Chapter Four

Tess Carpenter breezed into the bakery, flung herself into a chair beside the window and propped her chin on top of her interlaced fingers. "Okay, Monahan, 'fess up. Tell me everything, and don't leave out even one teensy-weensy delicious detail."

Sara glanced up from the bookkeeping forms on the table in front of her to find her best friend regarding her with intense, nearly ravenous interest. She looked like a coyote stationed at the mouth of a prairie dog burrow. Especially when she licked her lips.

Sara took a careful sip of coffee. "I don't know what you're talking about."

Tess whipped her exuberant brown curls from side to side and pounded her heels against the tile floor, like a little kid having a temper tantrum. "Don't give me that. If you don't fill me in on the amazing reappearance of Ryder Sloan within ten seconds flat, I am positively going to *explode* with curiosity."

Sara closed the file folder and pushed it aside with a sigh. She could see she wasn't going to get much work done during her midmorning coffee break today. "Oh. That."

"Yes, *that.*" Tess made a whirling, hurry-up motion with her hand. "Gimme the whole story. And *don't* leave anything out." She took a healthy chomp out of Sara's half-finished pastry and leaned back in her chair, arms folded, eyes gleaming, lips smacking.

Sara fiddled with her crumpled napkin. "There's not much to tell, really."

"Oh, come on." Tess lurched forward to wag a scolding finger at Sara. "Don't play coy with me, kid. You were eager enough to spill all your romantic secrets back in the old days. Remember how you'd moon over Ryder while we played records and tried on makeup up in my bedroom after school?"

"Shh!" Sara made a frantic hushing gesture. The bakery had gone unnaturally silent all of a sudden, as if customers and employees alike were hoping to pick up some choice crumbs from Tess and Sara's conversation.

Loitering in front of the nearby display case, Doc Thomson seemed to be taking an unusually long time to make his selection, even though he'd ordered the exact same bran muffin every single morning for the last thirty years. And Susan, the baker's daughter, was liable to rub a hole right through the shiny glass top of the next table if she kept on wiping it so industriously with that damp towel.

Call her paranoid, but Sara was even beginning to suspect that old Mrs. Appleby up by the cash register might not be quite as deaf as she pretended to be. Right now she was adjusting her hearing aid like a satellite dish, perhaps hoping to tune in a signal.

Sara tilted her head close to Tess's. "I did not *moon* over Ryder," she insisted in a low, indignant voice.

"Oh, no? What's this, then?" Tess clasped her hands to her heart, donned a goofy, lovesick expression and fluttered her eyelashes like demented butterflies. "'Ooo, he's just so utterly scrumptious! Whenever I'm near him, I could just swoon!'" She burst into laughter at Sara's outraged expression. "Sound familiar?"

Sara drummed her nails against the tabletop. "I never talked like that, and you know it."

"Close enough. But never mind. Come on, give." She made a coaxing curl with her fingers. "Where's Ryder been hiding out all these years, anyway?"

Sara shrugged one shoulder. "Beats me." She tore a couple of little pieces off her napkin.

Tess frowned, puzzled. "What do you mean? What did he tell you?"

"He . . . we . . . didn't get around to discussing it."

"What?"

Sara cringed as all heads in the bakery swiveled in their direction. She tore some more pieces off her napkin.

"What do you mean, you didn't discuss it?" Disbelief rang through Tess's voice. "What'd you talk about all evening, the weather?"

"Would you please keep it down? And just how do you know Ryder and I talked at all last night?"

Tess made a rude noise with her lips. "Get real. How do you *think* I know? Listen, the local grapevine could leave CNN in the dust. Two seconds after you let Ryder in your front door, word was all over town." She helped herself to another bite of Sara's pastry and said with her mouth full,

"I could barely restrain myself from interrogating you before now."

"Your willpower is admirable." Sara cast self-conscious glances around the bakery. "Sorry to disappoint you, but I don't have any fascinating news bulletins to reveal about Ryder Sloan."

Tess uttered a word she would have washed out her children's mouths for saying. "For cryin' out loud! You didn't find out where he's been? What he's been doing? Why he left? If he's married?"

Sara continued to shred her napkin into confetti. "You ought to go work for CNN yourself."

"Sa-a-a-ra..."

"Okay, okay." She and Tess had been closer than sisters ever since kindergarten. Tess had been there to pick up the pieces when Ryder broke her heart. Her friendship, loyalty and support had helped Sara through some tough times. Confiding in her old pal now seemed the least she could do.

Although there were a few things Sara had no intention of mentioning to Tess. Like how Ryder had caught her off guard with that startling, disturbing kiss.

She reached for her coffee, only to discover her cup was empty. She set it back down and took a deep breath. "There's really not much to tell," she hedged. "He said something about being a documentary filmmaker."

"Ryder? No kidding?" Tess's cocoa brown eyes widened in surprise. "Good for him!" A mischievous smile tugged up the corners of her mouth. "Wouldn't you just love to see crabby old Principal Keeler's face when he hears that? Remember how he blew his stack in the school cafeteria that day and called Ryder a worthless, good-for-nothing hooligan who'd never amount to anything?"

"I remember." Instinctively, Sara's temper began to simmer on Ryder's behalf. People had always been so unfair to him, so quick to judge without bothering to look past that rebellious, sullen exterior of his.

"So, where's he been living?" Tess helped herself to the rest of Sara's pastry. "Mind if I finish this?"

Sara waved it away. "I don't know where he's been living. We didn't get into that."

"Mmm." Tess polished off the pastry and licked her fingers. "Let's cut to the important stuff. Is he married?"

Her question jabbed Sara like a needle. "How should I know?" she replied, exasperated.

"How should you *know?*" Tess gaped at her. "For heaven's sake, you bump into the great love of your life for the first time in ten years, and you don't even bother to find out whether or not he's married?"

Sara plucked off another napkin fragment. "He's not the great love of my life."

"No? Then why are you sitting there playing Loves Me, Loves Me Not with your napkin?"

Sara crimped her lips together as she quickly swept the mound of tattered paper into her empty coffee cup. "Ryder means nothing to me anymore."

"Baloney." Tess shook her head sadly. "Boy, you are the world's worst liar. Not to mention the world's worst investigative reporter." She tapped her foot impatiently until Sara returned from disposing of her trash. "I don't suppose you bothered to find out why Ryder's come back to Hideaway Bay, did you?"

Sara tucked the file folder into her shoulder bag. "He says he's come back to sell his father's house."

"Do you believe him?"

Sara let her bag drop onto the table with a clunk. "How should *I* know?" She glared at Tess. "Look, if you've concocted some crazy theory that Ryder's come back here to whisk me off into the sunset with him, forget it. Our relationship ended long ago."

A smugly infuriating smile teased Tess's mouth. "Maybe Ryder doesn't think so."

Sara yanked her shoulder bag into place. "What Ryder Sloan thinks is no concern of mine. I'm not interested in picking up where we left off. So don't go getting any crazy ideas into your head otherwise." She marched toward the exit, noting with dismay that all eyes in the bakery were following her.

The bell over the door jingled when Sara hauled it open. "And that goes for all the rest of you, too," she announced in a loud voice.

As she fled the bakery, the last thing she glimpsed was Tess's amazed, ear-to-ear grin.

The instant he spotted Sara coming out of the bookstore just before noon, Ryder's heart soared and got all fluttery, as if a flock of birds had taken off inside his chest.

He couldn't exactly call this chance encounter an amazing coincidence—not when he'd been cruising up and down the streets of Hideaway Bay for the last twenty minutes, scanning the curbs for her parked car.

But Sara didn't need to know that.

Ryder was pleased to discover he hadn't lost his knack for "accidentally" bumping into her. Not surprising, perhaps, considering all the practice he'd had years ago.

He lengthened his stride to catch up with her. His director's eye took in all the little details of Sara's appearance—at least, those he could observe from behind. Softly flowing hair...bulky turtleneck sweater with sleeves pushed up to reveal her slender forearms...plaid wool skirt swirling around her calves as she walked down the sidewalk. With her low-heeled suede boots and armload of books, Ryder would have cast her immediately in the role of well-dressed college student.

She strode purposefully down the sidewalk, head held high, shoulders straight, refusing to be distracted by any window displays in the storefronts she passed. She kept her gaze firmly focused ahead of her, as if making a beeline for an important goal only she could see.

Ryder murmured into her ear as he came up behind her. "Carry your books home from school?"

Obviously, Sara had been so absorbed in her thoughts, she hadn't heard his approaching footsteps. With a gasp, she whirled to confront him. "You!" Her cheeks went pale as ice, then flushed fire-engine red. "What are you doing, sneaking up on me like that?"

Trite, but true. She was beautiful when she was mad. "I wasn't exactly tiptoeing," Ryder pointed out. "As a matter of fact, I think a flying saucer could have landed in the middle of Main Street and you wouldn't have noticed. Those must have been some pretty deep thoughts you were all wrapped up in."

Sara hugged her books to her chest and scowled at him. "My thoughts are none of your business. And I don't appreciate your following me."

Ryder spread his hands, Mr. Innocence. "Hey, this is a small town. We're bound to run into each other once in a while."

Her skeptical stare was unwavering. "Not if I see you coming first."

"Sara, you're not giving me a fair chance. Here, let me take those."

"I can carry my own books, thank you."

"Humor me. I'm trying to relive my youth."

Sara rolled her gorgeous green eyes. "You never c carried anyone's books home from school, and you k it."

"Well . . . okay. I was afraid it would ruin my tough- image. So how about letting me make up for it now?"

"Oh, all right," she mumbled, giving in with ill gr probably just to avoid a wrestling match over the boo

As Ryder took them from her arms, he noticed by titles they were all books on child raising. How like S even after six months of on-the-job training, to keep doing her homework!

Ryder found her devotion to her niece and nephew just touching, but positively heroic. And who better t Ryder himself understood the depths of Sara's love loyalty?

"Those kids are lucky to have you," he said gruffly.

Sara glanced up at him with a start. "Well . . . thank The irritation and mistrust on her face melted a little.

Ryder knew an opening when he saw one. "How ab having lunch with me?"

Immediately, she backed up a step. "I can't. I've b running late all day, and I have an appointment at one, then I have to pick up the twins. . . ."

"All the more reason to have lunch with me right no Ryder pointed out reasonably.

She consulted her watch as a diversionary tactic. don't think that would be a good—"

"Sara," he told her in a stern voice, "you have to ea

She set her chin at a stubborn angle. "Look, Ryde told you last night, I'm not interested in dredging up old—"

"I dare you," he said, lowering his face so it was m inches from hers.

Sara held her ground, though alarm flitted across her face. She blinked. "I beg your pardon?"

Ryder moved even closer, close enough to see those little gold flecks amid the green of her eyes. "In fact, I *double* dare you," he drawled. "To have lunch with me."

Sara swallowed. "Don't be ridiculous." Her eyes were huge. "I'm not going to have lunch with you just because you—"

"Chicken?" Ryder asked with a taunting arch of his brows. Maybe he was being childish, but he'd never known Sara Monahan to back away from a challenge. Besides, he was desperate.

She saw right through him, the way she always had. "Nice try, but it won't work." She grabbed her books back.

"Sara, for Pete's sake—"

As she swung away from him, one of her books slid to the ground.

Both of them went for it at once, with predictable results.

"Ouch!"

Sara rubbed the top of her head and aimed a dirty look at Ryder, who was gingerly exploring the bump on his own noggin. He felt like an idiot, a clumsy oaf, a complete—

Then, all at once, Sara smiled at him.

And what a smile it was, radiating like a sunrise to light up her face. It spread outward from her parted lips, crinkled up the tip of her adorable nose, and put a sparkle in her eyes.

Then, even more amazingly, she started to giggle.

As the ridiculousness of their situation dawned on him, Ryder began to chuckle.

Sara giggled even harder, pressing fingertips to her uptilted lips.

Ryder threw back his head and laughed out loud. He spied a patch of blue sky overhead, and noticed the low coastal clouds were burning off. The sun was finally coming out.

"Boy, what a pair we make, don't we?" Sara shook her head ruefully. "You'd think we were five years old or something."

"Playing tug-of-war over a pile of books."

"I guess we both got what we deserved." She winced as her fingers checked the sore spot on her head again.

Ryder jerked his thumb in the direction of the café. "Come on. Let me buy you lunch."

His invitation sobered her quicker than a cold shower. "I don't—"

"Please."

She glanced up and down the street, at the sidewalk, at the sky. "All right," she said finally. "But on *two* conditions."

"Name them."

She held up one finger. "First, we go Dutch."

"Okay."

Another finger. "Second, we don't talk about the past."

Ryder hesitated.

"I mean it," Sara said. "If even one word about our relationship escapes your lips, I'm outta there. If you so much as use a *verb* in the past tense, I'm leaving."

There was a lot he wanted to explain. And plenty of questions he was itching to ask her. But at least this was a first step on the road to proving to Sara that he wasn't the scoundrel she thought he was. "Agreed."

The instant their deal was sealed, Sara started having second thoughts. Ryder was nothing but trouble. She should be giving him as wide a berth as possible, yet here she was, about to have lunch with him.

"Want to put your books in the car first?" he asked, heading in the direction where she was parked.

It didn't surprise Sara in the least that Ryder had already spotted her car. He'd always been a keen observer, alert to his surroundings. His eyes used to dart rapidly from side to side whenever he entered a room or turned a corner, like a soldier scouting out enemy territory. Always on the lookout for trouble, that was Ryder.

And here was Sara, walking right into it.

"Does the Sea Breeze Café still serve the best seafood in town?" Ryder asked while Sara dumped her books in her car.

"The Sea Breeze Café *never* served the best seafood in town," she replied. "But it's cheap and it's close by." She slammed the car door. "Come on, let's go."

She told herself she'd only agreed to have lunch with Ryder because they were creating a scene in public. She'd sensed people peeking out at them from shop windows, had seen heads swivel curiously in their direction as people passed them on the sidewalk. Ryder's reappearance had created quite a stir, and Sara's reaction to it would undoubtedly be the topic of dinner conversations all over town.

Better just to give in and have lunch with him, than to prolong their argument in full view of Main Street.

Yeah, right.

The only flaw in that reasoning was that Sara had never worried much about what people might think. She'd never allowed the curiosity or disapproval of others to guide her behavior.

Heaven knows, if public opinion had ever influenced her choices, she would never have gotten involved with Ryder Sloan in the first place.

Sara still couldn't believe he was back. Ryder! Walking right beside her, holding open the door of the café, resting his hand ever so lightly on the small of her back to usher her inside.

Warmth spread outward from the base of her spine.

Ever since Ryder had stepped out of the fog yesterday, a dreamy sense of unreality had enfolded Sara in its arms. While performing the most mundane task, the astonishing fact of his return would strike her like a dizzying blow to the head.

All at once, she would forget how many scoops she'd already counted into the coffee filter, or stare uncomprehendingly at the car keys in her hand and forget where her next appointment was. Once or twice she'd actually pinched herself to make sure she was truly awake.

For so long, Sara had assumed she would never lay eyes on Ryder again. He could have been dead, for all she knew.

But the living, breathing, flesh-and-blood male now seated across the booth from her was definitely no ghost.

"Crab salad," Sara told the waitress, and immediately forgot what she'd ordered.

"I'll have the grilled salmon." Ryder handed their menus back to the waitress with a brief, friendly smile. And just that small interaction was evidence to Sara of how much he'd changed. The Ryder Sara had known had masked his insecurities behind a terse, stony facade. He'd avoided eye contact with most people, afraid they were secretly looking down on him. And he'd rarely smiled at anyone but Sara.

This new Ryder was obviously more comfortable with himself, more at ease with others. Despite her resolve not to ask any questions about the last ten years, Sara couldn't dodge a tiny dart of curiosity. What combination of events and experiences during that time had instilled in Ryder this new air of confidence and self-worth?

When he shoved up the sleeves of his sweater, she noticed he was wearing a Rolex watch. The sweater itself was an ivory wool fisherman's sweater—not the kind of sweater any fishermen around *here* ever wore, but the imported kind you ordered from one of those expensive mail-order catalogues.

His coal black hair and deep blue eyes were a vivid contrast to the creamy wool. No matter how much she tried to deny any attraction to him, Sara had to admit, he looked incredibly sexy. Scrumptious, as Tess might have put it.

She took a hasty sip of water, resisting the urge to dash the glass's contents into her own face.

"You must be pretty successful at your work." The words slipped out of her mouth before Sara could yank them back. Oh, well, they had to talk about *something.* Filmmaking seemed as safe a subject as any.

"I do all right." Unless Ryder's tendency to downplay his accomplishments had also changed, that must mean he was even more successful than Sara had thought.

"You said you make documentaries?"

"That's right. Educational films, news documentaries, stuff for public and cable television, that sort of thing." He toyed with his spoon. "Nothing you've ever seen, I'm sure. Though I *have* had nibbles from a couple of big-time producers down in L.A. that I'm hoping will pan out." He shrugged. "Actually, I've had a lot more success in England so far than I have in this country."

"England?" Of all places on earth, the land of aristocracy and afternoon tea was the last place Sara would have

imagined him. "Is that where you went when you lef— She choked back the question too late. Damn.

Heat flooded her face.

Ryder shook his spoon at her. "Uh-uh-uh," he chide "Remember our deal? No talking about the past, only tl present." His eyes glowed at her from beneath his dai brows. "And maybe the future."

"You and I haven't *got* a future," Sara retorte crunching on an ice cube from her water glass.

Ryder's brows lifted. "Who said I was talking abo *us?*"

She smiled sweetly at him. "Why else would you I making such a pest of yourself?"

He grinned back at her, hoisting his water glass in sa lute. "Touché."

His grin touched Sara as intimately as a caress, lade with the kind of unspoken messages that even a mei glance can convey between two people who know eac other very, very well.

She felt her pulse accelerate in response. How she' missed talking with Ryder, confiding in him, exchangin all those meaningful glances!

How she'd missed the way he used to look deep into he eyes right before he kissed her, as if searching for any ol jections, as if he were still unsure of her feelings even ai ter a thousand kisses....

Sara wiped damp palms on her skirt. Here she was breaking her own ground rules by wallowing around in th past like some sentimental spinster! She would not allo herself to be seduced by the past, any more than she ir tended to allow Ryder to seduce her in the future.

She picked at her crab salad when it came, her appetit having mysteriously vanished.

"There *is* something I wanted to talk to you about."

Sara dropped her fork with a clatter when Ryder spoke. Her nerves were as tautly strung as piano wire. "Have you forgotten our deal? We agreed that—"

"It's not about us," he said quickly. "It's about my father's house."

"Oh." She cleared her throat. "What about it?"

Ryder pulled out his wallet to pay the bill. *His* half of the bill, that is. "I don't know if you've been by it lately, but the place has deteriorated into even more of a dump than it was originally."

"I guess that's bound to happen, after ten years of neglect." Darn it, that came out sounding all wrong! As if she were reproaching him for neglecting *her* for ten years.

Ryder let it pass. "Yeah, I guess I should have made some arrangements before I— Well, never mind." He dropped a few bills onto the table. "Anyway, I'm planning to fix the place up before selling it."

"Sounds like a big project." And one that would likely keep him hanging around Hideaway Bay for a while...

Ryder nodded. "I could probably handle most of the work myself, but it sure would make it easier to have some help."

Sara's lips twitched in distaste. "Ryder, you know I couldn't hammer a nail straight if my life depended on it."

He laughed, a delicious sound that went straight to the pit of her stomach. "Not *you.* All the time you spent hanging around the garage where I worked, and you still couldn't tell a distributor from a dipstick. I need someone a little more mechanically oriented."

"Who did you have in mind?"

"That's where I'm hoping you can help me. I thought I'd hire some high school kid to help me on weekends, and maybe after school for a couple of hours. Know anyone who might be interested?"

"Hmm." Sara tapped her chin with her finger. "What you ought to do is ask at the high school. Denise Gordon is the guidance counselor there. She could probably help you find someone."

"Would you mind introducing me to her?"

"Well..."

"Come on, Sara," he said in that cajoling tone she'd always found so impossible to resist. "Schools make me nervous, remember? I'd probably get so flustered, I wouldn't even be able to find my way to her office."

"Oh, you wouldn't have any trouble at all," Sara told him with an impish smile. "It's right next door to the principal's office."

"Very funny. Look, if you come with me when I talk to her, maybe she'll take it as a character reference. Otherwise, if she starts asking around town about me, she's liable to expel any student found working for me."

Sara twisted her lips as she dug her share of the lunch bill out of her purse. "I think you're exaggerating."

"Oh, yeah? What if she talks to one of my former teachers?"

Sara paused. "Okay. I'll introduce you. But I have a business appointment in exactly two minutes—"

"Great. The high school's right next door to the grade school. I'll meet you when you pick up the twins." He scooped up the check along with their money. "I'll go pay this up at the front register."

Ryder seemed to be in an awful hurry all of a sudden, as if *he* were the one late for an appointment instead of she. He whisked Sara out of the café before she even had time to regret agreeing to meet him later. "See you at three," he said cheerfully, ducking to brush a quick kiss on her cheek.

Sara stared after him as he sauntered off down the sidewalk, hands stuffed in his pockets.

Typical Ryder. Always running out on her.

She touched her fingertips to her cheek. The imprint of his kiss still burned.

Chapter Five

Ryder was whistling as he drove to the grade school at t minutes to three. Somehow, miraculously, he'd pe suaded Sara to introduce him to the school guidan counselor. Not that he actually felt incapable of introdu ing himself, but this small favor from Sara was a perfe excuse to see her again.

The perfect way for Ryder to get his foot in the door. (at least his big toe.

He was glad for another chance to prove to Sara wasn't the heartless cad she thought he was.

Was that why he'd come back to Hideaway Bay? T prove something to Sara? To set things right with her?

Maybe this whole thing was all about Ryder's eg Maybe the knowledge of how Sara must despise him ha nagged at him all these years, eating away at his co science and festering in his soul.

Maybe he just couldn't stand it that she held such a low opinion of him.

Ryder had been sensitive to the opinions of others while growing up, that was true. But as an adult, he'd learned to shrug off criticism. As a filmmaker, he'd learned to dismiss the occasional unfavorable review as irrelevant to what he was attempting to accomplish with his work.

Sara, it seemed, was the one critic on earth whose opinion really mattered to him.

And once he'd convinced her he wasn't really such a bad guy, then what?

Unfortunately, Ryder hadn't yet written the end of that particular script. Because deep down inside, he wasn't sure how he wanted it to turn out.

He was taken aback by the traffic jam he found in front of the grade school. Twenty years ago, when Ryder himself had been a student at Hideaway Bay Elementary, nearly all the kids had *walked* home from school.

Now, he had to park halfway down the next block, and walk back past mothers leaning on their car doors and chatting while they waited for the school bell to ring. He recognized a couple of them, and noticed that quite a few more recognized *him,* judging by the turned heads and silenced chatter.

He spotted Sara standing near the flagpole at the front entrance to the school, deep in conversation with an attractive woman who used her hands a lot while speaking. As Ryder drew closer, he realized who the woman was. Ohhh, boy.

"Hello, Tess," he said.

Tess's hand froze in midgesture, while her dark brown eyes grew as big as teacups. "Well, well, well," she said slowly, lowering her hand to her hip and giving Ryder a thorough, head-to-toe once-over that made him want to crawl behind the nearby shrubbery. "Ryder Sloan, as I and breathe." She shook her curls. "I never would l believed it, if I hadn't seen for myself."

"How are you?" he asked lamely. He'd always be bit overwhelmed by Tess's outgoingness, her vivacious assurance. You never knew what was going to come ou her mouth next.

She lowered her eyelids to half mast and studied hin if reserving judgment on him for now. "How am I? married. Two kids."

"Tess and her husband Dan own the drugstore. Da pharmacist, who grew up in Oregon," Sara told Ry Her eyes twinkled as if she were amused by his awkw encounter with Tess.

"Uh, really?" he said, reluctant to tear his gaze f Sara's lovely green eyes. He forced his attention bac Tess. "How old are your kids?"

Her face lit up as if he'd just asked the correct ques on "Jeopardy!" "Alex is ten, and Jenny is eight." jabbed Ryder playfully in the ribs with a sharp, lacqu fingernail. "So, you planning to stick around town good this time?"

"Tess!" Sara looked horrified, but Tess only laug "Well, if you'd just go ahead and ask him yourse wouldn't have to."

Ryder couldn't help grinning. "I see *you* hav changed much," he said to Tess.

"Oh, no, I'm still just a simple, small-town girl," said with an airy wave of her hand. "But *you!* Sara's t giving me the lowdown on this brilliant, successful ca of yours, and I must say, I'm totally impressed."

Knowing Tess's penchant for exaggeration, Ry translated that to mean she'd managed to pry as man two words from Sara on the subject. "Well, thanks. But I wouldn't exactly call it brilliant—"

Thankfully, the school bell rang at that moment, distracting Tess from her inquisition. Kids began to pour out of the redbrick school like a surge of fans onto the field after a home team victory. Within seconds, the three of them were surrounded by excited shouts, bouncing lunch boxes and pinwheeling arms and legs.

Tess shaded her eyes with her hand. "There's Jenny...and here comes Alex. Oops! Looks like he's about to get into some kind of scuffle with his best friend Eddie. Gotta run." As she dived into the mob, she hollered back over her shoulder, "Talk to you again soon, Ryder."

He lifted his hand in response, feeling both dazed and relieved as he watched her go.

Sara touched his elbow. "Sorry about that," she told him. The pink stain of embarrassment still lingered on her cheeks. "One thing Tess has never been is shy."

Ryder stroked his jaw. "She does have a talent for saying exactly what's on her mind, doesn't she?"

"Sometimes I'd like to install a little checkpoint between her brain and her mouth, to monitor what comes out."

"But she's a good friend."

"The best." Sara nodded emphatically. "I never appreciated how good a friend she was, until..." Her voice trailed off as her cheeks flamed pink again. "Well, until you went away," she mumbled, pretending to be suddenly absorbed in looking for the twins.

"Sara," Ryder said, placing his hands on her shoulders. Once again, that helpless feeling of guilt descended on him. God, what he wouldn't do to make things up to her!

The muscles in her shoulders knotted immedia though she didn't shrug his hands off. But she wou turn around and look at him, either.

Then her nephew rushed up, and Ryder knew his presence was probably forgotten for the time being.

"Aunt Sara, I gotta get a new lunch box." Nich crossed his arms and pushed out his lower lip, as if paring for an argument. His shirt was untucked, sneaker was untied, and he had a smudge of dirt o chin.

Sara knelt so they were eye-to-eye, marveling at sweet wave of tenderness that flooded her each time caught sight of the twins. Over Nicholas's shoulder, could see Noelle approaching at a more sedate pace, down, heels dragging. Oh, dear.

Sara set her concern aside for a moment to focu Nicholas. "You need a new lunch box, huh?" She cou resist ruffling his hair, even though he would probab mortified by this display of affection in front of schoolmates.

"Noelle, too," he said, not budging an inch. "Non the other kids bring their lunch in sacks."

Sara bent down to tie his shoelace. "Well, we'll just to see about buying some lunch boxes, then, won't we

Nicholas persisted as if Sara had said no instead of Obviously, he'd prepared his arguments well in adva and wasn't about to let them go to waste. "We had lu boxes in Chicago," he said matter-of-factly, "but they burned up in the fire."

Sara caught her breath. Tears prickled her eyelids, she managed to blink them back. "How 'bout if w shopping this afternoon?" she suggested in a voice wavered only slightly.

"'Kay." Nicholas shrugged one narrow shoulder, as if new lunch boxes were a matter of indifference after all.

Sara bit her lower lip as Noelle came shuffling up to them. "Hello, sweetheart. How was school today?" she asked brightly.

Noelle had tied her sweater around her waist, but it drooped now so that one sleeve dragged on the ground. She mumbled something at her feet.

"What'd you say, honey?" Sara brushed her niece's bangs out of her eyes.

"I gotta be in a play," Noelle said in a faint, unhappy voice.

"A play?"

"Yeah!" Nicholas chimed in. "Our class is doin' a play called *Sleeping Beauty,* an' I get to help make the scenery!" He gave his sister a superior yet sympathetic glance. "Noelle just gets to be one of the good fairies."

"Why, Noelle, that's wonderful!" Sara straightened the sagging sweater and used the sleeves to pull Noelle closer to her. "I'm so proud of you."

Noelle's lower lip trembled. "But I don't *wanna* be in a play," she said mournfully.

"Sweetheart, why not?"

"We hafta 'memberize a bunch of words, then say them in front of people."

"Well, you can do that," Sara told her. "I'll help you memorize the words, and we can practice the play together. It'll be fun!"

"But I'm *scared!*" Noelle wailed.

"Hey, you know what?" Ryder crouched beside Sara and spoke to Noelle. "It's okay to be scared. *Everybody's* a little bit scared to be in a play. In fact, they even have a name for it."

Sara wasn't sure who was more startled, she or Noelle. She'd completely forgotten Ryder was standing behind her.

Noelle crooked a finger in the corner of her mouth and stared at him with enormous blue eyes. "They do?" she finally said in a tiny voice.

"Sure! They call it stage fright." Ryder tapped his chin. "Let me see, I'll bet when you think about saying your lines in front of all those people, you get... butterflies in your tummy."

Noelle blinked, then nodded.

"And your hands get all sweaty?"

"Uh-huh."

"And you feel like throwing up?"

Noelle bobbed her head vigorously.

Ryder slapped his knee. "That's it, then. You've got a perfectly normal case of stage fright."

Noelle's finger slipped out of her mouth. She gaped at Ryder in awe. "What do I do?" she asked breathlessly.

"Well, you practice your lines a lot with your Aunt Sara." He winked at Sara, who was observing this exchange with bewildered astonishment. Recently, Noelle had been completely tongue-tied around strangers.

Obviously, the famous Ryder Sloan charm had an equally potent effect on females of all ages.

"Then, you just take a deep breath, go out there and give it your best shot," Ryder said. "Doesn't matter if you're scared. Doesn't matter if you forget your lines. As long as you do your very best, that's the only thing that counts."

"It is?" Noelle was hanging on every word as if Ryder were some mystical prophet. Or the world's slickest con man, Sara thought cynically.

"Yup." Noelle's tiny hand disappeared completely when Ryder enfolded it between his. "That's all anybody can ever ask of you, and that's all you can ever ask of yourself. As long as you do your best, you can hold your head up high and never apologize to anybody."

Noelle stood up a little straighter. Gratitude flickered in Sara like a candle flame. What a shame that Ryder himself hadn't been able to follow that advice while growing up!

He shook Noelle's hand. "My name's Ryder," he said solemnly. "What's yours?"

"Noelle Monahan." She ducked her head. One shoe crept up to rub the opposite calf.

"An' I'm Nicholas!" her twin announced, not about to be overlooked.

"Good to meet you, Nicholas." Ryder extended his hand, which Nicholas shook after a moment's hesitation. His chest puffed up like a bantam rooster's.

"Congratulations to you, too," Ryder said. "Building the scenery for a play is a very important job."

Nicholas swelled up even further. "That's what my teacher Mrs. Hennessy says."

"Well, Mrs. Hennessy is absolutely right."

Noelle tugged on Ryder's sweater. "Will you come see my play?" she asked shyly.

Sara could hardly believe her eyes and ears. Was this the same bashful, timid little girl she invariably had to coax into saying hello when introducing her to someone new?

Then the implications of Noelle's question dawned on Sara. Heat flooded her cheeks.

"Honey, Ryder's very busy," she said, instinctively edging between Ryder and her niece, as if to shield Noelle from any empty promises. "Besides, he's only visiting Hideaway Bay for a little while. He'll probably be gone by the time your class puts on the play."

The look Ryder shot her might have been indecip able to most people, but not to Sara. He was surpri annoyed, hurt. But he smiled warmly at Noelle. " course I'll come to your play," he told her. "I woul miss it for the world."

His expression dared Sara to challenge him.

For the sake of the children, she swallowed her ann ance. "We're going to walk over to the high school, can introduce Ryder to someone," she told the tw "Then I'll take you shopping for lunch boxes."

Ryder and Nicholas kept up a lively stream of chatte the way next door to the high school, and Sara coul help appreciating how Ryder skillfully made sure to clude Noelle in the conversation, too.

As they climbed the front steps of the two-story b building, an avalanche of memories came crashing d on Sara, sweeping her into the past like a time mach She'd had occasion to walk these locker-lined corrido number of times over the past ten years. But none of th times had been with Ryder.

Sara hadn't really known Ryder while both of them been students here. He'd graduated—barely—several y ahead of her, and their friendship hadn't begun until a that. Sara *had* known his reputation, of course. She kn he was trouble, she knew to steer clear of him.

Then, right after she'd gotten her driver's license sophomore year, she'd been driving home after study at a friend's house, when the car broke down. It was n thirty in the evening, and early enough in the spring t dark as midnight at that hour. The friend lived a few m outside town, and the stretch of road where Sara's p ents' car had chosen to quit running was unlit and serted.

Sara tried to restart the engine a dozen times, but to no avail. "Just peachy," she muttered, pounding the steering wheel in frustration. It was a long walk back to town from here. And the night was full of all sorts of creepy things—owls, bats, foxes, skunks. When she stepped out of the car, she heard millions of frogs croaking in stereophonic sound. Yuck.

Thank goodness her father always kept a flashlight with a fresh battery in the glove box. After a few muttered curses, Sara managed to figure out how to open the hood. She skimmed the flashlight beam over the car's innards a few times before her shoulders slumped in despair. Hopeless, just as she'd figured it would be. The engine was as big a mystery to her as an atomic reactor.

"Need some help?"

Sara screamed and whirled around, heart catapulting to her throat. The wildly zigzagging flashlight beam flickered back and forth across his face like strobe lights in a disco. It took a few moments before she could hold it steady enough to see who he was.

Uh-oh.

Ryder Sloan.

Sara didn't know whether to be relieved or more scared.

"God, you startled me!" she gasped. Beneath her flattened palm, she could feel her heart thumping like a jackhammer in her chest.

"Sorry." He flicked his long hair out of his eyes with a jerk of his head.

"Wha—what are you doing way out here, anyway?" Sara's mouth was dry as dust. She licked her lips nervously.

Ryder hesitated, as if he didn't want to answer. "Coming back from Beacon Point."

"On foot?*"*

He shrugged. "I like to walk."

"What on earth were you doing out by the lig house?"

Once again, Sara had the feeling he wasn't going to swer. "Sometimes I just like to go out there and think," said finally.

"By yourself?"

"Yeah."

She was on the verge of asking him what he thou about, when she recalled that this was Ryder Sloan she w standing here chatting with. Ryder Sloan, who got in fi fights, who'd set a new school record for being expell who'd even been thrown in jail overnight one time, af he'd stolen some food from Oceanside Market.

A hoodlum. A worthless punk. Nothing but troub That's what Sara's parents thought. That's what t teachers at school thought. That's what everyone in to thought.

So how come Sara wasn't scared anymore?

"Lemme see that flashlight."

When she handed it to him, his callused fingers brie touched hers. Sara's skin felt strange, electrified. "He hold this for me." When he handed it back, showing h where to aim the beam, she deliberately brushed his fi gers again. He didn't seem to notice.

He smelled salty, like the ocean, as she stood next him, holding the flashlight while he tinkered with som thing in the engine. Sara had no idea what.

"There." He let the hood slam shut with a ban "Oughta do it." He dusted off his hands.

"Gosh, thanks." Sara took a deep breath, noticing f the first time how the night smelled of grassy fields a sweet clover. "Um, can I give you a ride back to town?

Her pulse quickened again at this daring offer. What would her parents say if they found out?

Ryder seemed taken aback. He scratched his head, scuffed his toe on the gravel shoulder, gazed up at the stars. "Uh, no," he said. "Thanks. I'd just as soon walk."

"Well... okay." Sara backed toward the driver's side. "Thanks again for fixing the car."

"Sure."

She felt vaguely let down by his rejection. Excited by this brush with the forbidden. Curious about what Ryder Sloan thought about, all by himself out on Beacon Point at night.

She waggled her fingers in farewell as she pulled back onto the road, leaving him standing there alone on the shoulder.

Ryder Sloan hadn't seemed dangerous at all! Just helpful and nice and... kind of shy.

Funny how she'd never noticed before how sexy-looking he was.

Just wait until Tess heard about this amazing encounter! After Sara had first sworn her to secrecy, of course.

"Sara? Sara!"

Twelve years later, Ryder's voice yanked Sara out of her trip through the time machine. "Where are you going? Isn't this the place?"

Sara blinked. She curved her palm over her forehead to check if she felt feverish. How else to explain this dizzy, disoriented feeling?

She backtracked slowly to where Ryder and the twins had stopped, outside a door marked Guidance Counselor. "Sorry," she mumbled. "Guess I wasn't paying attention."

But she certainly intended to pay closer attention from now on. She couldn't allow the seductive pull of memories to blur the line between past and present. Ryder Slo was part of her past, part of a closed book Sara h slammed shut forever.

Reluctantly, she led the way into the guidance coun lor's office. She still thought this scheme of Ryder's to up his father's house was just an excuse to stick arou Hideaway Bay and torment her.

As far as Sara was concerned, the sooner Ryder l town and hightailed it back to Kathmandu or wherever was he'd come from, the better.

"Hey, Ryder, wanna come shopping with us for lun boxes?" Nicholas asked eagerly.

Sara groaned. Like it or not, it looked as if she was g ing to be stuck with Ryder for a while.

Chapter Six

Ryder pounded the last nail into the new floor joist, rolled back on his heels and backhanded a film of sweat from his brow. Overhead, he could hear his new helper, Shane, ripping out that old section of drywall that Ryder's father had once punched a fist through in a drunken rage.

Ah, memories. Ryder picked up his plastic water bottle and chugged down a long stream of cool, refreshing liquid. Sometimes it was tough being back in this house. This house filled with ghosts.

The ghost of his unhappy mother, before she'd fled town with a visiting artist who'd come to paint scenes of the picturesque harbor and quaint Victorian homes.

The ghost of his father, who'd sought refuge from his pain at the bottom of a whiskey bottle, who'd taken out his bitterness, disillusionment and frustration on his only son.

And the ghost of Ryder himself, haunted by fear, guilt, by loneliness, by the belief in his own inadequac Was it something he'd said or done that had driven mother to abandon him? If only he were a better so maybe Pop wouldn't drink so much, wouldn't hit him often.

Ryder squeezed his eyes shut and gave his head a sha shake to clear it. No point in wallowing around in the pa He was beginning to understand why Sara was so dead against it.

Sara.

At the thought of her, Ryder's pulse picked up its temp the same response she'd stirred in him ever since that d so long ago when she'd brought him the cookies. He fixed her broken-down car one night out on Beacon Poi Road, and the very next afternoon she'd shown up at t garage where he worked, bearing a plate of home-bake chocolate chip cookies to thank him.

No one had ever baked anything for Ryder before. Th were the most delicious, mouthwatering cookies he'd ev eaten. And from that day on, he'd been hopelessly stuc on Sara Monahan.

With an impatient grimace, Ryder levered himself to h feet. He was never going to get this house renovated if h sat around wasting time and mooning about Sara.

When he'd set foot inside these dilapidated walls for th first time after his ten-year absence, Ryder's plans ha nearly crumbled along with the ceiling plaster. The plac was such a wreck, he almost decided to put it on the ma ket just as it was, and let some other poor sap worry abo fixing it.

But some stubborn, determined streak wouldn't let hi give up so easily. Now, with every newly hammered boar every replaced fixture, every brush stroke of new pain

Ryder felt as if he were repairing a little piece of himself, too.

Working on the house had become a sort of therapy, so that Ryder jumped out of bed each morning, eager to get started on that day's project.

Each new section of drywall, each coat of plaster did more than just cover up a hole in the wall or water damage on the ceiling. It also made those ghosts seem farther away, less substantial. Ryder was hoping that by the time he finished renovating the house, those ghosts would have vanished completely.

He was calculating some measurements at his makeshift worktable, a couple of planks laid over two sawhorses, when he heard a car pull up to the curb outside. When he craned his neck to peer out one of the sparkling new windowpanes, a jolt of anticipation ricocheted through him.

It was Sara's car.

Ryder hastily combed a hand through his hair and wiped his face with his shirtsleeve. As he stepped out onto the front porch, both passenger doors opened and the twins spilled out.

Nicholas charged ahead up the front walkway. "Hi, Ryder! Is this your house?"

Ryder grinned. "Sure is. What do you think of it?"

Nicholas's mouth fell open as he tilted back his head and looked the place up and down. "Wow! It's nice!"

Ryder chuckled. Chunks of siding hung askew, the front steps had been temporarily patched with scrap lumber, and the whole place needed paint. Bad. "How'd you like to be my real estate agent, Nick?"

"Hey, yeah!" He scrambled up the steps.

Noelle hung back, peering shyly at Ryder throug dangling screen of blond hair as she attempted to bo hole in the ground with the toe of her shoe.

"Hi there, gorgeous." Ryder crouched down on heels. "What have you got there behind your back?"

She blinked at him with big blue eyes that were goin melt quite a few hearts someday. In fact, Ryder's c heart was already starting to go mushy. "We brought something," she said breathlessly.

"You did?" He reared back in surprise. "Well, come up here on the porch and show me what it is."

She hesitated for only a second before marching up steps at a dignified, ladylike pace. Glancing over the of her head, Ryder saw Sara hanging back at the far of the walkway. She wore a tan linen blazer over a j green dress that matched her eyes. And she looked as if were sucking on a lemon.

Noelle brought out the object from behind her back a presented it to Ryder. "I made this for you."

"You did?" Ryder took the folded piece of red co struction paper and examined it carefully.

"It's a invitation!" Nicholas informed him.

"Why, so it is." On the cover was a crayon drawing a woman lying on a bed, wearing a crown. Ryder flipp it open. Inside was carefully printed The Second Gra Class Of Hideaway Bay Elementary School Invites You Our Play *Sleeping Beauty.*

"It's next month," Nicholas said, pointing a chub finger at the date and time written at the bottom. "A guess what? I get to be in the play after all, 'cause Jimr Thomson has the chicken pox, so I get to be a talking tr instead of him."

"Yeah? Good for you!" Ryder high-fived him. "Not good for poor Jimmy Thomson, though."

"He gets to miss a whole *week* of school." Obviously, Nicholas considered the chicken pox a small price to pay for such a vacation.

Ryder fingered the invitation, noting all the detail that had gone into the picture. The crown even had jewels on it. "Did you really make this yourself, Noelle?"

She nodded. "Teacher helped us with the writing. But I drew the picture all by myself."

"Well, I think it's about the best drawing of Sleeping Beauty I've ever seen in my entire life." To Ryder's surprise, a lump rose in his throat. Noelle's thoughtful gesture had strummed a strange, wistful chord inside him. He couldn't believe she'd gone to all this effort just for him.

He swallowed, but that wistfulness lingered. "Thank you for inviting me," he told her. "No one's ever given me a special, handmade invitation before."

Noelle's eyes shone up at him, touching Ryder's heart. "Are you gonna come to our play?" she asked.

Ryder glanced up and saw Sara standing at the foot of the steps. His eyes locked onto hers. She gave a quick, nearly imperceptible shake of her head.

"Of course I'll come to your play," he said, catching the annoyed crimp of Sara's mouth before he looked back at Noelle. "I wouldn't miss it for the world."

"Yay!" Nicholas crowed.

Ryder tugged gently on a lock of Noelle's hair. He'd never realized before how silky-soft a child's hair could be, as fine as spun gold. "Thank you for making me the invitation, sweetheart," he said. "I'm going to keep it forever."

He heard Sara's footfall on the steps. She cleared her throat. "I should have called first," she said. "But the kids went over to Tess's house to play after school, and when I picked them up, they were all excited about inviting you to their play, so..." She gave Ryder a not very convincing smile. "I hope we're not interrupting you."

"Not at all. Fact is, I was just about to knock off work for the day, anyway."

"Well, we won't keep you." She began to retreat down the steps. "Come on, kids. Time to go home and fix dinner."

On impulse, Ryder said, "I was just about to whip up some dinner myself. How about if the three of you join me?"

"Yeah! Can we, Aunt Sara?"

"Please?"

Sara nibbled her lower lip. The last thing she wanted was to spend any more time with Ryder, forced to make companionable chitchat in front of the twins. But they both seemed so enthusiastic about the idea....

Three pairs of eyes regarded her expectantly, two with eagerness, one with a gleam of challenge.

Sara knew when she was outnumbered. "Are you sure we wouldn't be imposing?" she asked, trying to ignore the flash of triumph that briefly lit up Ryder's face.

"Absolutely not." He scratched his head. "I *am* going to need a couple of assistants, though." He gave Nicholas a friendly punch in the shoulder and tousled Noelle's hair. "Whaddaya say, guys? Either one of you any good at peeling carrots?"

"Me! Me!" Nicholas jumped up and down, stretching his hand skyward as if frantically signaling that he had the right answer.

Ryder clapped his palms together and rubbed them briskly. "Terrific! Noelle, I bet you know how to spread butter on bread for garlic toast, don't you?"

She nodded enthusiastically.

"Great! Shall we adjourn to the kitchen, then?" As the twins raced past him into the house, Ryder called, "Be careful where you step! There are lots of tools lying around, and I might not have gotten every single nail swept up."

He turned back to find Sara watching him with skepticism. "What's wrong?" he asked, arching his brows in innocence.

Sara pursed her lips. "It's just that I've never seen this domestic side of you before, Ryder. Is there no end to the talents you've acquired over the last ten years?"

He winked at her. "Stick around, and maybe you'll find out."

"*You're* the one who has trouble sticking around," she muttered, putting as much distance between them as possible while she edged past him into the house.

The instant she crossed the threshold, Sara was struck by an unsettling sense of déjà vu, as if she'd stepped through a portal into the past instead of Ryder's doorway. Vivid images flooded back of the first time she'd ever come to visit Ryder in this house.

She'd come to offer her condolences upon the death of his father. It was several months after the incident when Ryder had fixed her broken-down car out on Beacon Point Road. During the intervening weeks, Sara had caught an occasional glimpse of him around town, but they hadn't spoken since the day she'd gone to the garage where he worked to thank him.

She hadn't forgotten him, though. Couldn't seem to get him out of her mind, in fact. At odd moments, she would see his handsome, moody face looming out of the darkness, and remember what his fingers had felt like when they'd brushed against hers.

At night, she would lie awake in bed, imagining Ryder lying awake somewhere, too. Perhaps even thinking of *her.*

And then Ryder's father had died. He'd been working out on a fishing boat one drizzly, overcast morning when a large ocean swell knocked him off balance. He'd toppled over the side of the boat and drowned before the rest of the crew could rescue him.

He'd been stinking drunk at the time.

And so Sara had dressed in her gray skirt, white blouse and gray cardigan sweater—the closest outfit she had to what she considered proper funeral attire—and knocked timidly on the door of the house Ryder had shared with his father.

When Ryder opened it, surprise shimmered quickly across his stormy features, like the lightning flashes in the thunderclouds overhead. Then, like the lightning, it vanished.

"Better come on inside," he said, his expression once again guarded, wary. "It's cold and wet out here."

So Sara had entered Ryder's house for the first time, and stood there dripping raindrops onto the filthy braided rag rug, uncertain of what to say, wondering if coming here had been a mistake after all.

But somehow she'd found the words, and although Ryder didn't actually say so, she'd known he appreciated her coming. In Sara's mind, that visit had always marked the beginning of their friendship. Within weeks, they were inseparable.

Ryder told Sara later on that she was the only person in town who'd bothered to pay a condolence call.

Now, years later, Sara stood in the same living room taking stock of the changes. The braided rag rug had apparently been relegated to the scrap heap. The grime-smudged windows had been washed until the glass sparkled, and the dark, dingy walls had been freshly painted a creamy off-white. The whole house seemed airier, lighter, as if it had finally shaken off a bad case of depression. Lots of work still remained to be done, but there was an atmosphere of cheerfulness, of hope around the place.

The same thing could be said of Ryder. Once, he'd been a troubled, lonely teenager with a chip on his shoulder. But he'd transcended his unhappy roots and grown into a man who could be proud of his success, a man who was finally at ease with himself.

Being in the same room with him, however, made Sara distinctly *un*easy.

She widened the distance between them, and tried to focus on her surroundings instead of the sentimental feelings Ryder aroused inside her.

"You've certainly worked miracles on this place," she said, stepping gingerly around scattered tools, scraps of lumber, paint cans. "I figured you must have been busy, considering I haven't seen you around town for a few days."

Ryder massaged the sore muscles in his lower back. "Sometimes I think it would have been easier to tear the whole place down and start from scratch," he said. "But I have to admit, the work is pretty satisfying."

The last part of his sentence was nearly drowned out by a muffled crash from upstairs. Sara glanced at the ceiling, then arched her eyebrows at Ryder and made a wry slant of her mouth. "Termites?"

Ryder smiled. "My new assistant."

"Oh, so you did find someone through the high school?" Sara cringed and ducked her head as another ominous crash filtered down from above.

"Shane Mathis. Know him?"

"I know his mother slightly."

"He's got more brute strength than finesse at this point. But he's been a big help getting some of the muscle work done." He cupped his hand to his mouth and hollered up the staircase. "Hey, Shane! Come on down here."

Moments later, a tall, gangly youth trudged downstairs.

"Shane, this is Sara Monahan, an old friend of mine." Ryder's introduction jarred Sara a bit. Old friends? Is that what they were? Once upon a time they'd been so much more, yet this guarded truce they seemed to have arrived at amounted to so much less.

Sara stuck out her hand. "Nice to meet you, Shane."

Shane appeared momentarily nonplussed by her gesture. Then he shook a fringe of dark hair out of his eyes and briefly gripped her hand. "Hey," he mumbled.

"Why don't you go ahead and knock off for today," Ryder suggested, "and I'll see you tomorrow morning around eight, all right?"

Shane's narrow jaw dropped slightly, as if the idea of being somewhere at eight o'clock on a Saturday morning was a completely foreign concept to him. But he closed his mouth and gave an affirmative jerk of his head. "Sure."

"Goodbye, Shane," Sara called as he ducked out the door. The teenager reminded her strongly of Ryder at the same age, with that same wary, sullen expression, that same screen of dark hair concealing his eyes from the world.

"S'long," Shane muttered over his shoulder.

Yep. Just like Ryder. Sara wondered if Ryder himself was aware of the resemblance. Then she caught him studying the door with a regretful, faraway look in his eyes, and knew that he was.

His gaze shifted to Sara, and for an instant they exchanged a glance of such perfect understanding, it nearly took her breath away. For the length of a heartbeat, it felt as if they were the old Ryder and Sara again, able to communicate volumes with a mere look, a gesture, a touch.

The illusion was shattered by a loud series of metallic clangs emerging from the kitchen. Ryder hunched his shoulders and winced. "Oops! Guess we'd better go see what the help is up to."

Sara hurried after him. "We could always call out for pizza."

"No, we can't. I don't have a telephone."

Too bad, Sara thought. All at once, the prospect of sharing dinner in the cozy confines of Ryder's kitchen seemed like a very unwise idea, indeed.

"More wine?" Ryder positioned the bottle over Sara's glass and raised his eyebrows inquiringly.

She hesitated, then replied, "Sure, why not?" with the reckless air of a drunken reveler, even though she'd made her first glass last all through dinner. "Stop, that's enough," she said when he'd poured barely a splash.

Ryder himself wasn't much of a heavyweight when it came to drinking. Not after what he'd seen booze do to his father. "Noelle? Nicholas? Some more lemonade?"

"No, thank you," they chorused.

Ryder struggled not to smile. Both twins wore identical reddish orange mustaches, courtesy of the spaghetti sauce.

"What's for dessert?" Nicholas asked.

"Nicholas!" Sara sent Ryder a sheepish, don't-kids-say-the-darnedest-things glance. "Where are your manners?"

"Oops!" Nicholas covered his mouth in embarrassment. "Sorry."

"You're not s'posed to ask for dessert till someone asks if you want any," Noelle reminded him in a loud stage whisper.

Ryder chuckled. Were all kids this charming? He was a rookie when it came to dealing with children, but the more time he spent around Nicholas and Noelle, the more exceptional they seemed to him. A warm glow of affection spread through him, filling some of the empty places inside him.

"Well, I'm afraid I don't have too much to offer in the dessert department," Ryder said. "How about an apple?"

The twins looked at each other, shrugged. "Okay," they both said after some silent vote had been taken.

Ryder got two apples from the refrigerator, washed them off and handed them to the kids. "Did you want one, Sara?"

"No, thanks." She pushed her chair back from the kitchen table. "Let me help you clean up this mess."

"Mess? What mess?" Ryder shaded his eyes with his hand and made a big production of scanning the kitchen. "I don't see any mess in here, do you, guys?"

Noelle and Nicholas giggled.

Sara propped her hands on her hips and narrowed her eyes in mock exasperation. Worms of limp spaghetti strands wriggled down the front of the stove. Carrot peelings decorated the sink in orange streamers. The first experimental batch of garlic toast was scattered across the counter like lumps of charcoal. And a graffiti artist had scribbled all over every available surface with spaghetti sauce.

Ryder couldn't remember a more enjoyable meal in his life.

"Well, maybe there's a *tiny* bit of cleanup to be done," he conceded with a wink at the twins. He lobbed Sara a sponge. "Want to start with this? Or would you rather have a shovel?"

"This'll do fine for now," she replied. Her eyes sparkled at him in a way that made his blood go fizzy.

"We can help," Noelle offered as she and her brother started to climb down from their chairs.

"No, no," Sara and Ryder said in hasty unison.

"You helped cook dinner," Sara said diplomatically. "Now it's Ryder's and my turn to clean up."

"'Kay." They sat back down and munched happily on their apples.

The two adults exchanged rueful, relieved glances.

Normally, Ryder would have insisted that Sara sit, too, while *he* cleaned up. But tonight, he didn't want her to feel like a guest. He wanted her to feel like . . . family.

Ryder had never had a real family. Or, if he had, it had disintegrated when he was too young to remember what it was like. Tonight, for the first time, he'd shared in all the little domestic rituals that most people took for granted. Preparing dinner, sitting down at the table together to eat and discuss the children's day at school, cleaning up afterward.

Considering it was something Ryder had never done before, the whole routine had felt amazingly right to him. Comfortable. Intimate. Something he might even be able to get used to.

For the very first time in Ryder's life, this house felt like a home to him.

In harmony with his thoughts, Sara commented, "I didn't realize you'd actually moved in here."

Ryder plunged his hands into the soapy dishwater and handed her another plate to rinse. "Well, once I got this place fixed up to the point where it wasn't a safety hazard anymore, I decided I was wasting money renting a room at the boarding house."

Sara crinkled her brow. "The boarding— Oh, you mean Mrs. Litchfield's place." Amusement trickled into her voice. "It's called the Ocean View Bed-and-Breakfast now."

"Bed-and-Breakfast, huh?" Ryder's mouth twitched in a rueful half smile as he handed her a fistful of dripping silverware. "Well, whaddaya know. Hideaway Bay has finally gotten trendy."

Sara rinsed the silverware, then stacked it in the dish drainer. "Oh, we get lots more tourists than we used to. There's even a harbor cruise during the summer."

"No kidding?" Ryder cocked his eyebrows in surprise. "You mean people actually pay to ride some old tub around the bay?"

"Ten bucks a head."

He let out a low whistle. "Maybe I'm in the wrong line of work."

Sara mumbled something under her breath.

Ryder threw her a questioning look as he handed her the last of the silverware, savoring the feel of her soapy-slick fingers against his. But Sara avoided his eyes, briskly wiped her hands on the dish towel and said, "Come on, kids, time to hit the road."

Dinner had been delayed by a series of mishaps that had hampered the elaborate preparations, so that it was nearing nine o'clock now. Two pairs of eyelids drooped at half-mast.

"Thanks for dinner," Sara told him as she helped the twins into their jackets. "What do you say to Ryder?"

"Thanks for dinner," they mumbled sleepily.

Ryder followed as Sara herded them toward the front door. "Thanks for coming," he told them. "I sure enjoyed your company." He was surprised to discover how much he meant it. "I hope we can do this again soon."

Sara must have deciphered the yearning in his voice. She sent Ryder a puzzled glance that was a mixture of sadness and surprise. Then she gave a sharp shake of her head, as if deciding she'd been mistaken.

Ryder walked them to the car and waited while Sara buckled the drowsy children into their seats. When she started around to the driver's side, he captured her wrist.

She flinched, as if his fingers were live wires. "Ryder..."

He drew her back into the concealing shadows of the spreading maple tree beside the curb. She came reluctantly, but she came.

"Ryder, don't do this. Please, I—"

"Shh..." He wove his fingers through her hair, tilting her face up to meet his. "I've been wanting to do this all evening."

Sara swallowed. "The twins," she said. "We can't—"

"The twins are sound asleep." Ryder knew Sara was right, that this was a mistake. He also knew that he had to kiss her, before the craving that had been building in him for hours drove him right over the edge.

He slid a hand beneath her blazer, around her narrow waist. When he pulled her close, he could feel her heart racing beneath the thin silk of her dress.

Sara's lips parted, whether in protest or invitation, Ryder couldn't be sure. It didn't matter.

He kissed her, gently at first, holding himself back with heroic effort. She seemed determined not to respond, but then her soft lips began to move beneath his, seeking the old familiar rhythms of the passionate duet they'd played so many times before. Her hand alighted on his chest, tentative as a dove.

Ryder moved his mouth over hers, worshiping, exploring, reacquainting himself with all her sweet, hidden secrets, rediscovering the flame of desire that burned higher and hotter within him as their kiss deepened.

Sara was everything he'd ever wanted, everything he could never have. Rather than dull his passion for her, ten years of separation had only stoked it higher.

He inhaled deeply, like a man desperate for oxygen, drawing into his lungs that special fragrance of hers, the one that made him think of a grassy, flower-strewn meadow on a summer day. Her lips were warm and yielding, her breath coming as fast as his was.

A tiny whimper caught in Sara's throat, and that sound catapulted Ryder back over the years to the first time he'd ever kissed her, when she was seventeen and Ryder was still mystified by how the prettiest, most popular girl in town had come to be his best friend.

He'd been crazy about her for over a year then, although his instinctive caution had prevented their relationship from evolving into anything beyond their unlikely friendship. But on that fine summer day when Sara had packed a picnic lunch for them to share out at Beacon Point, Ryder had finally screwed up the courage to let her know how he felt.

Not with words, of course. That wasn't his style. But after the sandwiches and fruit and cookies were all gone, after Sara settled back on her elbows, closed her eyes and turned her face to the sun, Ryder knew it was now or never.

Heart thudding in his ears, he scooted himself next to her on the picnic blanket, took a deep breath, and brought his lips to hers.

Sara's startled green eyes had flown open at the instant of contact. And to Ryder's great delight, astonishment and relief, she'd kissed him back.

She'd made the same tiny whimper then that she was making now. Ryder opened his eyes, and saw that Sara's eyes were open, too—inky pools in the dark night. He felt himself slipping into those pools, drowning, sliding toward something he was desperate to reach.

Yet somehow, he was still afraid to let go.

Beneath her palm, Sara could feel Ryder's heart galloping as rapidly as her own. The contours of his body were achingly familiar, yet strangely different. His chest was broader, more solid, the muscles more well-defined. It was like coming back to a place you'd once called home, only to find strangers had been living in it.

She shouldn't be kissing him. But, just as she'd ignored the warnings of her well-meaning parents years ago, Sara went right on kissing him, ignoring the alarm bells that bitter experience was sending out from her brain.

He was so strong, yet so gentle! There had always been a tentative quality to Ryder's kisses, the only time he ever seemed unsure of himself. His newfound boldness excited Sara as much as the touch of his hands on her body. Desire spilled through her, hot and urgent.

She slid her hand to the side of his face, feeling the pulse drumming along his jaw, the play of his facial muscles as he moved his tongue inside her mouth. When she curled her fingers through the hair at the nape of his neck, she was briefly surprised to find it so much shorter than her fingers remembered. More changes.

She felt a bump, and dimly realized that Ryder had backed her up against the trunk of the maple tree. Her mind was awhirl with sensations, desires, emotions. How astonishing that embers which had lain dormant for a decade could explode so quickly into this fiery passion!

Perhaps those embers hadn't been as dormant as Sara had thought.

Ryder's cheek was rough against her hand, his mouth hard upon hers. Desire crashed through her in a blaze of smoke and sparks. Dear heaven, how she wanted him!

Like cracking open Pandora's box, Sara allowed certain memories to struggle out of that carefully secured prison where she'd kept them boarded up all these years. Memories of Ryder's hands stroking her bare flesh. Memories of that rapturous, earth-shattering union when they'd finally become as one and Sara had been so certain she'd found the love that would last the rest of her life.

Memories of how Ryder had deserted her the very next day.

Sara had gone to his house, looking for him, only to find the door locked. Ryder had never bothered locking doors.

She'd gone to the garage where he worked, only to discover that Ryder had given notice that very morning, mumbling something about leaving town right away.

Ryder's boss had studied Sara with a mixture of puzzlement and pity. "I kinda thought he might be taking you with him," he'd said.

Recalling the shock, the pain, the utter devastation of that discovery doused Sara's passion like a bucketful of water.

She'd been a young, naive fool back then.

Now she was ten years older. She was no longer naive, thanks to Ryder. And she'd be damned if she'd let him play her for a fool again.

She wrenched her mouth from his, using both hands to push him away. "No!" she whispered, disgusted with her own weakness for him. "I won't let this happen again!"

Ryder reached for her. "Sara..."

She stepped aside so she was no longer trapped between him and the tree. "Don't kiss me again, Ryder."

His hands clenched into fists at his sides. "You can't hide from what you feel for me, Sara. From what we feel for each other."

She pulled a piece of bark from her hair, and flung it aside. "Can't I? Just watch."

"It's wrong to deny it."

"Is it?" Sara impatiently yanked the front of her blazer closed. "You weren't so concerned about right and wrong ten years ago, when you skipped out on me after you'd finally made your conquest."

Ryder's voice simmered with banked emotion. "You know that's not how it was."

"All I know is that I made the biggest mistake of my life by getting involved with you in the first place." Sara pivoted on her heel and marched back to the car. "And I don't intend to make the same mistake again," she said in an angry stage whisper, just before she slid into the driver's seat.

She closed the door with a muffled yet resolute *thunk*.

Ryder stood at the curb, watching until the red taillights disappeared in the distance. His shoulders slumped, and every muscle in his body began to ache with weariness. Back inside the house, he closed the door with a hollow *click* that echoed in the utter silence.

All at once, the place that was so recently filled with warmth and laughter seemed as empty and desolate as that strange, secret yearning place inside Ryder's chest.

Chapter Seven

"Aunt Sara, Ryder! Lookit the sea lion!" Nicholas jumped up and down, pointing frantically over the boat railing. Beside him, Noelle stared raptly at the large, brown, sleek-coated mammal lounging on the platform of a bobbing red buoy, seemingly indifferent to the tour boat chugging by.

"I see him, Nicholas," Sara called over the steady throb of the engines. The brisk autumn breeze off the bay whipped her hair about her head. "He looks like he's waiting for someone to throw him a fish, doesn't he?"

"Yeah!"

Sara tugged the collar of her jacket more snugly around her neck, and settled back into her seat. Beside her, on the row of molded plastic chairs attached to the pilothouse, Ryder chuckled. "Sure gives you a brand-new outlook on things, seeing them through kids' eyes."

"Yes, I've discovered that myself."

Sara still couldn't get over the way Ryder and the twins had hit it off. During the past couple of weeks, ever since the night he'd cooked them dinner, Ryder had become a near constant presence in their lives. Every time Sara turned around, it seemed, there he was, inviting himself over for a meal, or suggesting some outing that aroused the children's enthusiasm so that Sara didn't have the heart to say no.

Ryder was the first person besides Sara that Noelle and Nicholas had formed any strong attachment to since their parents' deaths. Which made it difficult, if not downright impossible, for Sara to steer clear of Ryder the way she'd intended to.

In the past dozen days, the four of them had been to the ice-cream parlor and a movie matinee, had taken a nature hike up at Redwood National Park, and paid a visit to the small Hideaway Bay Maritime Museum. Ryder had had dinner at their house three times, and had driven them all into Eureka for pizza twice.

Sara had been more places with Ryder in the last two weeks than during their entire youthful courtship. She and Ryder had never exactly dated in the traditional, dinner-and-a-movie sense. Sara had perceived even back then that Ryder was embarrassed by the differences in their social and financial circumstances. Taking her out in public, where people were bound to whisper about him and wonder what a nice, proper girl like Sara Monahan saw in a no-good hooligan like him, would have been excruciating for Ryder.

He would have taken her out on conventional dates, of course, if Sara had insisted on it. But she'd been more than content to spend their time together sharing a picnic, or taking a walk through the woods, or sitting hand-in-hand on the bluffs overlooking the ocean.

Lately, it seemed as if Ryder were trying to make up for all those movies and restaurants he'd never taken Sara to. It seemed almost as if he were . . . courting her again.

Except for two things.

First, the constant presence of two pint-size chaperons.

Second, the fact that Ryder hadn't so much as made a move to hold Sara's hand. Not since the night in front of his house when he'd kissed her. When, against her better judgment, Sara had kissed him back.

Not that she was complaining, of course. She'd made it perfectly clear that night that she had no intention of getting involved with Ryder again, and she'd meant it. She could hardly object if he abided by the rules she herself had laid down.

But it bothered her that she couldn't quite figure out what Ryder's angle was—what he hoped to accomplish by spending so much time with her and the twins.

Almost as if they were some kind of . . . family.

"Bye, Ryder!"

"See you later!"

"So long, you two."

The affection on Ryder's face as he watched the twins vanish into the house touched Sara's heart. On impulse, she asked, "Would you like to come in for some hot chocolate?"

Ryder propped his hand on the door frame above her head and shifted his weight to one leg. "Thanks, but Shane's coming by to work for a few hours this afternoon." He rolled his eyes. "At least, I *think* he is. He was supposed to show up yesterday, too, but he never did."

"I'll give you a rain check on the hot chocolate, then." Sara felt a faint twinge of disappointment. Lately, she'd found herself searching for excuses to prolong their partings.

A lock of black hair slipped across Ryder's forehead as he brought his face close to hers. For a second, Sara thought he was about to kiss her. Her mouth went dry... her pulse started to race.

But all he did was touch a finger to the tip of her nose, and give her one of those intimate, devastating smiles that had always turned her knees to mush.

"I had fun with you and the kids today," he said in a low voice that made her senses tingle.

"I—we had fun, too," Sara agreed, feeling slightly short of breath.

"I'm glad we got to take that boat tour, before it shuts down for the season."

"Yes."

Sara could feel the heat flowing off his body, enveloping her in that seductive aura that inevitably drew her toward him whenever they were alone together. It was a complex blend of desire and memories and hope, and she was finding it more and more difficult to resist.

In Ryder's eyes, she saw a mirror image of the same attraction she was fighting. His lips parted. He brought his hand to her cheek. "Sara..."

She held her breath.

The strong planes of his face shifted, revealing some internal struggle. After a moment, he gave his head a sharp shake, like a man coming out of a trance. Whatever he'd been about to do or say, he'd obviously changed his mind.

He dropped his hand. "Well, I'd best be going." He took a step backward, then snapped his fingers. "Something I was going to ask you."

"Yes?"

He cocked his head at that same cajoling, irresistible angle the twins used when requesting some special favor they expected Sara to refuse at first. "Would you mind if I left your phone number with my agent, just in case he needs to get hold of me?" He shrugged one broad shoulder. "I haven't bothered installing a telephone at my father's house, since I'll only be there temporarily."

Sara's stomach dropped like a plummeting elevator. "Sure. That's fine." Her facial muscles felt paralyzed.

She must have done a good job of concealing her reaction, though, since Ryder just said, "Thanks. I sure appreciate it." He winked in farewell. "See you later."

Sara's normal practice was to watch him leave by peeking out one of the narrow curtained windows on either side of the front door.

Today, however, she was too agitated to spy on him.

Ryder's mention of his agent had caught her off guard. He'd never seemed too concerned before that his agent might have a hard time contacting him. Why this sudden desire to make himself available for phone calls?

I'll only be there temporarily.

Well, that said it all, didn't it? Obviously, Ryder's sentimental journey back to his hometown was drawing to an end. He'd conquered and laid to rest whatever old demons had lured him back here, and was ready to pick up the reins of his career and move on.

Somewhere along the way, in the whirl of movies and pizzas and sightseeing excursions, Sara had half forgotten that he had a big, exciting career waiting for him out there beyond the narrow horizons of Hideaway Bay.

With an ominous sinking sensation, she realized that in recent days she'd come to count on Ryder's presence, even though deep down inside she knew better. Some foolish, misguided corner of her heart had dared to hope that *this* time, Ryder might stay. . . that *this* time, their relationship might have a chance.

Only *this* time, it wasn't just Sara who was going to get hurt.

Dread descended over her when she considered the twins. How would Ryder's inevitable departure affect Noelle and Nicholas, now that they'd become so fond of him?

Everything important in the children's lives had burned up in that fire six months ago. Everything they'd depended on. Sara had done her best to rebuild their shattered sense of security, of permanence, of faith in the future. She'd tried to teach them how to trust again.

Except that now they were all too eager to place their trust in someone Sara knew couldn't be counted on. Someone to whom commitment meant saying whatever the other person wanted to hear. Someone who'd broken her own heart once, who could very easily break the twins' hearts now.

In the back of her mind, Sara had wondered all along whether Ryder might be getting too close to the twins. But how could she have cut short their budding friendship, once she saw what a positive influence Ryder was on them? He'd magically coaxed Noelle out of her shell of shyness. And Sara couldn't even remember the last time Nicholas had had a nightmare.

Now, it was clear she'd let things go too far.

"How could I have been so blind?" she muttered, sitting down on the staircase with a thud. "How could I have made such an awful mistake?"

It was her duty to protect Nicholas and Noelle, to shield them from any further emotional harm. But she'd let them down, by allowing their friendship with Ryder to continue.

And as a result, her precious niece and nephew were now on a collision course with yet another heart-shattering loss. They were crazy about Ryder. And even though they'd made great strides in their recovery after their parents' deaths, they were still so fragile emotionally.

It would devastate them to lose someone else who'd come to mean so much to them.

No use cautioning the twins not to count on Ryder's continued presence—that his time here was limited and one morning they were going to wake up and discover he'd vanished from their lives for good.

How could Sara's warning have any effect on the twins, when she herself couldn't even follow her own advice?

She'd conveniently managed to forget that Ryder would never be content settling down. She'd deceived herself into hoping there might be the tiniest chance he would stay in Hideaway Bay for good this time.

Worst of all, she'd lowered her emotional defenses and allowed Ryder back into her life again.

Time was running out. Ryder would leave soon. And then Sara would have to pick up the pieces of *three* shattered hearts.

She dropped her head into her hands.

She knew what she had to do now.

Moments later, a tear trickled through her fingers.

"Hey, man! I already got my mom hassling me, my teachers hassling me—I don't need *you* hassling me."

Shane Mathis kicked at a roll of linoleum, flipped a dark curtain of hair from his eyes, and scowled at Ryder.

Ryder leaned back against the kitchen sink, crossed his arms and repressed a grin. Only a seventeen-year-old could produce such an injured, outraged look of persecution.

Shane's sullen slouch, the surly, indignant twist of his mouth, reminded Ryder of himself at that age.

Still, it wouldn't do the kid any good to go easy on him.

"As long as you're working for me," Ryder said calmly, "I expect you either to show up when you say you're going to, or else let me know ahead of time that you won't be here that day."

Shane jammed his hands into the back pockets of his jeans. "Look, I told you, I just forgot, okay? What's the big deal?"

"The big deal is, when you make a commitment to do something, people count on you. And when you let them down, after a while they don't trust you anymore."

Shane snorted. "So what?"

Irritation pricked Ryder. Even when he'd been Shane's age, he'd always kept his word. He'd never treated anyone dishonestly or promised more than he was willing to deliver. And *still* people had regarded him with suspicion, had written him off as untrustworthy and unreliable.

It irked him to watch Shane shrug off a bad reputation as something of no consequence.

"Maybe you don't care now," Ryder told him, trying not to let anger show in his voice. "Maybe you even think it's cool to act irresponsibly and just take off with your buddies whenever you feel like it—never mind your obligations."

Shane's jaw jutted forward. He shifted all his weight to one leg in a belligerent stance.

"But some day, when you're out of school and your mom isn't supporting you anymore, you're going to need a job. And no one's going to hire you if they think you're a screwup, if they know they can't count on you."

Shane scuffed his toe against the unfinished kitchen floor and mumbled something.

Ryder bent forward from the waist. "What's that?"

Shane flung his arms in the air. "I said, I get enough lectures in school, man."

"Maybe you ought to start paying attention for a change."

Ryder felt for the kid. Though he knew Shane would never believe it, Ryder understood what a tough time he was going through. Frustrated by school, fighting with his mother, bored with life in the town he'd grown up in. And as if all that weren't bad enough, his bloodstream was churning with all those teenage hormones.

That awkward transition zone between youth and manhood was an anxious, uncomfortable place to be.

But that didn't mean Shane shouldn't be held accountable for his choices.

Under Ryder's thoughtful scrutiny, Shane's face grew red. "Hey, I don't need all this hassle. And you know what? I don't need this job, either."

"Okay." Ryder pushed himself away from the sink so he could reach in his back pocket for his wallet. He extracted a few bills. "Here's your pay for this week." He held it out. "That squares everything between us, I think."

As it finally dawned on Shane what Ryder meant, his eyes widened. He didn't touch the money. "Look, I didn't mean— I mean, I kinda need— Oh, man." He dragged a hand through his long, floppy hair. "You're firin' me 'cause I missed one day of work?"

Ryder folded the bills and tucked them into Shane's shirt pocket. "First off, I don't have a problem with your missing a day of work now and then. What I have a problem with is when you don't bother letting me know you won't be here."

Shane opened his mouth as if to protest, but Ryder went on before he could speak. "Second, I'm not firing you. You just quit, remember?"

Shane's narrow face took on the expression of a shoplifter caught red-handed. "Geez, I didn't mean I was *quitting!* It was just like, you know..." He swallowed and looked utterly miserable.

Ryder waited.

Shane nervously rocked from side to side. "Um, look, I'm sorry I didn't let you know I wasn't gonna be here yesterday."

"Okay."

Shane swallowed as if he were tasting something bitter. "I screwed up. I shouldn't've done that."

"Okay."

He squinted at Ryder through a dangling curtain of dark hair. "So...can I still keep working for you?"

"That's up to you," Ryder said. "Your choice. But—" he held up a warning finger "—if you decide to stay, I'm gonna hold you to your responsibilities. Next time you're not showing up as scheduled, you tell me ahead of time. Agreed?"

Shane nodded, looking relieved.

"Okay." Ryder hoped he hadn't come on too heavy-handed with the kid. He hated to give him a hard time for just one mistake, but Shane had to learn that his actions had consequences.

Ryder pointed at the roll of linoleum. "How about helping me with this? Ever lay linoleum before?"

Shane shook his head.

"Well, I haven't done it for a while, either. Maybe together we can figure it out."

"Sure." Shane crouched down and immediately started to unroll the linoleum.

"Whoa, wait a sec. First we need to take some measurements. Easier that way."

"Okay." Shane scrambled to his feet again and practically stood at attention.

"Oh, by the way," Ryder said, rooting through his toolbox for the metal tape measure, "you know that painting I had you do upstairs last time?"

"Yeah?" Shane's Adam's apple bobbed up and down. His expression turned wary yet resigned, as if he expected to get chewed out for something, but was accustomed to it.

"I just wanted you to know, you did a great job," Ryder said, noting the surprise, then the pleasure that lit up Shane's eyes. "You've got a real knack for painting. Nice, even strokes, no missed spots, and most impressive of all—" Ryder winked "—you even cleaned up the mess afterward."

Shane shrugged, embarrassed but obviously pleased.

"Here, hold this end of the tape measure." Ryder backed across the floor. "Maybe you could get a job painting, once all the work on this place is done." He jotted down a measurement on a scrap of paper. "I'd be happy to write you a letter of recommendation."

"Hey, thanks." Shane's shoulders expanded out of their characteristic slouch. "Maybe I'll do that."

Pretty ironic, Ryder thought, *me trying to straighten the kid out, pretending to be some kind of role model or father figure.*

He just wished *he'd* had someone who cared enough to make him toe the line when he was Shane's age. His own father's idea of instilling motivation was a sharp clout on the side of the head.

Somehow, Ryder had managed to drag himself out of the hellish quagmire of his upbringing, to overcome the obstacles that fate had strewn in his path.

He was lucky, and he knew it. A lot of kids who got off on the wrong track never managed to find their way back. If Ryder could lend a helping hand to a kid like Shane, provide a little direction and advice to someone as troubled and confused as he'd once been, he was more than glad to do it.

Then he thought about Sara, and the dangerous game he was playing by spending so much time with her and the kids.

A game that in the end could have no winners, only losers.

The last thing Ryder wanted was for Sara and the children to get hurt. It wasn't fair, the way he'd gotten so tangled up in their lives. But he couldn't seem to help himself. The time he spent with the three of them satisfied some mysterious, powerful longing deep inside him, and made him eagerly anticipate his next chance to see them.

Ryder had spent his entire adult life avoiding attachments, unwilling to sacrifice the freedom to move on for the dubious rewards of staying put.

Now, for the first time, he was starting to wonder what he might have missed along the way.

What were these strange, urgent instincts that had begun to tug at him lately? The first, tentative growth of those roots he'd never had the desire to put down?

Or chains...chains that would anchor him permanently to Hideaway Bay, when what he really wanted was to sail free and unfettered as the wind...

Ryder let his automatic measuring tape rewind with an impatient *snap!*

Maybe Shane wasn't the *only* one who needed some sense drilled into him.

Chapter Eight

Ryder leaned back in his chair, crossed his ankles on the front porch railing and took a long, thirst-quenching swallow of beer.

It wasn't much of a porch, really, not like the spacious, roofed porch at Sara's house. What he ought to do was build a nice redwood deck in the backyard. Get some patio furniture, one of those fancy gas-powered barbecue grills, and—

Wait a second.

Ryder dropped his feet to the ground with a thud. All he'd intended to do was fix this place up so it was habitable, make whatever repairs were necessary before putting it up for sale. And that was still all he planned to do.

Wasn't it?

He took a swallow of beer, observing how the setting sun had painted the horizon with vibrant strokes of purple, orange and crimson. Against this radiant background, the cypress trees lining the bluff above the harbor stood out like black lace scrimshaw. An osprey circled lazily above the water, spotted a fish, and abruptly plummeted like an arrow, nose-diving toward its prey.

Ryder wondered where he'd ever gotten the idea there was no beauty to be found in his hometown.

He shifted forward in his chair so he could massage the sore muscles that sanding hardwood floors had strained in his lower back. With an exaggerated groan, he got to his feet. Might as well go see what he could scrounge up for dinner.

A pair of headlights came around the corner. Ryder was about to push open the front door, when the car drew close enough for him to recognize it in the fading light.

All at once, he forgot his complaining muscles, his rumbling stomach.

Sara stepped out of the car. Ryder hadn't seen her for several days, and was caught off guard by the surge of pleasure that poured through him. Once again, Sara had come to *him,* rather than the other way around.

Progress? Maybe. But toward what goal, he wasn't certain.

She wasn't exactly rushing into his arms. As she came up the front pathway, in fact, she strongly resembled a woman being forced to walk the plank at sword point.

Ryder resisted the sudden urge to haul her into his embrace and ply her with long, hot kisses and seductive caresses. He could tell being swept off her feet was the last thing on Sara's mind.

"Well, hello," he said. "This is a pleasant surprise."

"I was on my way over to pick up the twins at Tess's, and I just thought I'd...stop by."

The last fading rays of sunset scattered reddish gold glints through Sara's hair. She looked as if she'd just come from a late-afternoon meeting, wearing a stylishly tailored burgundy dress that made her look every inch the successful businesswoman. Despite the cream-colored blazer she wore over it, she shivered.

Or maybe it wasn't the cool evening air that was making her shiver.

"Come on inside," Ryder said. "I've got beer in the fridge. Would you like one? Or a soda, maybe?"

"No, thanks," Sara replied, stepping quickly past him into the house. "I can only stay a minute."

Ryder shut the door behind them. "I could give you an abbreviated version of the grand tour—show you how the place is coming along."

"No, that's all right," she said, hugging her elbows across her rib cage. "That's, um, not why I came."

Ryder folded his arms as dread settled in his chest. She had a reason for coming here, all right. And he had a feeling he wasn't going to like it one bit.

"Come on, Sara. Spit it out. You look about as comfortable as I used to feel, sitting in your parents' front parlor."

She gave a nervous little laugh, along with a dismissive flip of her hand. "That hardly ever happened, and you know it."

"Yeah, every time your father came home from work and found me waiting out front for you. He'd drag me inside and give me the third degree, while your mother wrung her hands and brought me something to drink and tried to pretend she didn't mind me sitting there on her antique sofa."

Sara's eyes grew soft and regretful. "They were just doing what they thought was best for me. Trying to protect me."

"Yeah." Even though Sara's parents had never been anything but perfectly polite toward Ryder, they hadn't been able to conceal their disapproval, their worry, their distaste. And after all these years, it still hurt.

Sara took a deep breath. "Ryder...I came here to talk to you about Noelle and Nicholas."

"They're all right, aren't they?"

"Yes. I mean, no. I mean—"

Ryder's apprehension increased. It wasn't like Sara to sound so unsure of herself.

Then, she squared her shoulders, hoisted her chin and met his gaze head-on. All softness, all regret was gone from her eyes. "I want you to stay away from the twins from now on," she said.

Sara forced herself to watch as a storm of turbulent emotion shimmered on the flat planes of Ryder's face, then vanished. He lowered his eyelids a fraction of an inch, as if trying to draw a shade over whatever was going on inside him.

She would have felt a whole lot better if he'd exploded at her.

Instead, he calmly took a broom and began to sweep up some of the sawdust littering the unfinished living room floor. "Why do you want to keep me away from the twins all of a sudden?" he asked in the same tone of voice he might have used to inquire about the weather outside.

"It—it's what I think is best for them, Ryder." Sara's fingernails dug into her palms. She knew perfectly well what kind of painful emotional button she was pushing. While Ryder was growing up, all the so-called respectable people in town had warned their children away from him. "I—I shouldn't have let things go this far, I should have spoken up earlier. If only I'd known how—"

Her throat clenched up tight as a fist. She swallowed. Dear heaven, this was even harder than she'd feared it would be! "Please," she said miserably, hating the fact that she had to hurt him this way. Hurt *all* of them this way. "Try to understand."

"Maybe if you explained it to me." Ryder's knuckles were bone white as he swept. The broom made a steady, controlled, whisking sound against the floor.

Sara had spent days refining her explanations, working out all the logical points she wanted to make. Now, faced with the unhappiness Ryder was trying to conceal, the unhappiness she'd caused him, all her carefully reasoned arguments went flying out the window.

"I just don't want them to get too attached to you, that's all," she blurted out.

Sweep, sweep, sweep.

"I mean, I realize it's too late already. Nicholas tries to imitate everything you do, and Noelle gazes up at you like you're a combination superhero and Prince Charming."

"Oh, come on." Ryder bent down to whisk the pile of sweepings into a dustpan. "Aren't you exaggerating a little?" But he looked pleased.

"Ryder, they're both crazy about you," Sara said helplessly.

He emptied the dustpan into a brown paper sack. "I— To tell you the truth, Sara, I'm kinda fond of them, too." He cleared his throat, sounding embarrassed.

"I *know* you are. But that isn't the point."

"No? Then what exactly *is* the point?"

Sara grew even more flustered. She'd never been able to concentrate while Ryder was scrutinizing her with those thoughtful, blue laser eyes. "It's just that— The twins are extremely vulnerable right now. They've suffered so much tragedy, so much loss, and I—I just can't sit still and watch while they set themselves up for more sorrow."

Ryder ran his thumbnail up and down the window frame, as if he were a building inspector checking for splinters. "You think I'm going to wind up hurting them, is that it?"

"Yes." Sara raked a hand through her hair, casting about for a way to soften the harshness of that one word. "They're just now learning to trust again, Ryder. To allow themselves to depend on people, after losing the two people in the world they depended on most."

Ryder dragged a hand over his face and shook his head in sympathy. "Poor kids. I can't begin to imagine the horror they've gone through."

"No." Sara's throat cinched tight in a sudden spasm. She felt as if she were strangling on her own words. "And that's why I can't—why I *won't*—allow Nicholas and Noelle to grow any more dependent on you than they already have. I can't stand by and watch them suffer yet another painful loss."

Ryder's eyes narrowed, and his mouth turned grim. "You think I'll run out on them, the way I ran out on you." He stepped toward her. "That's what this is really all about, isn't it, Sara?"

A flicker of resentment ignited inside her. "Let's just say I know from previous experience that other people's feelings are of no concern to you, once you decide it's time to pick up and leave."

A muscle tightened in his jaw. "That isn't true."

"Don't try to rewrite history, Ryder. I was there, remember?"

"Remember? Oh, I remember, all right. For ten long years, I haven't been able to *stop* remembering."

Before Sara could react, Ryder's hands were on her shoulders, pulling her close. "I remember how you were the only good thing in my life. I remember what it felt like to touch you. To kiss you." His gaze dropped to her mouth. "To make love to you."

He gently stroked her hair as he continued. His voice, his eyes, his touch mesmerized her. "During all those years, I never stopped thinking about you, Sara." He tucked her head under his chin, and his breath stirred wisps of hair at her temples. "God knows, I tried," he whispered.

Sara felt herself sinking into the familiar, seductive lure of his embrace. She lifted her hands hesitantly, finally letting them settle against his broad, strong back. How could something that felt so good, so right, be so completely wrong?

But it wasn't just her own happiness at risk anymore. As soon as Sara remembered the twins, her spine stiffened along with her resolve. For the children's sake, if not her own, she couldn't allow Ryder to reel her in like a fisherman making short work of some poor, defenseless salmon.

She pushed him away. "How touching," she said, retreating behind a shield of sarcasm. "And were you also thinking about me the day you left town without even telling me goodbye?"

Cobalt sparks glittered in his eyes. "I *was* thinking about you," he said. "Although not in the sense you mean."

Sara knew it was pointless—dangerous, even, to prolong this conversation. But ten years' worth of unspoken accusations seemed determined to force their way out of her mouth. "You were thinking of *yourself,* Ryder. How you didn't want to get trapped here. Trapped by your past." Her voice wavered slightly. "Trapped by *me.*"

Ryder would never forgive himself for the pain that s haunted Sara's eyes, like a visual echo of her long-ago guish. He should have spoken to her before he left to explained the reasons why he had to go.

"It wasn't just myself I was concerned about," he t her now, years too late. "I was worried that, if I did leave, *you'd* become trapped here, too."

A ripple of confusion crossed her face. "What on ea are you talking about?"

Ryder captured her hand. It felt limp and ice-c against his skin. "You were so young. Your whole life in front of you. With your brains and talent and fam background, you had a brilliant future ahead of you." squeezed her fingers for emphasis. "You had a chance really *be* somebody, Sara." Ryder's shoulders sagge little as he recalled his own sense of inadequacy. "I did want to ruin it for you."

Sara blinked. "I still don't have the foggiest idea w you're talking about."

"That night, remember? Our last night together?"

She crimped her lips into an impatient line. "Do I member the first and only time we made love, Ryder? vaguely." Sarcasm etched her tone like acid. "Somewh by the beach, wasn't it? Out at Beacon Point?" pressed a pensive fingertip to her chin and frowned at ceiling. "Or am I thinking of someone else?"

Though he knew she was only putting on an act, the i of Sara making love with someone else set jealousy s mering in Ryder's blood. "I'm talking about what you s afterward," he explained with a thin veneer of com sure.

"Hmm." She tilted her head to one side and feig concentration. "What did I say…'Thank you'? Or, 'I really enjoyed myself'?"

Ryder gnashed his teeth. Though he understood that Sara was only mocking their lovemaking because she was hurt, his gut reaction was that she was blaspheming something sacred.

He released her hand. "You started talking about the future. Our future."

"Oops!" She covered her mouth and hunched her shoulders in a sheepish gesture. "Guess that was a no-no, huh? Nothing guaranteed to scare a guy off like a little postcoital chitchat about commitment, is there?"

And this was something else Ryder would never forgive himself for—turning his sweet, trusting Sara into such a cynic.

He plowed doggedly ahead. "You started talking about not going away to college in the fall. About staying in Hideaway Bay to be with me."

"Did I?" Now he saw genuine bewilderment on her face. "I suppose I may have. So what?"

"Sara, don't you see?" How was it possible for two people to have such completely different interpretations of the same event? "I couldn't let you give up college for me. It wouldn't have been fair." Ryder struggled for the words that would make her understand. "How could I tie you down, when it was your chance to soar in life?"

Sara looked as stunned, as offended as if he'd slapped her. "So you decided to do what *you* thought best for me, and never mind how *I* felt about it?"

Frustration churned inside him. "You were barely out of high school. Settling down with me might have seemed like a wonderful romantic adventure at the time, but eventually, you would have grown to hate me."

"Don't presume to tell me what I would or would not have done, Ryder." Sparks flashed from her eyes. "On the basis of one little comment, you decide I'm about to throw my life away? That poor little Sara is too dumb and naive to make her own decisions, so you have to make them for her?''

''I never thought you were dumb and naive,'' Ryder protested. ''But I could see the stars in your eyes.''

''Oh, please.''

''No, listen to me.'' Ryder ran a finger beneath his collar. He was starting to feel the uneasy panic of a man fighting for his life. ''Look, we both could have stayed in Hideaway Bay, gotten married, had a couple of kids. But the timing was all wrong. We were barely more than kids ourselves!''

''For heaven's sake, you make it sound like I begged you to marry me!'' Sara retorted indignantly. ''I never even brought up the subject.''

''Maybe not, but can you deny that we'd have eventually wound up together, if I hadn't left town?''

Her lips welded together in a tight, quivering seam. ''Would that have been so terrible?'' she finally burst out.

Ryder dragged his hands through his hair. ''Sara, we had no money, no education, no prospects. Where would we have lived—here? In the dilapidated dump I inherited from my father?''

Sara's chin came up a notch. ''My parents would have helped us out.''

''Your parents would probably have disowned you if you'd married a no-account like me.'' Ryder's brows dipped together. ''Besides, I would never have agreed to take any handouts from them. A man's got to be able to support his own wife, before he's got any business getting married.''

Sara gave a scornful wave of her hand. ''I wasn't some kind of hothouse flower. I could have supported myself.''

"Working some minimum wage job? And what about when babies started coming along?"

Though she had no comeback for that, she continued to glare at him, too stubborn to admit he had a point.

Ryder sighed. "Sara, we'd both have cheated ourselves if we hadn't gone out into the world and reached for something more."

She fixed him with a steady, skeptical gaze, like a prosecutor confronting a defendant on the witness stand. "You had every right to leave town if that's what you wanted," she informed him coolly. "But don't try to turn running out on me into some kind of noble gesture. It was a cowardly, sneaky thing to do." Her voice wobbled slightly. "You didn't even have the guts to say goodbye to my face."

Ryder brought his hand up to touch her cheek. "I knew if I saw you again," he said gently, "if I had to tell you goodbye, I could never bring myself to leave."

Sara jerked away from him. "So you decided it would be preferable to shatter my faith in you? To torture me with questions about why you'd left, about what I'd said or done wrong to drive you away?"

"That was never my intent." The bitter edge to her voice slashed Ryder with a blade of guilt. "I did what I thought was best," he said, knowing it was true, yet wondering why that didn't seem enough now.

"Yes, well, now *I* have to do what *I* think is best. For the twins. For me. For all of us."

Sara's temples throbbed. She backed toward the door, nearly tripping over a discarded piece of lumber. All at once the old house seemed oppressive, as if walls, ceiling and floor were slowly collapsing toward her. Old memories, old hurts assailed her from all sides.

She had to get out of here.

But not before she accomplished what she'd come for.

"Stay away from Noelle and Nicholas, Ryder. I won't let you hurt them." She struggled to breathe through the heavy weight of the past, which had settled on her chest like an anvil. "And while you're at it, stay away from *me*, too."

Ryder's eyes were bleak with sorrow and regret. "The last thing on earth I want is to hurt you or the twins, Sara." His voice sounded hoarse, as if the words were being ripped from his throat. "For God's sake, I hope you believe me."

Sara's hands were shaking. "Believe you? How can I do that, Ryder?" She made a choked sound that was half laugh, half sob. "I stopped believing in you long ago."

With that, she fled through the front door, stumbling down the steps, nearly tripping over the curb in her haste to reach the sanctuary of her car. She slammed the door and locked it as if a menacing pursuer were hot on her heels.

Ryder didn't come after her.

Maybe after this, she'd really, truly seen the last of him. Maybe now he was finally out of her life for good.

Exactly what she wanted, right?

So why did tears smear her vision as she drove away from Ryder's house for what was probably the very last time?

Chapter Nine

"Geez, you can really be a dope sometimes, you know that?" Tess Carpenter flipped a hamburger over on the grill and threw her best friend a disgusted look.

Sara's arm jerked, nearly knocking over the root beer can which rested on the picnic table next to her elbow. It had been almost a week since she'd seen Ryder and talking about him still made her jittery. "Thanks a lot," she said indignantly, trying to mask her hurt feelings. "I knew I could count on your support."

Tess made an elaborate shrug. "Hey, what are friends for? To set you straight when you've done something *reeeally* stupid."

Sara drummed her nails on the plastic blue-and-white checked tablecloth. "I fail to see how you can call trying to protect the twins *stupid.*"

Automatically, she glanced toward the far end of the Carpenters' backyard, where the twins and the two Carpenter kids were taking turns swinging on an old tire t to the limb of a shady oak tree. The Carpenters' dog frisky boxer named Max, was making an eager effort participate.

"You're not trying to protect the twins," Tess sa "You're trying to protect yourself." She pointed her me spatula at Sara like an accusing finger.

"Protect *myself?* From what?" Sara demanded sco fully. "Ryder? He can't hurt me. I got him out of my s tem a long time ago."

"Liar."

"I am not."

"Are so."

"Am not."

"Are so."

They glared at each other, chins set stubbornly, har clamped on hips, for about five seconds before they bu into giggles.

"Maybe you're right," Sara admitted when they fina stopped laughing at themselves. "I guess Ryder can still under my skin a little. But that's *not* why I told him to s away from Nicholas and Noelle."

Tess flung out her arms as if she were throwing hers on the mercy of the court. "For Pete's sake, give the g a break, would you? Stop treating him like a criminal.'

Sara squinted at her suspiciously. "What are you, pr ident of the Ryder Sloan Fan Club?" She cocked her he and began to tick off direct quotes on her fingers. ' creep, a coward, a no-good louse I was better off witho Isn't that what you once called him?"

Tess groaned. "Sara, that was ten years ago. Go grief."

"And during the few short *weeks* he's been back in town, you've completely revised your opinion of him, is that it?"

Tess peeked under a burger to check its progress. "Hey, all I know is what I see. And since Ryder's come back, he's tried to set things straight with you, gotten to be buddies with the twins, and in general acted like a pretty decent guy."

Tess plopped herself down onto the picnic bench next to Sara. "Seems to me you're being too hard on Ryder. Maybe you're trying to get even with him for the way he once hurt you. Subconciously, of course," she hastened to add at Sara's expression of outrage.

Sara sat up stiffly. "I told you, I'm only trying to shield the twins from any further unhappiness. I don't want them getting any more attached to Ryder than they already are. He's bound to get bored here soon, and when he leaves town, it'll be devastating for them."

Tess slapped her palm against the table. "What are you going to do, require a lifetime commitment to stay in Hideaway Bay from anyone who wants to befriend Noelle and Nicholas?"

Sara flicked a stray lock of hair from her eyes. "Don't be ridiculous."

"*You're* the one who's being unreasonable." Tess gazed past Sara's shoulder toward where the kids were playing, and her animated features grew soft with tenderness and sympathy. "I know the twins have been through a terrible tragedy, Sara, and I know you're doing your level best to protect them from any future harm."

Tears prickled the back of Sara's throat. "I can't bear for them to get hurt again."

Tess hugged her. When she drew back, her own eyes were glistening. "Honey, don't you see? The best thing you can do for those kids is to let them lead normal lives. And, unfortunately, part of normal life is getting hurt by people from time to time."

Sara jumped to her feet and began to distribute paper plates, dealing them around the table like a champion poker player. "It's just that I know for certain Ryder isn't going to stick around—"

"You don't know any such thing." Tess followed in Sara's wake, passing out napkins and plastic silverware. "For all you know, Ryder's back for good this time."

I'll only be there temporarily, he'd said, referring to his father's house.

Sara forced a skeptical laugh. "Come on, get real," she scolded Tess. "Ryder? He's got a filmmaking career now, and from all the signs a very successful one. The clothes he wears, that fancy watch, the expensive car he drives..." Sara shook her head. "Once his agent calls to offer him some juicy new project, that'll be it. He's not about to stay put out here in the boondocks." She cupped a hand behind her ear and pretended to listen. "Hollywood beckons."

Tess ripped open a package of hamburger buns. "Look, don't you think this business of fixing up his dad's house is just a ruse? He could have *hired* someone to make repairs and put it on the market. The fact that he showed up in person means he must have some other reason for coming back here, don't you think?"

Sara growled with exasperation. "I suppose you have some romantic delusion that Ryder's come back to sweep me off my feet, pledge his undying love and swear he made a terrible mistake by running out on me."

"Sure, why not?" Tess grinned at her. "Seems as likely a reason as any for him to come back."

"You're dreaming."

"And you're not being fair to Ryder."

"I told you, I have to consider the—" Sara cut short their debate when Tess's husband, Dan, emerged from the back door carrying a big ceramic bowl draped with a cloth napkin.

He crossed the patio, set the bowl on the table and wiped his hands on the front of his checkered barbecue apron. Then he whisked off the napkin with a flourish. "Voilà!" he said. "Another fabulous batch of Dan Carpenter's world-famous potato salad."

Tess poked her finger into it and licked the results critically. "Mmm. Little too much onion, don't you think, dear?"

Dan clapped his hand over his heart and looked wounded. "I'm a pharmacist, remember? I always measure in the exact amount of everything." He frowned. "Let me taste that."

Tess swatted his finger away. "I'm sure you did quite enough tasting while you were mixing it up. Besides, I was just teasing. The potato salad's delicious."

Dan was a big, friendly man with thinning brown hair and a waistline that was just starting to push over his belt a little. Sara had often wondered how anyone with such large hands could possibly perform the delicate measurements required of his profession.

"Teasing?" he accused his wife in mock horror. "You dare to tease about my potato salad?" Now he narrowed his eyes, bared his teeth and looked ferocious. "*Nobody* teases me about my potato salad."

"Dan . . ." Tess began to retreat around the table.

He raised his hands like grizzly bear paws and began to stalk her.

Tess grabbed the spatula and held it out in front of her like a sword. "I'm prepared to use this, I swear!"

With a roar, Dan lunged at his wife, bundled her into his arms and growled into her neck while Tess squealed, "Stop! That tickles!"

Four kids and a dog came racing across the backyard to see what all the commotion was about.

"Mom, what's Dad *doing* to you?" eight-year-old Jenny cried.

Max whimpered, ran in circles, sniffed the ground at Tess's feet.

Tess, laughing so hard she couldn't speak, finally managed to shove Dan away. Max began to bark at him. Tess rubbed her neck and peered accusingly at her husband. "Good heavens, didn't you shave this morning? I feel like I've been attacked with sandpaper."

"That'll teach you to mock my potato salad." He winked at his son, Alex, who grinned back. "Here, my sweet, let me kiss it and make it better." He planted a loud, juicy smack on Tess's cheek.

"Oh, stop it," she said. But she was beaming.

And that was another thing Sara liked about Dan Carpenter. He was the only person in the world who could make Tess blush.

The sound of a throat being cleared immediately caught the entire group's attention. Everyone turned toward the redwood gate at the side of the house.

Ryder stood there, his hand resting on top of the open gate, looking embarrassed. "Er, I knocked at the front door, but no one answered," he said. "Hope I'm not interrupting anything."

Everyone seemed to spring into action at once—everyone except Sara, who stood rooted to the brick patio like one of Tess's potted plants. Her heart hammered against her ribs, her skin felt alternately as hot as the barbecue coals and as cold as the ice in the drinks cooler.

Ryder. Had she really believed she might never lay eyes on him again?

Had she really believed that's what she wanted?

"Ryder!" The twins' glad cry of welcome was nearly drowned out by Max's excited barking as he galloped across the yard to check out the newcomer.

"Well, well, you must be the famous Ryder Sloan." Dan was already approaching Ryder with his hand extended.

Tess fluffed up her hair and straightened her T-shirt. As she skirted around the picnic table past Sara, Sara's hand clamped down on her wrist like a shackle. "You invited him," she said in a voice as cold as metal.

Tess twirled one of her curls around a finger and tried not to appear guilty. She failed. "Well, um . . ."

"All the time we've been sitting here talking about him, you knew he was going to show up any minute, didn't you?"

Tess gulped. "Well, he did say he'd *try* to stop by. . . ."

Sara freed her prisoner. "Tess, how could you? After I explained how I wanted to keep him away from the twins, and then you go and invite him to dinner!"

Tess shrugged. "That was before I heard he was persona non grata."

Sara's gaze traveled across the yard. All four kids were clustered around Ryder, competing for his attention while he chatted with Dan. Even Max was slobbering all over Ryder's hand as he scratched under the dog's chin. Terrific.

Sara sighed. "You could have warned me before he got here."

Tess pursed her lips and made a scornful noise. "Why? So you could ruin a perfectly nice barbecue by hustling the twins out of here? No way. Dan would never forgive the insult to his potato salad."

Now Noelle and Jenny each had Ryder by the hand and were dragging him toward the patio. Sara's stomach fluttered in nervous anticipation.

"Hey, Ryder, wanna play some basketball with me and my dad?" Alex asked, skipping backward. "We just put up a hoop last week."

"He's gonna push us on the swing," Nicholas informed the older boy.

Alex made a face. "Aw, swings are for sissies."

Nicholas's mouth fell open. He was obviously aghast at this information, coming as it did from someone he admired and looked up to.

Alex, bless his heart, caught his mistake right away. "I guess they're not really for sissies. But let's play basketball instead, okay?"

Dan settled the argument by saying, "Fellas, I think it's about time to eat. We'll have to save the fun and games for later."

Sara leaned over and spoke out of the side of her mouth. "How is it your kids appear to be such pals with Ryder?"

"Oh, didn't I mention it?" Tess quickly busied herself sliding hamburgers onto buns with the expertise of a short-order cook. "We ran into him at the park Thursday afternoon."

"Gosh, no, you didn't mention it," Sara said sarcastically. "Along with a few other things."

"Do Noelle and Nicholas like ketchup on their burgers?"

"Hmm? Oh. Noelle yes, Nicholas no." Sara's forehead crinkled. "What on earth would Ryder be doing at the park?"

"Well, actually, he was driving by on the way from the hardware store, and I waved at him."

"Flagged him down, you mean."

"Whatever. Anyway, he tossed a football around with Alex for a while, and showed Jenny how to do a backward flip off the jungle gym."

"No wonder you're such a big fan of him all of a sudden." Sara's heart was thudding so hard, it was difficult to breathe. Ryder and his entourage were almost here.

"Hey, I figure anyone who's so good with kids can't be all bad," Tess said, setting the plate of burgers on the table. "Something maybe *you* oughta keep in mind. Ryder! How nice you could make it!"

"Hello, Tess. Sara." He nodded somberly in Sara's direction, their eyes meeting across the picnic table, over the heads of four bouncing children and one cavorting boxer.

She nodded back, unsmiling, her nerves vibrating like guitar strings. Had Ryder himself conspired in this "accidental" encounter as an excuse to see her and the twins again?

His black hair was shiny with moisture, curling over the collar of his red polo shirt as if he'd just stepped out of the shower. He must have been working on the house all day.

Sara hadn't seen him in nearly a week, and noticed that he looked thinner, as if he hadn't wasted much time eating meals lately. His eyes were a deep, incandescent blue in contrast to the shadows beneath them. Didn't look as if he'd wasted too much time sleeping lately, either.

"Here. I'll let you add the fixings to your own hamburger." Tess thrust mustard, ketchup and a dish of sliced tomatoes and onions into Ryder's hands. "Kids, it's chow time! Everyone up to the table. No, not you, Max."

"Care for a beer, Ryder?" Dan said, raising his eyebrows in question.

"Sure. Thanks."

"I wanna sit next to Ryder!"

"Me, too!"

When the seating arrangements were finally worked out to everyone's satisfaction, Sara found herself sitting at the far end of the table from Ryder, on the opposite side. But her awareness of his presence was so strong, the unspoken bond between them so powerful even after all these years, they might as well have been locked in an intimate embrace.

Though she did her best to ignore him, his every word and gesture registered on her internal radar screen. She noticed he took two scoops of potato salad. She noticed every time he lifted the can of beer to his lips. She noticed whenever he teased the children and made them laugh.

And she knew with instinctive, unerring certainty that Ryder noticed everything *she* did, too.

Tess's mischievous eyes darted back and forth between them as if she were a spectator at Wimbledon. "So tell us, Ryder," she said, crunching off the end of a carrot stick, "how did you ever get to be a filmmaker? I never noticed you running around with a home movie camera while we were growing up."

Sara aimed a kick at Tess's ankle. In light of Ryder's poverty-stricken upbringing, she considered that remark pretty tacky. Home movie camera, indeed!

Tess neatly dodged the kick and smiled expectantly at Ryder, though Sara knew that smile was really meant for her.

Ryder didn't seem to take offense. No doubt he'd learned it was pointless around Tess. "Well, strangely enough, it happened in Afghanistan," he said. "I was working with an international relief group during the war, when our encampment came under attack."

Tess propped her chin on her fist and regarded him with rapt fascination. "Oh, my heavens! It must have been terrifying."

"Afghanistan?" It took Sara a few seconds to realize that incredulous question had come out of her own mouth. During all the time Ryder had spent with her and the twins, she'd deliberately *not* asked any questions about the period after he'd left town. Maybe she'd been trying to prove that she hadn't spent all those years wondering about where he'd gone and what he was doing.

But this tantalizing glimpse of Ryder's past was so astonishing, so unlikely, Sara couldn't resist pursuing more details. "What on earth were you doing in Afghanistan? Is that where you went when you—er, when you moved away from Hideaway Bay?"

"First I headed for San Francisco." Though Ryder appeared to be addressing the group at large, Sara knew his story was really aimed at her.

Her face burned, and her hand shook a little as she pushed some potato salad around her plate with a plastic fork. She wasn't sure if she was ready to hear all this.

Ryder glanced around at the kids and said carefully, "When I was in San Francisco, I got into a little, er, trouble, with some gentlemen who were, uh, being rather too persistent in their attentions toward a lady."

Translation, Sara thought, *he got into a brawl with some guys hassling a woman in a bar.*

Typical Ryder. Always rushing to the defense of the underdog. Even when *he* was the underdog.

"Exactly how many of these gentlemen were there?" Dan asked, cocking one wry eyebrow.

"Uh, four, as I recall." Ryder cleared his throat sheepishly. "Anyway, while I was getting stitched up in the emergency room, the doc happened to mention he was leaving the next week to go work with this medical relief group in Afghanistan."

Ryder took a swallow of beer, then shrugged. "Sounded like as good a place as any for me to head next. So I tagged along, made myself useful repairing equipment, building shelters, that sort of thing."

Tess made an impatient rolling motion with her hand. "So what happened after you were attacked?"

"Oh. Well, there were some journalists there, including a team from the BBC. When the cameraman got wounded, the reporter lobbed the camera at me and asked if I knew how to use it." Ryder scratched his head, bemused. "I figured I didn't know until I tried, and even now I can't remember exactly how I did it. It's all a blur. But I guess I got some pretty good footage, and it got lots of airplay in Britain. Afterward, the BBC hired me on as a cameraman."

"And from there, you went on to documentary filmmaking," Tess prompted.

"Yup." Ryder hoisted one shoulder. "Just sort of worked my way up, I guess."

"Tess tells me you've been very successful," Dan said, sneaking another spoonful of potato salad.

Ryder sent her a sideways grin. "Tess exaggerates."

"*My* wife? Naw, no way." Dan nudged her in the ribs.

Tess pretended to get all huffy. "Now, wait just a second. Ryder, you told me in the park the other day that you've won all kinds of awards in Europe."

"A few," he conceded.

"And you've made lots of money."

Sara attempted to kick her in the ankle again, and missed.

"I've done okay."

Sara could see that, despite the self-confidence Ryder had gained over the years, he was still uncomfortable accepting praise or crowing about his own achievements.

Part of her wished Tess would shut up. But, now that she'd tasted a little sip of information about Ryder's life outside Hideaway Bay, Sara found herself parched with thirst for more.

Tess wasn't letting up. "And some big-time American producers have shown interest in your work, right?"

Ryder kneaded the nape of his neck. "There've been some nibbles."

"Wow! That's fantastic." Tess widened her eyes and chewed her lower lip. "So, how much longer until you're off to start your next film?"

Instinctively, Sara's glance sped down the table to meet Ryder's eyes. Every cell in her body tensed, and her heart seemed to stop beating.

A muscle shifted in Ryder's jaw, betraying his discomfort. But he kept his eyes focused straight at Sara. "I don't really have a definite timetable yet," he replied slowly.

Sara lowered her gaze and let out her breath, feeling as deflated as a limp balloon. No matter how hard she fought against it, that tiny, foolish fragment of hope persisted that Ryder might someday declare his intention to stay here for good.

His vague, noncommittal answer settled heavily in the pit of her stomach, like her half-eaten hamburger.

"Well, I certainly hope you won't forget about all your friends back in Hideaway Bay after you leave," Tess said meaningfully. "Isn't that right, Sara?"

This time, Sara didn't even bother trying to kick her.

Chapter Ten

The streets of Hideaway Bay were nearly deserted as Ryder strode along them, even though it was only nine-thirty on a Saturday night. Most folks looking for excitement would have driven over to Eureka, where there were restaurants and movie theaters and places to go dancing.

His hometown's lack of anything remotely resembling nightlife had driven Ryder crazy when he was a teenager. Now, though, he found the dark, quiet streets strangely peaceful.

The autumn night held a nip in the air, a warning that winter was on its way despite the unseasonably warm weather they'd been having lately. Ryder filled his lungs with the same mingled tang of salt and fish and fresh-cut lumber he so strongly associated with his growing-up years. Even though the last lumber mill in Hideaway Bay had closed down when he was a kid, when the wind was blowing from the right direction, you could still catch a whiff from the mill in Eureka.

How he'd detested this particular combination of smells when he was growing up! To Ryder, it had seemed to symbolize everything he wanted to escape, swirling around him, taunting him with constant reminders of his destiny—to be trapped in this town forever.

But now he found the unique, fragrant mixture somehow reassuring and familiar. Now it just smelled like . . . home.

He cut across the vacant lot on the corner of Fourth Street and Harbor Avenue, following the same route he'd taken so many times before. The route to Sara's house.

And, like all those other times, his chest once again expanded with that queer, tingling pressure the moment he set foot on the block where she lived.

He wanted to sprint the last part of the way because he couldn't wait to see her.

He wanted to slow his steps to a crawl, to make this final leg of the journey last as long as he could, because the anticipation was so enjoyable.

Even though Sara might very well slam the door in his face the moment she saw him.

Ryder knocked softly, assuming the twins were asleep. He stuffed his hands into the pockets of his leather jacket and glanced around the neighborhood while he waited.

Out in the night, an owl hooted somewhere. A horn honked down on Main Street. The sea breeze whispered through the tall cedar tree in the front yard.

Ryder removed a hand from his pocket and was preparing to knock again, when the porch light snapped on and the door cracked open.

"I'll only stay for a moment," he said quickly. "But I need to explain something."

A sigh drifted out. "Come in, then." Sara sounded resigned as she opened the door wider.

Ryder stepped into the entry hall and closed the door behind him with a soft *click.* "I waited till I figured Noelle and Nicholas were asleep," he said. "So they wouldn't know I was here."

Sara nodded. "Thank you." Her arms were folded across the front of her sweater like a barricade.

Ryder paused, wondering if she would invite him into the living room to sit down. Apparently, however, her hospitality had reached its limits as far as he was concerned.

"I'm sorry to drop by so late," he began, "but I had to come see you—to tell you—to explain that I didn't know you and the twins were going to be at Tess's this afternoon."

"No?" Sara tilted her head and rubbed her temple with her fingertips, as if trying to soothe away a migraine.

"No. I...ran into Tess in the park a couple days ago, and she invited me to the barbecue, and I— Well, I guess I was lonely. I wanted some company. Her two kids are nice, and I just thought, why not?"

Sara nibbled her lower lip. "You hardly have to apologize for accepting a social invitation, Ryder." She moved to the hall tree and began to straighten the jackets hanging there.

"Well, I just didn't want you to think I'd deliberately ignored your wishes. About staying away from the twins, I mean."

Sara's back was to him, so Ryder couldn't see her face or read her eyes. The only clue to her feelings was her silence and the tense hunch of her shoulders.

"I...guess I'd better be going." Ryder's spirits slumped a little as he reached for the doorknob. Not that he'd expected to change anything by coming here, but Sara's distant attitude was clear proof she wasn't about to relent and allow him back into their lives.

Then, as he opened the door, Sara said, "I've been thinking about what you told me the other day."

Ryder closed the door and turned around. "What do you mean?" he asked cautiously.

She plucked at the sleeve of Noelle's blue jacket, avoiding his eyes. "The reasons why you left town. Why you left me behind."

"Oh." He cleared his throat.

"I decided that...maybe some of what you said was true." Her voice was so faint, Ryder had to strain to hear. Obviously, this wasn't easy for her.

"We *were* awfully young," she went on, examining the jackets closely, as if searching for lint. "Maybe it *is* for the best that we both got to live our own lives."

Relief flowed through Ryder. "Sara." He turned her around and drew her into his arms. "Sweetheart, I'm so sorry things couldn't have worked out differently..."

And he *was* sorry—not for that long-ago decision, but for the fact that he'd hurt her. For the fact that he'd destroyed her trust along with any possibility of ever rebuilding the magical relationship they'd once shared.

Deep inside, Ryder knew it was just as well. This way, there was no risk of hurting Sara again if he left Hideaway Bay.

When he left, he corrected himself.

Sara let her forehead drop against Ryder's chest. No matter how hard she tried to keep him at an emotional distance, somehow she always wound up back here in his arms.

"I'm still mad at you, though," she said, her voice muffled against the front of his shirt. "For the way you left without saying goodbye."

Ryder eased her back so he could see her face. "That was wrong of me. Cowardly. Completely unforgivable." A lock of black hair fell across his forehead, making him look more like the rebellious youth Sara had once fallen in love with.

"Sneaky," she agreed slowly. "Despicable. Dishonest."

Ryder's eyes were focused somewhere deep inside hers. "I hope you'll give me a chance to make it up to you," he said. His eyes were as blue as the sea, as mesmerizing as the horizon, lulling Sara like ocean waves....

She inhaled sharply, suddenly short of oxygen. "I, um, think one of the twins is calling me."

"I didn't hear anything."

She swallowed. "I should go upstairs anyway. I—have to get up early for work tomorrow."

"Tomorrow's Sunday."

"But I—"

"Sara."

Somehow, the narrow space between them had evaporated. Sara moved back into Ryder's arms as irresistibly, as inevitably as the tide comes in. His heat, his scent, the hard contours of his body enveloped her. She pressed her face into the curve of his neck and breathed deep as if her life depended on it. She smelled leather and a salty, delicious mixture of sweat and the sea.

When Ryder tipped her head back to kiss her, she tasted his desperate, passionate longing.

All caution, all regret, all doubts were blown away like a puff of dandelion seeds in the wind. This was Ryder. That was all Sara needed to know.

He cradled her face between his hands like a fragile, priceless treasure as he moved his mouth over hers. His lips were gentle, exquisitely tender, maddeningly unhurried. But Sara felt a tremor reverberate through his body, as if he were restraining himself only with great effort.

Moving in slow motion, as if she were drugged or dreaming, Sara slid her hands beneath Ryder's jacket and wrapped her arms around his narrow, muscled rib cage.

His breath was hot against her face, coming faster now, stirring the fine wisps of hair near her temples.

"Sara," he murmured against her lips. "Oh, Sara..."

He curled his tongue into her mouth, and she welcomed it eagerly with her own—seeking, yearning, aching for something she didn't dare to name.

Her knees were melting, threatening to buckle under the weight of her desire. Dear heaven, how could this possibly be wrong? How could she have doubted that she and Ryder were meant for each other, when he was the only man on earth who could make her feel this way?

With a moan of pleasure, Sara slid her flattened palms inch by inch up the towering curve of his back, reacquainting herself with that broad, solid, reassuring expanse. She traced the hard ridge of his spine, greeting each vertebra like an old friend, as the play of his straining muscles transmitted itself through her fingertips.

"Ryder," she whispered when their lips briefly parted, and the sound of his name was like a wish.

Then his mouth came down on hers again, hard this time, and Sara had to clutch his shoulders with all her strength to keep her knees from collapsing.

She couldn't get enough of him, couldn't get close enough to him, couldn't wait to satisfy the incredible, aching need building inside her. Ryder's heart hammered a wild counterpoint to hers, filling Sara's ears with the rhythm of pounding drums.

She heard a brief, muffled utterance when he scooped her up in his arms. She clasped her hands behind his neck, closed her eyes and pressed her cheek against his heaving chest.

She was floating in his arms, lighter than air even though her limbs felt leaden with desire. At that moment, Sara knew she couldn't have summoned the will to protest, even if Ryder had headed up the staircase.

He carried her into the living room instead, sweeping aside the magazine she'd been reading as he eased her onto the sofa, never breaking their embrace as he lowered himself beside her.

"Sara," he said in a low, ragged voice, "Sara, I want you. I want you so much...." His words disappeared into her mouth as their lips melded together once more.

Ryder peeled off his jacket as if it were ablaze. Sara tangled her fingers through his hair, drawing him closer, deepening their kiss. She'd never sensed this ravenous hunger inside him before, or experienced it within herself. Even the passion they'd shared so long ago seemed dim and distant by comparison.

Somehow she was lying on the couch, with Ryder above her. His hands ignited wildfires of desire as he slid them along her body, stroking, kneading, arousing her flesh.

He dragged his mouth from hers. "Sweetheart," he said with a groan, "I need you... I need to touch you...."

He slipped one hand beneath her fuzzy pullover sweater. The sudden brush of his callused fingers against her bare skin made Sara arch her back.

"You feel so good," he murmured into her ear. "So right..."

She'd taken off her bra when she'd changed into the sweater earlier. Now, she squirmed with pleasure when Ryder cupped her breast in his exploring hand. He pressed his abdomen against her, proving in no uncertain terms that he wanted her as much as she wanted him.

Sara breathed faster. The room was spinning, her skin was on fire, she could barely draw enough air into her lungs....

When Ryder stroked her hardened nipple with his thumb, something inside her shattered.

Maybe it was her illusions. Maybe she'd been deceiving herself as to where all this was headed. But all at once, it was crystal clear to Sara that she was on the verge of making a terrible mistake.

I want you, Ryder had said.

I need you, he'd said.

Not one word about love.

Not that a declaration of love would prove anything. Didn't Sara have the emotional scars to prove it? Even if Ryder mouthed the right words, he wasn't talking about the same kind of love Sara meant. The only kind of love she would settle for.

The forever kind of love.

Once before, she'd made love with Ryder, believing his words. How could she possibly make love to him now, knowing he wasn't planning to stick around this time, either?

She wrenched her head aside and yanked down her sweater. Ryder pushed himself onto his elbows and peered down at her in confusion at her sudden resistance.

"What's wrong, sweetheart?" His eyes were like twin blue flames, still burning with need. His mouth glistened.

"*This* is wrong," Sara said, pushing against his broad chest. "Now, let me up."

He rolled away from her into a more or less upright position, and raked his hair back from his forehead.

Sara scooted as far away from him as possible. She felt dizzy, light-headed, numb.

Not to mention like a fool.

"We can't let this happen," she said, wishing her heart would stop beating so fast. "We're not two kids groping in the back seat of a car anymore. This is serious."

"It was *always* serious," Ryder said, his jaw wedged at a stubborn angle as if daring her to deny it.

Sara straightened her sweater with trembling hands. "I just can't go through this again, Ryder. I *won't* go through it. It hurts too much when you leave."

There it was again, that pitiful, ridiculous, hopeful corner of her heart crying out to him. *Tell me you* won't *leave, Ryder! Promise me this time you'll stay. Just give me an excuse to surrender to what I feel for you....*

Ryder remained silent.

After a moment, he shoved his hands against his knees and levered himself to his feet. "It's late. I should be going." He picked up his jacket.

Sara felt sick with disappointment as that poor, foolish blossom of hope withered and died. "Guess so," she agreed. She reached for the knitted afghan draped over the back of the sofa, and wrapped it around her. She was cold, so cold, chilled to the bone.

Let Ryder see himself out. He certainly ought to know the way by now.

But Sara couldn't let him leave without informing him of the decision she'd been wrestling with before he arrived. "Wait."

Ryder halted in the living room doorway.

"I won't stop you from seeing the twins anymore," Sara said through her teeth. With a pang, she recalled how overjoyed they'd been when Ryder showed up at the barbecue. "You're too important to them already." How could she deprive her niece and nephew of his friendship, when it meant so much to them?

Tess's words came back to Sara, how the twins needed to lead a normal life, and how normal life inevitably meant getting hurt now and then. "Much as I want to, I realize now that I can't protect Noelle and Nicholas forever."

Ryder drew his mouth into a grim, resolute seam. "The last thing I want is to hurt them. Or you."

"All I ask is that you tell them goodbye before you go. Explain why you're leaving."

An odd look passed over his face, and for an instant he appeared hesitant, as if he didn't want to make that particular promise.

Finally, he nodded. "All right." He peered curiously at Sara from beneath his dark brows. "What made you change your mind?"

"Tess," she replied, and that was all the explanation he was going to get out of her.

As soon as he realized that, he scratched his chin thoughtfully. "Well, I'll have to thank Tess, then." He turned to leave, then tapped the side of his skull as if an idea had just alighted there. "Oh, by the way, I'll pick you up Friday night at seven."

Startled, Sara whipped her head toward him. "What?"

"The play, remember?" Ryder snapped his fingers as if bringing her out of a hypnotic trance. "Sleeping Beauty? Fairies and talking trees?"

Oh, God, the play!

The twins would be heartbroken if Ryder didn't show up. But there was no reason on earth that Sara had to sit next to him. The school had a *big* auditorium.

"Don't bother picking me up," she said. "I—I've made other arrangements."

Ryder made a pistol of his thumb and forefinger, and cocked it at her. "Seven o'clock sharp," he said with a wink.

"Ryder! Ryder, don't you dare—"

The click of the front door closing behind him was his only response.

Sara slid the papers from the lawyer back into the red-white-and-blue mailing envelope that had arrived that afternoon. Then, she propped her elbows on the kitchen table, covered her face with her hands, and burst into tears.

The papers were from her brother's lawyer in Chicago, informing her that Brad and Diana's wills had been probated. A trust account had been set up to provide for the twins until they were old enough to inherit their parents' estate. Until they turned twenty-one, Sara, as their legal guardian, would control the trust account.

Just a bunch of dry old legal papers and dull financial documents. But somehow, seeing Brad and Diana's lives reduced to this unfeeling, convoluted legalese had struck Sara anew with the shock and horror that they were dead.

Her beloved big brother. Her warm, loving sister-in-law. Gone forever. Sara's shoulders shook with sobs. Tears seeped through her fingers.

A faint noise, like a tiny peep of protest, caused her to lift her face from her hands.

Nicholas stood in the kitchen doorway, his face pale, his eyes big as dinner plates. He looked scared.

Sara hastily grabbed a paper towel from the roll on the counter and mopped at her eyes. "It's okay, honey. Come on in." She blew her nose, then gave him what she hoped was a reassuring smile.

Nicholas tiptoed cautiously into the kitchen. "Aunt Sara, how come you're crying?" His lower lip trembled, and he appeared to be teetering on the verge of tears himself.

"'Cause I miss your mommy and daddy," she answered truthfully. She held out her hand. "Sometimes, it makes me sad enough to cry."

Nicholas slipped his hand into hers. "You miss them, too?"

"Of course I do," Sara choked out in a half laugh, half sob. She slid an arm around Nicholas and pulled him close, wondering if perhaps she shouldn't have made such an effort to conceal her own grief from the twins.

She'd assumed the sight of her own sorrow would only add to the burden of theirs, but maybe the knowledge that someone else shared their terrible loss would have been comforting.

Sara pressed her cheek on top of her nephew's tousled head. "I loved your mommy and daddy, too," she told him, struggling to keep her voice from breaking. "Crying's nothing to be afraid of, Nicholas. Whether it's your own crying, or someone else's."

Sara could tell her nephew was upset, because otherwise he would never have tolerated her embrace for so long. She pulled him up onto her lap, suspecting with a wistful tug at her heart that this was probably one of the last times he would sit still for it. Pretty soon he would be too big.

"I wish my mom and dad weren't dead," he said in a small, quavering voice.

Sara hugged him tight, swaying back and forth with her arms wrapped around him. "Me, too," she managed to whisper.

Nicholas sniffled. "I try not to cry, but sometimes I just can't help it."

Sara kissed the top of his head. "It's okay to cry, sweetie."

"It is?" He peeked up at her through strands of unruly blond hair, his inquisitive blue eyes shining with unshed tears. He was the spitting image of her brother.

"Sometimes, crying can even make you feel better," Sara told him, smoothing his hair back from his forehead.

Nicholas scrunched up his face. "It can?"

"Sometimes."

"Not always?"

"No," Sara admitted. "Not always."

Nicholas thought about that. "Boys aren't s'posed to cry, anyway," he said, sitting up straighter.

"Oh, really?" Sara smiled and tapped the tip of his button nose. "And where, pray tell, did you get that idea?"

Nicholas shrugged. "At school, I guess. That's what the other kids say."

"They do, huh?"

"Otherwise, you're a sissy." He delivered this piece of second-grade wisdom with an emphatic bob of his head.

"You know what, Nicholas?" Sara hugged him. "I don't believe that. There's nothing wrong with either girls *or* boys crying."

Nicholas looked skeptical. "I bet *Ryder* doesn't cry."

"Hmm." Sara had to admit her nephew had a point. Ryder was a master at shoving his emotions down so deep, sometimes he himself didn't know they were there.

"Well, some people cry on the inside instead," she explained.

"Oh."

She gave Nicholas one last hug before he squirmed out of her lap. "Now, what would you like for dinner tonight?"

"Macaroni and cheese!"

"Again?" Sara rolled her eyes. "We just had that two nights ago!"

"But it's my *favorite,*" Nicholas insisted, scuffing his sneaker on the linoleum and looking so disappointed and adorable that Sara knew she couldn't deny him macaroni and cheese if he asked for it seven nights a week.

"Okay, okay," she said, throwing up her hands in surrender. "But you have to promise to eat all your vegetables, too."

He eyed her with suspicion. "What kinda vegetables?"

"Mmm..." Sara pressed a fingertip to her chin. "Spinach."

Nicholas made a horrible face.

"Brussels sprouts?" she teased.

"Yuck!"

"How about...green beans?"

"Okay," he agreed quickly, obviously relieved to be offered something less objectionable than the first two alternatives.

"Good." Sara picked up the envelope from the lawyer, along with the rest of the day's mail. "I'm going to go upstairs and change my clothes, and after that I'll teach you how to cook macaroni and cheese, okay?"

"Yeah!" Luckily, Nicholas apparently didn't regard cooking as something *else* boys didn't do.

Sara wondered if that was because Ryder had cooked dinner for them once.

As she walked upstairs to change out of her business clothes, she resolutely shoved the thought of Ryder out of her head. Or tried to, anyway. She ought to have been more successful at it, considering all the practice she'd had lately trying not to think about him.

The door to the twins' room was halfway closed. As Sara passed by, she heard the murmur of conversation coming from within. She halted, frowned, made a detour to check on Noelle. Who on earth could she be talking to?

Sara paused at the door, listening. Then she smiled. Noelle was playing with her dolls, acting out all the roles in some imaginative story she'd created. Sara hovered out of sight and eavesdropped shamelessly.

"Nicholas! Quit climbing that tree and get in here!" Noelle's bossy tone made Sara smile.

"Aw, Noelle, do I have to?" She gave her brother's voice an annoying whine.

"Yes. Because it's time to wash up for dinner. Now hurry up!"

"Oh, okay." Sara heard a few thumps, as if the Nicholas doll had fallen out of the tree.

"Noelle, Nicholas, time for dinner!" Sara had to bite back a giggle. Was that breathy, saccharine voice supposed to be hers?

"Okay, Aunt Sara." The Noelle voice was obedient and eager-to-please this time, instead of bossy.

More thumps. Apparently the dolls were trooping into the house.

"Noelle, how come there's four places set for dinner?" the Nicholas doll asked in a loud whisper.

"Because we're having company, silly."

"Who?"

"Ryder's coming for dinner."

Sara caught her breath at this unexpected plot development.

"He *is*?"

"Uh-huh. I invited him, and we have to be 'specially good while he's here and eat everything on our plates."

"How come?"

"Because then he'll like us, and maybe he'll come here to live with us. And then he and Aunt Sara can get married, and he can be our uncle."

Sara's hand flew to her mouth to stifle a gasp. Her eyes blurred with tears.

"Won't that be wonderful?" the Noelle doll was saying enthusiastically.

"Yeah!"

"Noelle, Nicholas, it's time for dinner," sang the saccharine voice.

"Ding, dong."

"Oh, now who can that be?"

"I'll get it," said the Noelle doll. *Thump thump thump thump.* "Why, hello, Ryder! Won't you please come in?"

"Thank you, Noelle. My, what a pretty dress you're wearing." Despite the lump in her throat, Sara had to choke back laughter at Noelle's hearty, baritone imitation of Ryder's deep voice.

"Aunt Sara, look who's here! It's Ryder!"

"Oh, my, what a surprise! Ryder, I didn't know you were coming!"

"Hello, Sara. Boy, that food sure looks delicious! You're the best cook in the whole world, I'll bet."

"Well, if you lived here with us, you'd get to eat my good cooking every night," the Sara doll simpered.

The real Sara crept softly away from the door as the Noelle doll chirped, "And then we could all be a family!"

Sara caught her breath. Dear God, this is exactly what she'd feared might happen! The twins had gotten too attached to Ryder, had come to count on him to be part of their lives.

Part of their lives? Ha! Who was she kidding? Sara kicked off her heels so violently that they flew across the bedroom and crashed into the wall. The twins were counting on Ryder to be their *uncle* someday, for heaven's sake!

She whipped off her blouse with such agitation that a button popped off. She cursed Ryder for coming back to town. She cursed herself for allowing him into their lives.

And she cursed herself *again* for her own terrible weakness where Ryder was concerned. The weakness that kept leading her straight back into his arms, stirring up futile hopes that somehow, magically, they would all live happily ever after.

"You've got to *do* something," Sara pleaded with her reflection in the mirror above the dresser. "You've got to prepare the twins somehow, make them understand that Ryder is only in town temporarily. That the four of us are *never, ever* going to be a family!"

Then, for the second time that day, Sara dropped her face into her hands and burst into tears.

A few minutes later she dried her eyes, sighed at her bleary, puffy-lidded reflection, and marched back downstairs to teach Nicholas how to cook macaroni and cheese.

Chapter Eleven

Friday night, after a dinner of pork chops and applesauce, Sara hustled Nicholas and Noelle into their coats. She finally gave up on Nicholas—no way were the branches of his tree costume going to fit through his coat sleeves. Hopefully, the costume would keep him warm enough.

Eyes darting every few seconds toward the grandfather clock in the living room, Sara buttoned up Noelle's coat over her costume. "You look pretty as a princess," she told her niece, skillfully dodging a swoop of the silver-glittered magic wand.

"I'm not a princess, I'm a fairy, 'member?"

"Yes, I know. Sleeping Beauty's the princess. But you look beautiful anyway." She tucked a sequined ruffle inside before buttoning the last button.

"How 'bout me?" Nicholas asked indignantly.

Sara rose to her feet, thinking fast. "You look very... treelike, Nicholas."

He beamed at her. "Thanks!"

Sara jammed her arms into her own coat, glancing once more at the clock. Quarter of seven. That ought to allow plenty of time to make their escape before Ryder showed up.

She made a hasty inventory. Purse, car keys, Nicholas's coat...

"Okay, let's go." Sara herded the budding actors across the entry hall, opened the front door...

And found Ryder standing there, knuckles raised in the air as if he'd been about to knock.

Sara's heart sank and fluttered wildly at the same time, like a wounded bird.

"Ryder!" The twins bounced with excitement.

Ryder scratched his head, jerked his eyebrows up and down like yo-yos, and made a big production of seeming bewildered. "Do I know you two?" he asked.

"It's *us!* Nicholas and Noelle!" Nicholas cried.

Ryder's jaw dropped. "Why, so it is! I didn't recognize you." He touched Noelle's star-studded headpiece. "I thought you were a beautiful fairy."

Noelle giggled with delight and tapped him with her magic wand.

"And I could have sworn Nicholas was a tree."

"It's just my costume!"

"Well, it sure fooled me. I'll bet your Aunt Sara went to an awful lot of work to make it." Ryder arched his brows at her in a parody of innocence. "Leaving kind of early for the play, aren't you?"

"I, um, had to get the kids there ahead of time," Sara muttered, knowing full well Ryder saw right through her plan to avoid him.

"Gee, we'd better get going then, hadn't we? My car's right out front."

Sara opened her mouth to protest, to insist that she and the twins go in *her* car, but Noelle and Nicholas were already tumbling out the door and racing out to the curb where Ryder's sleek, European sedan was parked like a waiting limousine.

She snapped her mouth shut.

The twinkle in Ryder's eye turned to a gleam of admiration. The rugged angles of his face shifted briefly to reveal an inner yearning that made Sara's skin tingle.

"You look fabulous tonight," he told her in a husky voice. From behind his back, he brought out a single red rose. "You deserve at least a dozen long-stems, but I thought they'd be too awkward to hold in your lap during the play."

Sara was absurdly touched by his old-fashioned, romantic gesture. Somehow, even the corniest rituals had always seemed incredibly sweet and poignant when Ryder performed them, as if Sara were the first woman on earth to be the recipient of such thoughtfulness.

She remembered the first time he'd given her flowers. It was springtime...they'd been walking past a meadow strewn with wildflowers. Ryder had climbed over the fence and picked her a whole bouquet of violets and daisies and buttercups.

Sara had to blink back tears as she reached for the single red rose. "Thank you." Then she winced as a thorn pricked her finger.

It figured.

"Shall we go?"

As Sara reluctantly accompanied Ryder to his car, she couldn't helping noticing that *he* looked rather fabulous tonight himself. His dark suit was perfectly tailored to fit his broad shoulders and long, lean torso. No doubt it had been custom-made by an exclusive tailor in some exotic place like Paris or Hong Kong.

Ryder's handsome, chiseled features were cleanly shaven, his dark hair swept back from his forehead. Sara caught a subtle whiff of some musky, expensive after-shave. He wore a silk tie and, unless she was mistaken, Italian leather shoes that must have cost a fortune.

Ryder Sloan had certainly come a long way from his leather-jacket-and-jeans days. Sara felt as if she were being whisked off to a Hollywood movie premiere, instead of the second-grade play.

"Ryder, are you Aunt Sara's boyfriend?" Nicholas asked when they arrived at the car.

Ryder chuckled.

Sara groaned.

Next time, she had to remember to sneak out the *back* door.

Ryder folded his arms. He unfolded them. He tapped his foot on the floor. Then he wiped his sweaty palms along the seams of his trousers.

He hadn't been this antsy since the first time one of his films had been up for an award.

He didn't know how Sara could stand it. Whenever it was Nicholas's or Noelle's turn to speak a line of dialogue, Ryder's stomach started performing backflips. His mouth went dry. He dug his nails into his palms, sending up a silent prayer that they would remember their lines.

But then, the next time he glanced sideways at Sara, Ryder noticed the rose she held in her lap was quivering as if a stiff breeze were blowing through the school auditorium. Proof that Sara's stomach was performing some gastrointestinal gymnastics of its own.

When it was Noelle's turn to speak again, her poor nervous aunt dug her fingers into her thigh and silently mouthed the words like telepathic cue cards.

Ryder slid his hand over and took hold of Sara's curled-up fingers. She glanced up at him, startled, then gave him a crooked, jittery smile. Ryder squeezed her hand. Sara squeezed back.

They watched the rest of the play like that, clutching each other's hands for support, sagging with relief at each successfully delivered line, just like all the other nervous parents in the darkened auditorium.

It was one of the most nerve-racking experiences in Ryder's life.

It was also one of the most eye-opening.

Never before had he been filled with such a potent, overwhelming mixture of pride and affection and downright fear. Was this what being a parent was all about?

As applause filled the auditorium while the cast took its final bow, Ryder felt exhilarated. Relieved. Completely drained.

Sara was clapping wildly as the lights came on, biting her lower lip, her eyes sparkling with tears. It occurred to Ryder that Sara, too, must be experiencing a whole gamut of unfamiliar emotions as she embarked on this challenging new journey of raising her niece and nephew.

All at once, Ryder wondered what it would be like to join Sara on that journey. To share with her the joys and heartaches, the triumphs and disappointments of raising those two wonderful kids.

Nice fantasy, but that's all it could ever be. Ryder's line of work wasn't exactly compatible with a wife and children. Oh, he knew colleagues who lived that way. Conducted their marriages by telephone. Touched base at home every few months—maybe even made it home for Christmas, if their schedules permitted.

But they also missed anniversaries and birthdays and Little League games. Not to mention other important events, like school plays.

That wasn't the kind of husband and father Ryder wanted to be. Or rather, what he *would* have wanted to be, if his life had turned out differently.

As it was, he had no business indulging in such whimsical fantasies. What if he started to believe in them? What if he actually persuaded himself to try out the role of family man, only to discover he wasn't cut out for it?

He would never, *ever* risk hurting Sara and the twins that way.

And that's why any tempting ideas about settling down had to remain in the same fairy-tale category as the play he'd just watched.

As children spilled out from backstage, Ryder watched their parents greet them with hugs and kisses and exclamations of praise and pride. Just a few moments ago, Ryder himself had been filled to overflowing by those same emotions. But now his insides echoed hollowly with a strange, yearning restlessness that felt amazingly like envy.

Noelle came skipping down the aisle to where Sara and Ryder stood waiting, her round cheeks flushed pink, her fairy headgear slipping sideways.

Sara opened her arms, bundled her niece into them and swung her around in the air. "Oh, Noelle, I'm so proud of you! You were wonderful!"

Noelle positively radiated excitement. "I remembered all my lines! 'Cept that one part where Teacher had to whisper to me."

"You did a great job, sweetheart," Ryder assured her. "You were the best fairy I ever saw."

"An' I wasn't hardly scared at all!" She hugged herself with glee.

Ryder met Sara's glance, saw that her eyes were moist and her lips trembling. He understood what an important milestone this play had been for Noelle, how difficult it must have been for her to overcome the fears and shyness that had plagued her since her parents' deaths. Tonight was proof of the long, healing strides she'd made, thanks in large part to her loving aunt.

Now Nicholas came charging down the aisle, creating somewhat of a hazard with his protruding branches. Sara burst out laughing. "I'd give you a big hug," she said, "but I'm afraid I'd get splinters!" She touched his cheek, his face being about the only accessible part of his anatomy. "You were terrific, Nicholas. I'm awfully proud of you."

"Didja hear Chad Bowman sneeze?" Nicholas let out a child-size guffaw. "It was when we were s'posed to stand still and not make any noise, but he said one of my leaves tickled his nose."

"Gosh, no, we didn't hear any sneeze at all," Ryder said, just in case Chad Bowman's parents were lurking nearby. "You were a fantastic tree, Nick. In fact, if they gave out Academy Awards for Best Performance as a Member of the Plant Kingdom, you'd win hands down."

Nicholas grinned from ear to ear. Or, more accurately, from branch to branch.

"Both of you were just wonderful," Sara told them.

"The whole play was," Ryder said. "Say, I've got an idea." He clapped his hands together, then pretended to wince. "Ouch! Guess they hurt from applauding so much."

The twins beamed smugly at each other.

"I think this evening calls for a celebration, don't you?" Ryder said.

"Yeah!"

"Goody!"

Sara's response was a bit more reserved than her niece and nephew's. "What kind of celebration?" she asked warily, as if Ryder had proposed an orgy of drunken revelry.

"How 'bout if I take us all out for ice cream?"

More enthusiasm from the kids, increased foot-dragging on Sara's part.

"Ryder, that's really not necessary." But he could tell by the resignation scribbled across her face that she wasn't about to disappoint the twins, once they'd gotten their hearts set on ice cream.

For about two seconds, Ryder almost felt guilty.

"It would be my pleasure," he said, wishing it could be hers, too.

"It's getting kind of late...." She kept putting up a fight, even though both of them knew the battle was lost.

Ryder tapped his watch. "It's eight-thirty on a Friday night."

Sara glanced at the twins' eager expressions and sighed. "Isn't it a little cold out for ice cream?" she asked, making one last valiant try.

"We won't be eating it outdoors," Ryder pointed out.

"Please, Aunt Sara?" Noelle begged.

"Pleeeze?" Nicholas's plea sounded so desperate, even Sara had to smile.

"All right," she said, surrendering to the inevitable. "But Nicholas, you're going to have to take that costume off before you can manage a spoon."

The speed with which he proceeded to wriggle out of his tree costume right there in the middle of the auditorium would have been hilarious under other circumstances. But Sara wasn't exactly in a laughing mood.

Tonight, she'd discovered some troubling truths about herself.

Maybe it was the way Ryder's romantic gift of the rose had touched her heart earlier.

Maybe it was the closeness she'd felt to him all evening, holding hands during the play, sharing the same pride and nervousness as other couples in the audience, as if they were actually parents themselves.

Or maybe it was even that surprisingly touching moment when the Prince had awakened Sleeping Beauty with a kiss.

Whatever the reason, as the curtain had dropped at the end of the play, an emotional curtain had risen inside Sara, revealing some disturbing facts she could no longer deny.

She wished the magic of this evening could go on forever.

She wished Ryder was going to stay part of her life from now on.

And, oh, how she wished all four of them could be a family!

Back in the car, Ryder smacked his lips. "Mmm! I think I'll have me a hot fudge sundae when we get to the ice-cream parlor," he said as he started up the engine. "How 'bout you, Nick?"

"A banana split!"

"Noelle?" He glanced back over his shoulder.

"Umm . . ." She tilted her head and touched the top of it with her magic wand. "A strawberry ice-cream soda."

Ryder turned toward the front passenger seat. "How about you, Sara?"

She felt the last of her emotional defenses melt away under the warmth of his smile, the twinkle in his eye. And in that moment, she realized she loved him.

Me? she thought. *Oh, why don't you dish me up a double serving of heartbreak, please.*

And hold the cherries.

Waves crashed against the jagged rocks, sending geysers of water high in the air. Rivulets of foam spilled over the dark sandstone boulders as the ocean withdrew, readying itself for the next assault. Gulls wheeled overhead, their raucous cries piercing the thunder of the surf. A long-necked cormorant glided on a current of air toward its nest on a ledge partway up the cliff.

At the bottom of the cliff, the tide pools were an oasis of calm and quiet by comparison.

"Look! I found a starfish!" Crouched beside the edge of a pool, Noelle called over her shoulder to the others as she pointed to her discovery.

Nicholas came scrambling over the uneven terrain, pinwheeling his arms as he slipped on an algae-coated rock and nearly lost his balance. He flung himself down next to his sister. "Wow, neat!"

Ryder picked his way across the rocks and peered over the tops of two blond heads. "Yup, that's a starfish all right. Good job, Noelle." He ruffled her hair.

Noelle tilted back her head so she was looking at him upside down, squinting into the sunlight. "I never saw a real starfish before."

"You did, too," Nicholas contradicted. "At the 'Quarium in Chicago."

"Oh, yeah." Her excited smile dimmed a few watts.

"But this is your first *wild* starfish," Ryder pointed out, restoring her smile to full power.

"Uh-huh!"

"Aunt Sara, come see the starfish," Nicholas called. He dipped his hand experimentally into the water left behind by the receding tide. "Is it okay if we touch him?"

"Well, he won't hurt you," Ryder said. "But how would you like it if some giant creature came along and picked *you* up while you were just hanging out, minding your own business?"

Nicholas screwed up his mouth to one side, considering. "Not very much, I guess."

"I don't think *he* would, either."

"How do you know it's a *boy* starfish?" Noelle asked.

Ryder chuckled. "Good question, sunshine. Maybe I should have said *she* wouldn't like it."

"She who?" Sara came up behind Ryder.

Ryder winked at the kids. "Why, Susie Starfish, of course."

Nicholas and Noelle burst into giggles.

The sound of their laughter played against Sara's ears like the pleasant tinkle of wind chimes. Yet it also reverberated in her heart with an echo of sadness. Just as these mild, Indian summer days would soon give way to the blustery winds and chill rains of November, so too would Ryder be departing from Hideaway Bay.

And then the twins' joyful laughter would be replaced by tears of sorrow.

It was no use cautioning Nicholas and Noelle not to depend on Ryder's presence, that his time here was limited and one morning they were going to wake up and discover he'd vanished from their lives for good.

How could Sara expect two vulnerable seven-year-olds to heed her warnings, when she herself hadn't been able to hold Ryder at an emotional distance?

She was still reeling from the admission she'd finally made to herself last night after the play. Ten long years Ryder had been gone, and in all that time Sara hadn't managed to fall in love with anyone else. Then, he was back in town a mere few weeks, and *ti-i-m-b-e-r-r!* She fell for him like a chainsawed redwood.

She was hopelessly, helplessly in love, even though she knew she was headed straight for emotional destruction that would make her teenage heartbreak seem like minor growing pains.

Time was running out. Ryder would leave soon. And then Sara would have to pick up the pieces of *three* shattered hearts.

She made her way gingerly over the rocks, tagging behind the others as Ryder pointed out a sea urchin, some barnacles and a couple of hermit crabs.

Although the tide pools were a mere half mile from Sara's house, it was like a whole different world here. Cliffs rose up from the rocky shoreline to touch the sky. To reach the pools, they'd had to climb over an outcropping of boulders, dodging the ocean spray each time a wave hit.

Here in the crescent-shaped alcove formed by the cliffs and rocky outcroppings, it was peaceful—completely isolated from the sight and sound of other human beings.

A part of Sara wished they could stay here forever, cut off from the outside world with all its conflicts and complications. Just the four of them. A family.

Yeah, right. Swiss Family Monahan. Sara stumbled on a rock, nearly twisting her ankle. Even if the four of them *were* stranded on a deserted island somewhere, Ryder would figure out a way to build a raft and get back to civilization *quick*.

The thought of being stuck in the same place forever would drive *him* absolutely stir-crazy.

"I'm hungry," Nicholas announced, rubbing his stomach.

Sara pushed her dreary, depressing thoughts from her mind. Or tried to, anyway.

"Let's have our picnic!" Noelle cried.

"What do you think?" Ryder asked, cocking one dark eyebrow at Sara. "Think these two have worked up enough of an appetite?"

"I don't know about *them,* but *I* certainly have," she replied. She wished she could paint a picture of Ryder right now, to capture forever the way he looked at this very moment.

One sneakered foot was propped on a boulder, an arm draped perpendicularly across his muscular thigh. His pose made Sara think of an explorer scanning the horizon for the best route to glory and riches. His jeans were rolled up to his knees, and a lock of breeze-tousled hair curled roguishly across his forehead like a jet black comma.

No, not an explorer. More like a pirate.

"Let's go eat then," he said, spearing his arm toward the sky. "Onward, troops!"

The deep, vibrant blue of his eyes put the sky to shame. Sara's breath hitched in her chest. He was sexier by far than any movie idol she'd ever seen on the silver screen.

And, unfortunately, just as far out of reach.

Ryder rolled onto his stomach and propped his elbows on the picnic blanket. "That was delicious," he told Sara, who was lying on her back over on the distant reaches of the blanket.

"Gee, thanks."

"I mean it." Ryder scooted closer. The twins were down by the water's edge, building a sand castle. "Those sandwiches were great."

Sara lifted her sunglasses and peered at him skeptically. "Bread, ham, cheese, mustard. My special secret recipe."

Ryder laughed. "Well, they *were* good."

"Maybe you were just hungry."

"And maybe you don't give yourself enough credit."

She restored her sunglasses and wiggled further away from him. Another millimeter or so, and she'd be lying in the sand. "Cooking is *not* my strong suit."

"Are you kidding?" Ryder edged himself just a teeny bit closer. "Your cooking was what won me over in the first place."

Sara raised her sunglasses again. "I beg your pardon?"

"Don't you remember?" He stretched out his arm, drew a lazy knuckle down the curve of her jeans-clad hip. "That day you came by the garage where I worked, to thank me for fixing your car out by Beacon Point? You brought me a plate of chocolate chip cookies you'd baked." He inched closer, seductively stroking her thigh. "I think that was when I first started falling for you."

Sara stared at him, her face perfectly still. Then, the corners of her mouth began to twitch. Her eyes sparkled with mirth. Finally, she burst out laughing.

Ryder watched in bewilderment as she flopped back onto the blanket, unable to contain her merriment.

"Mind telling me what's so funny?" he asked. He'd just revealed something intimate and sentimental to her, and here she was, apparently finding it hilarious.

Sara wiped her eyes with a corner of the blanket and sat up. "Those cookies," she said, still hiccuping with laughter. "I didn't bake them myself."

"What do you mean, you didn't bake them?" Ryder swung himself into a sitting position. "I was certainly no expert on homemade cookies, but even *I* could tell they didn't come out of a package."

Sara scooped up a handful of sand and watched it drizzle through her fingers. "My mother made them," she admitted sheepishly.

"Your *mother?*"

"I told her my homeroom class was having a party."

"You're kidding."

"Nope."

Ryder braced his hands on the ground behind him, dropped back his head and gazed at a puffy white cloud sailing by. "You mean, all these years I've been deluding myself?"

"Guess that makes two of us."

Ryder glanced sharply at Sara. "What's that supposed to mean?"

Sara's tone had gone from amused to bitter-edged in the blink of an eye, like the sun slipping behind a cloud. She shrugged, dusted off her hands. "Just that I used to delude myself, too. Into believing that you and I had a future together."

Ryder scrambled to her side. She hunched her shoulders when he draped his arm around them, as if they were badly sunburned, but at least she didn't pull away. "Sara, I thought we finally agreed that you and I were too young back then to make any promises about the future."

He felt her shoulders lift and drop with a sigh. "I know. You're right." When she turned her beautiful, troubled face to study him, Ryder could read the question written on it as clearly as if it had been scrawled across the heavens by a skywriter.

And what about now? Sara's eyes were asking. *What does the future hold for us now?*

Ryder searched the depths of those gorgeous sea green eyes for his answer. But he couldn't give it to her, not the answer she wanted. Not yet.

Maybe not ever.

He couldn't trust himself to do what was right for Sara. For the twins. For all of them.

How could he promise to love them all for the rest of his life, when he'd seen for himself how easily such promises could be broken?

Like father, like son. And in this case, like mother, too.

A short distance down the narrow ribbon of beach, an artist had set up an easel. This sunny Saturday might be one of the last opportunities to paint outdoors before the autumn storm season arrived.

From the vantage point of this beach, you could see colorful fishing boats bobbing along the docks inside the harbor, and beyond that, the Beacon Point lighthouse jutting out into the Pacific. Top that off with the cypress-lined bluffs and spectacular ocean view, and it was no wonder this particular stretch of beach was such a popular spot for artists to set up shop.

Ryder's mother had run off with just such an artist, a man who'd come to Hideaway Bay to paint watercolors of the picturesque harbor and quaint Victorian homes. But the scenes of her hometown had lacked any such appeal for Ryder's mother. Ryder barely remembered her, but the vague image he carried with him was of a restless, unhappy woman who chafed constantly at the limited horizons of the life she'd chosen.

She'd resented her husband. Her child. The entire town. And she'd seized the first chance that came along to break free from the boredom and drudgery that had imprisoned her.

Ryder hoped that, wherever she was, she'd found the happiness that had so eluded her here.

He'd been hurt by her abandonment in ways he probably wasn't even aware of. But, in a strange way, he sympathized with her, too.

And that's what worried Ryder whenever he thought about building a life with Sara and the twins. He couldn't bear the thought of hurting them. But what if he took after his mother, and could never be satisfied settling down in Hideaway Bay?

What if those same restless urges that had driven him to leave town in the first place, that had sent him roaming the world for the last ten years, were destined to plague him for the rest of his life?

What if he was too much like his parents ever to play a continuing role in the loving, committed family life that Sara and the twins deserved?

"Think I'll go see how Nicholas and Noelle are coming with that sand castle," Ryder muttered.

He couldn't bring himself to look into Sara's eyes again, to read the pleading question for which he had no answer.

But as he plodded across the sand, Ryder felt Sara's gaze trailing him the whole way, like a spotlight illuminating all his inadequacies.

Chapter Twelve

Sara resisted the urge to throw her arms around the twins and smother them with farewell kisses. She wasn't sending them off on a two-month ocean voyage, for heaven's sake, just dropping them off at the Carpenters' house for dinner and a Saturday night sleep over.

Still, this was the first night they'd spent away from Sara since they'd come to live with her. The only restraint preventing her from at least hugging them goodbye was her fear of embarrassing them in front of their friends, Jenny and Alex.

She had to settle for, "Have fun, you two, and remember to mind Mrs. Carpenter," as she left them at the front door. Her niece and nephew immediately raced off after the Carpenter kids.

Noelle's voice drifted back down the hall. "Bye, Aunt Sara..."

Propped in the doorway with her arms folded, Tess grinned. "Gee, the kids don't seem nearly as nervous about this slumber party as you do."

Sara chewed on a fingernail. "I guess I still worry about them too much, huh?"

"You didn't sew their names and address into their underwear, did you?"

"No, of course not!"

"Then you're okay."

Sara managed a feeble smile.

"So," Tess said, glancing back over her shoulder to scout for any eavesdroppers, "how are things going with Ryder?" Her eyebrows bounced up and down suggestively, like Groucho Marx's. "Word has it, he's practically become part of the family."

Sara's heart constricted with a pang of dismay. How ironic that the twins, Tess—everyone in town, in fact—seemed to assume that Ryder was going to be a permanent part of the picture.

"I don't think that's what Ryder has in mind," Sara said.

Tess unfolded her arms. "Have you asked him?"

"Asked him what? What his intentions are? Please." Sara thought back to this afternoon at the beach, to the silence that had fallen with an ominous *thud* when the subject of the future had come up.

"Nothing would scare Ryder away any faster than my pressing him for some kind of commitment," she assured Tess.

"Oh, I doubt if Ryder scares all that easily," Tess said with the air of someone who has inside information. A mysterious smile danced about her lips.

But Tess hadn't seen the panic that had bolted through Ryder's eyes earlier this afternoon when the words *promise* and *future* were spoken.

"Just swear you won't make me wear one of those awful pink bridesmaid dresses with short puffy sleeves and a bow in the back," Tess said, rolling her eyes in horror.

Now *that,* Sara thought sadly, was a promise that was *easy* to make.

It was getting to be almost a habit, opening her front door to find Ryder standing on the porch.

A habit Sara was going to have to break.

"What are you doing here?" she asked, trying to ignore the fluttering in the pit of her stomach.

"I've come to whisk you off into the sunset," Ryder said. "Or at least, to *watch* the sunset." He hoisted a brand-new picnic basket with the price tag still dangling from the handle. "Bread, cheese, wine, fruit." In his other hand, he produced a portable stereo. "We've even got violin music."

"*Two* picnics in one day?" Sara crossed her arms. "Isn't that a bit excessive?"

"Ah, but this one is for adults only." His voice was a low, sexy rumble that made Sara's skin tingle.

Then she frowned suspiciously. "And just how exactly did you know the twins wouldn't be home this evening?"

Ryder licked his lips. "Uh, you mentioned it today at the beach... didn't you?"

Sara gave him a sour smile. "Why, no, I don't believe I did."

"Uh..." He lowered his arms. "Well, maybe Tess might have mentioned it."

"Tess?" All at once, the reason for Tess's mysterious smirk became crystal clear. "So, the two of you set this

whole thing up, is that it? The slumber party to conveniently get Noelle and Nicholas out of the way..."

"Sara." Ryder set his picnic props down and grasped her shoulders. "I'm crazy about the twins, and you know it." He drew her close, and murmured into her mouth, "Is it such a crime to want to be alone with you, just this once?"

Then he kissed her, for the first time in a week. Sara unfolded her arms, which she had stubbornly kept between them like a barricade. Ryder's mouth was warm...cajoling...and very, very persuasive. She had to rest her hands on his hips to keep her balance.

When he pulled back, she was dizzy, heavy-lidded, hungry for more.

"How about it?" he growled into the narrow space between their lips. "Will you come watch the sunset with me?"

A big neon Caution sign began to flash inside Sara's brain. But she was so tired of being cautious! For weeks, she'd tried to repress her desires and emotions where Ryder was concerned, and look where it had gotten her.

She'd fallen in love with him, anyway.

Tonight, for once, she wanted to throw caution to the wind. She wanted to be . . . reckless.

"All right," she agreed before common sense could change her mind. "Just let me change my clothes first."

"You look fine the way you are. Lovely, in fact." Ryder stepped past her to snatch her purse and a jacket from the hall tree in the entryway. "Come on, let's go. The sun won't wait for us."

"But—"

He handed Sara her things and pulled the door shut behind them. Then he tucked the portable stereo under his arm, picked up the picnic basket and took her by the hand.

He was like a force of nature Sara couldn't resist. Didn't *want* to resist.

For so long, she'd tried hard not to forget that her future would never include Ryder.

Tonight, for once, she *wanted* to forget, to allow herself to be swept along by the flood of feelings she'd kept dammed up for too long.

Tomorrow, or next week, or maybe even next month, she would have to clean up the wreckage and pay the price for this one night of abandon.

But sitting beside Ryder, with the sun slipping slowly toward the horizon and her hair streaming back in the crisp autumn air rushing through the car window, Sara believed with all her heart that tonight would be worth the cost.

She turned to study Ryder's handsome profile. "Where are we going, by the way?"

He shifted into high gear, then moved his hand over to cover hers. "Beacon Point," he answered. His teeth gleamed in the gathering dusk. "Where else?"

They sipped their wine and watched the stars come out. Across the windswept bluff, the lighthouse was silhouetted against the purple horizon, still maintaining its lonely sentinel's vigil nearly forty years after its rotating beacon had last warned passing ships away from the rocks.

Soft jazz, instead of violin music, drifted from the portable stereo. Sara leaned back against the gnarled trunk of an ancient cypress tree and sighed with contentment. She held her wineglass in one hand and stroked Ryder's hair with the other. He lay with his head in her lap, on top of the old bedspread that served as a picnic blanket.

"More bread? Cheese? Fruit?" he asked, popping one last grape in his mouth.

"No, thanks. I'm stuffed." Sara hadn't thought she'd be able to eat a bite, not with her stomach all aflutter in anticipation of what might happen this evening, when she and Ryder were finally alone together. But the beauty of the sunset, the refreshing sea breeze and the simple pleasure of Ryder's company had restored her appetite.

"Remember the first time I brought you out here?" Ryder asked, tugging on the drawstring dangling from the neck of Sara's jacket.

"Of course." She filled her lungs with the tang of salt and the scent of pine. "I remember how much it meant to me, that you finally trusted me enough to share this special place where you went to be alone, to think."

"You were the only person I ever brought here."

Although Beacon Point was a popular vista spot for tourists, artists and photographers—not to mention lovers, this secluded grove of Douglas fir and cypress was well off the dirt path that led to the lighthouse. A rocky ledge provided additional shelter from the wind, and helped conceal the cozy vantage point from anyone out on the sandy, grass-fringed headland.

I also remember the last *time you brought me out here,* Sara thought.

It had been a balmy summer evening, with the crash of ocean waves and the smell of suntan lotion filling the air.

It had been the night she and Ryder had made love for the first and only time.

The night before he left town and broke Sara's heart.

"You told me you loved me, but you didn't tell me goodbye," she said softly, unaware she was musing out loud until Ryder went rigid.

He rolled himself upright and took the glass from her hand. "Sara." In the last fading rays of daylight, his eyes were dark caves in the shadows. "Sara, honey, I'm so very, very sorry. . . ."

The anguish in Ryder's voice echoed in Sara's ears as he bundled her into his arms. She burrowed her face into the warm curve of his neck and circled her arms beneath his jacket. Ryder held her, rocking her, the two of them swaying back and forth on the ground beneath the trees.

"I'd give anything not to have hurt you," he whispered into her hair.

The pulse beat in his neck throbbed steadily, reassuringly against Sara's temple. He smelled of soap and leather, and his arms felt so good, so *right* around her that slowly, surely, her sadness seeped away into the darkness as his warmth banished the chill in her soul.

Ryder framed her face with his hands and drew back so he could peer into her eyes. "Sweetheart, I've never found . . . what we shared . . . with anyone else."

Sara's faint reply drifted away on the breeze. "Neither have I."

"We're so good together. . . ."

"Yes," she whispered. They always had been.

Ryder brought his mouth to hers. Sara rested her hand over his heart. He tasted like wine and forgotten dreams.

He kissed her gently, tentatively, just like that other night so long ago. When both of them were breathing rapidly, he broke the kiss and created a tiny gap between them, so that his breath was still warm against her lips.

"Let me make love to you," he said in a low voice that was both a promise and a plea.

Sara's heart leaped wildly. All the air seemed to rush from her lungs, leaving her powerless to speak. But she gave Ryder his answer by drawing his head, ever so slowly, down to hers.

In the pale light of the rising moon, she saw something wild and joyful explode in his eyes just before their lips came together.

And then all gentleness, all tentativeness was gone. They clung together, bodies straining and arching as if they could never get close enough to each other. They were two people who seemed determined to catch up with ten long years of unspent passion all at once.

Ryder skimmed Sara's jacket from her shoulders, then yanked off his own. He knew he should go slow, should give this momentous occasion the slow, sacred deliberation it deserved. But his every instinct urged him to whip off their clothes as if they were on fire. He was blind to everything except the consuming need to run his hands all over Sara's body and once again savor her soft, bare flesh against his.

The wary, insecure youth he'd once been had become a man who knew what he wanted. And the only woman he'd ever wanted was right here in his arms.

They rolled onto the blanket, knocking aside the picnic basket and portable stereo. Ryder slipped his hands beneath Sara's thin cotton sweater, and felt a surge of satisfaction as she arched against him.

He covered her mouth, her cheeks, her eyelids with kisses, as if trying to make up for all the pain he'd caused her. She tasted like honey, like wine, like cool, pure springwater on a sizzling hot day.

His thirst for her could never be quenched.

"Sara, it's been so long...."

His hand grazed the lacy fabric covering her breasts. A whimper of yearning escaped from her throat, only to become trapped between their lips.

Ryder raised himself to his knees and struggled out of his shirt, popping off a button in his haste. He forced himself to slow down as he helped Sara peel her sweater over her head. With shaking fingers, he unfastened the clasp of her bra.

Her breasts shimmered in the moonlight, her hair spilling across the blanket in a fiery red-gold halo. "Sara, you're so beautiful," he said, barely able to squeeze out the words past the frantic hammering in his chest.

Sara's eyes flared as wide as dark moons when Ryder brought his hands to her breasts. She responded in kind, tracing his ribs, outlining his chest muscles with her fingertips. Desire swelled inside him, and he knew he wouldn't be able to hold back for long.

"Kiss me again," Sara whispered.

He stretched out beside her on the blanket, stroking, caressing, kneading her soft, heated skin. Their mouths came together in an eager coupling.

Sara couldn't get enough of him, couldn't begin to satisfy the hunger that had starved her heart and soul for all those empty years. She longed to fill her senses with the smell, the taste, the feel of him.

She twined her tongue around his in a mingling of warm velvet and molten steel. The night air was cool against her skin, but the flames that burned inside heated her until she felt she must be glowing red-hot.

She tangled her fingers through Ryder's hair, clawing at his back and shoulders like a woman dangling from the edge of a cliff.

No one had ever made Sara feel this way before, and now she knew that no one else ever could. Ryder was the only man she'd ever loved, and if she never saw him again after tonight, she would still love him the rest of her life.

"Sara..." His voice was ragged, his mouth glistening with the moisture of their kisses. "I want you. Now."

I love you. Forever, she thought. But she also wanted Ryder with the same reckless, overpowering desire she saw etched in every taut, haggard line of his rugged face.

She reached for his belt buckle.

In seconds they were both naked, both reaching for each other, both exploring the delicious, long-lost secrets of each other's bodies.

Sara reveled in the delightful, bristly rasp of Ryder's skin as she skimmed her hands down the hard, lean length of him. When he shuddered in response, she felt a thrill of awe and feminine power unleashed inside her.

Ryder raised himself above her. When their eyes met, Sara felt as if she were peering into the depths of his soul, past the shutters he usually kept closed to conceal his innermost thoughts and emotions. It was as if she could clearly see for the first time all the hurts and disappointments and restless yearnings that had made Ryder the man he was today.

The man she loved.

The man she could never keep.

She saw desire and desperation in his eyes, too, and something else that looked an awful lot like . . . love?

Then his hands were on her breasts, stroking her nipples, radiating circles of exquisite pleasure like ripples from pebbles dropped into a pond. Sara writhed against him as a powerful need began to build within the core of her being, blotting out everything but the raging demand to satiate this frenzied desire.

The flush of her skin, the ragged pattern of her breathing, the wild, accelerating tempo of her heartbeat telegraphed her need as plainly as a spoken plea.

"Ah, Sara . . ."

With one quick, hard thrust Ryder was inside her. Rather than ease her craving for him, the union of their bodies only stoked an even more urgent longing inside Sara. She quickly matched her rhythm to his, clinging to him, whispering intimate words in his ear that she forgot as soon as she spoke them.

As they moved together, she sensed the passion and pressure mounting inside him, mirroring her own. She was on fire, she was cold as ice. She was empty with an aching hunger, she was filled with an agony of desire.

She flung her head from side to side as Ryder thrust harder, deeper, faster. "Darling," he ground out through clenched teeth. "Oh, Sara..." Her name became a tortured groan of pleasure as a grimace contorted his chiseled features.

And then Sara felt the earth whirling around her as she soared toward the heavens, swept along by an upwelling flood of unbelievable rapture. Fireworks exploded inside her as she cried out Ryder's name. The wind seemed to rush past her face as she sped through the stars, seeking his face in the darkness.

He was there, his familiar, precious features flushed with passion, his eyes glowing with some turbulent emotion Sara couldn't quite identify in her current dazed state. He smoothed her sweat-dampened hair back from her temples, looking so somber, so serious, that Sara had to smile.

"Not having second thoughts, are you?" she murmured when she finally caught her breath.

Ryder's furrowed brow arched in amazement. "About us? About this?" He drew her closer to him, into the crook of his arm. "No! I could never regret making love to you, Sara. Not when it feels this right." Then he shifted, and his mouth curved into a worried frown. "*You're* not having second thoughts, are you?"

"Not me," Sara answered dreamily, running a fingertip down the bold ridge of his nose.

Plenty of time for that tomorrow, she thought wistfully. Tonight, there was only Ryder. Only the two of them, together. No past, no future. Only the present.

Sara nestled deeper into his embrace and closed her eyes. The warmth of Ryder's body banished the chill of the night air. As her heartbeat slowed its thundering patter, she began to hear sounds again—mellow jazz still drifting from the stereo, the hoot of a far-off owl, the rustling of leaves as some small night creature scurried through the woods.

With her head on Ryder's chest, she could hear the steady thump of his heart, alive and reassuring. Behind all these sounds played the muffled background music of waves crashing against the rocks.

Their soothing refrain lulled Sara into a state of drowsy bliss. Tonight, at least, it felt as if she'd finally come to rest on a peaceful, enchanted, long-sought shore.

Something was tickling Sara's nose.

She crinkled the aforementioned nose, stirred, and opened her eyes.

She was gazing sleepily at the back of Ryder's head. They were nestled, spoon-fashion, in bed. Sara's bed. A spike of Ryder's dark hair had been tickling her nose.

It felt so natural, waking up with him like this, that for a moment Sara didn't even remember last night's glorious frenzy of lovemaking. But then, images and sensations crashed into her memory like the waves out at Beacon Point. Questing mouths, tangled limbs, the dizzying climb toward ecstasy, and then . . .

Oh, God. Sara's skin tingled, her cheeks flushed, her knees turned to water at the memory of it.

Ryder. She couldn't believe he was real, couldn't quite accept that he wasn't a dream. He was *here,* in her bed, his broad shoulders rising and falling in the slow, steady rhythm of sleep... his tall, muscular, naked body pressed back against hers in a parallel curve.

Sara tucked her arm more snugly around his waist. He certainly *felt* real. She didn't dare let herself consider what it was going to feel like every morning for the rest of her life, waking up and *not* finding Ryder here.

She didn't intend to spoil this one precious interlude together with bleak forebodings about the future.

The watery light of early morning trickled through the sheer curtains. Its pale, gray, diffuse quality informed Sara it was foggy outside. Neither she nor Ryder had given a thought to drawing down the shades last night. They'd been too wrapped up in each other, too eager for a repeat of that wild, delicious pleasuring they'd shared.

Ryder had shattered the speed limit driving back from Beacon Point. But once they'd reached Sara's bed, leaving a trail of discarded clothing in their wake, he'd taken it slow. *Very* slow. Exquisitely, mind-blowingly slow.

Sara curled her toes in delight, just remembering.

Ryder yawned, stretched, rolled over. His eyes creaked halfway open, providing a glimpse of blue sky on an otherwise foggy day. "'Morning," he croaked, yawning again.

Sara poked him in the ribs.

"Aack!" He recoiled.

"Do you always snap wide awake like this?" she teased.

Now he looked a little more alert. "Not when I've spent half the night making love to the sexiest, most beautiful woman in the world."

He grabbed Sara in his arms and nuzzled her neck until she begged for mercy. "There! Is that awake enough for you?" He propped an elbow on the pillow and rested his head on his fist, studying her with affection and amusement.

"No more complaints," Sara assured him. She loved the rasp of his whiskery face against her skin, the way his sleep-tousled hair stuck out in all directions.

She loved *him*, period.

"What time is it, anyway?" Ryder drew a finger lazily down the cleft between her breasts, licking his lips suggestively.

Sara shivered with anticipation. "There's a clock on the night table behind you."

He peered over his shoulder, and his eyes gleamed like a wolf's when he rolled back. "*Plenty* of time," he growled.

"Time for what?" Sara asked, innocently batting her eyelashes.

"I'll show you." When Ryder bent over her, Sara thought she would die of pleasure.

Before she could respond in kind, a loud hammering made her jump.

"What the hell is *that?*" Ryder grumbled, lifting his head.

Sara scrambled out from beneath him. "Someone's at the front door." She snatched her bathrobe from the closet.

"*This* early? Let 'em knock. Serves them right for interrupting me while I was right in the middle of—"

"Ryder, what if it's the twins?" Sara whispered loudly.

Panic drove the lust from his eyes. "Oh, geez." He leaped out of bed and frantically scanned the floor. "Where are my—"

"Over there." Sara pointed. She was madly scooping up her own garments, following the trail out into the hallway.

The hammering resumed, louder and more urgent this time.

"What on earth—" Sara paused halfway down the staircase to retrieve one last item of clothing. "I'm coming," she called.

At the foot of the stairs she searched wildly for someplace to stash the bundle of clothes in her arms. In desperation, she stuffed them out of sight beneath the antique hall tree.

More pounding on the door. Ryder was stumbling down the stairs behind her, hopping up and down on one foot while he dragged on a sock.

Sara checked that the sash of her robe was cinched tight. Then she tossed back her hair, fumbled with the lock, and threw open the door.

"Tess!"

Sara's mouth fell open in astonishment. She'd never known her best friend to leave the house without spending at least an hour assembling her outfit, fussing with her makeup, checking that every strand of hair was artfully arranged in place.

But this morning Tess's face was ashen, her eyelids smudged with worry, her mouth bracketed by deep creases. Her hair was a tangled mop of brown curls, and it looked as if she'd grabbed the first two items she'd found in her laundry hamper and thrown them on.

Instinctively, Sara reached for her.

"Noelle and Nicholas," Tess gasped. Now Sara noticed she was panting. "They're missing."

A blade of ice impaled Sara. "What?" She clutched Tess's wrist.

Tess gulped a mouthful of air. "The kids . . . they all got up at the crack of dawn, before Dan and I were awake." Her face crumpled. "I'm sorry, Sara, I'm so sorry! I should have kept my eye on them every second—"

"What happened?" Sara's facial muscles were frozen. She tightened her grip so that Tess winced.

"Alex and Jenny wanted to watch cartoons...they said the twins went out to play in the backyard." Guilt and fear made Tess's eyes look haunted. "By the time I got up, and went to check on them, they were gone!"

"How long ago did you discover they were missing?" Ryder's calm but concerned voice near her ear startled Sara. She dropped Tess's wrist.

If Tess was surprised to see Ryder there, she didn't show it. She glanced where her watch should have been, shrugged and spread her hands helplessly. "I don't—twenty minutes, maybe? Dan and I searched the house for them right away, then started looking around the neighborhood...."

"Have you called the police yet?" Ryder slid what he undoubtedly intended to be a reassuring arm around Sara's shoulders. It didn't help.

Tess shook her curls. "Not yet. I wanted to check here first. I thought maybe they decided to come home by themselves." The last vestige of hope drained from her face, leaving her gray and gaunt. "But they aren't here." It was a statement, not a question.

"We haven't seen them." Ryder squeezed Sara's shoulders. "I'll check around outside the house, though. Tess, you come in, call the police and report them missing. Sara, you get dressed. Then we'll all go look for them."

Tess slipped past them into the house. Sara stood rooted to the floor, paralyzed with dread. Losing Brad and Diana last spring made it all too easy for her to fear the worst now. Every news report she'd ever heard about missing children flashed through her mind in a kaleidoscope of terror.

Dimly, she realized her teeth were chattering.

"Sara." Ryder grasped her arms and gave her a little shake, trying to mask the worry lurking in his eyes. "Sara, we'll find them. They're going to be all right."

The determined, almost fierce note in his voice finally reined in her terror a little. "We've got to go look for them," she said through fear-numbed lips.

Relief blunted the harsh angles of Ryder's expression. "I'll check outside in the yard, while you get dressed."

Sara nodded. And that small voluntary movement seemed to open the floodgates of adrenaline inside her. All at once she couldn't bear to stand still, and cursed herself for wasting precious seconds while Noelle and Nicholas were lost out there somewhere, possibly scared, or hurt . . . or worse.

Her feet barely touched the steps as she flew upstairs to put clothes on.

Chapter Thirteen

Ryder did his best to stuff down the fear building inside him. At first, he'd truly believed the twins must have just taken a roundabout route home, and would turn up on Sara's doorstep before the adults even had time to mount an organized search. How many places were there for them to wander off to in a town this size, anyway?

But Ryder and Sara, Tess and Dan, and the police had been searching for over an hour now, along with various friends and neighbors.

No sign of the twins so far. No clue as to where they might have gone.

Sara gave him cause for concern as well, when she and Ryder happened to check back at the Carpenters' house at the same time. Her skin was pale and as cold as ice when he touched her, though her eyes burned feverishly.

"Have they come back here yet?" she asked breathlessly.

"I was just going to check on that myself." Ryder couldn't bear to watch Sara suffering through this nightmare. After all she'd had to endure in the past year...

Her gait as she hurried toward the house seemed jerky and unnatural. She moved like a marionette whose strings were about to snap.

Tess flung open the door the instant Sara's foot hit the first step. "Did you find them?" she called.

Ryder watched Sara's shoulders slump as if someone had pricked her with a pin and let out all the air inside her. Damn! Where the devil could the kids be?

He shook his head at Tess as he ushered Sara inside. "Obviously, they're not here, either."

Tess gave her head one brief, negative shake. "Sara, can I get you something warm to drink? Coffee? Tea? Brandy?"

"No. Thanks. I've got to go back out there and keep looking."

"But first, you're going to sit down and rest for a couple minutes."

"Ryder, I can't—"

"Yes, you can. You won't do the twins any good by collapsing from exhaustion." Ryder led her gently but firmly to the sofa, noting with dismay the erratic tremors that shuddered through her body.

Tess sat down in the chair across from them. She clamped her knees together and hugged her arms tightly around her midsection, as if trying to keep her limbs from flailing out in all directions. "Dan called a little while ago. Still nothing."

Sara nodded, her lips pressed into a tight white line.

Eight-year-old Jenny Carpenter peeked into the living room. "Come on in, punkin." Tess beckoned to her. "It's okay." She wrapped an arm around her daughter as Jenny leaned against Tess's chair.

Jenny had obviously been crying. Ryder noticed her brother, Alex, stationed by the front window. The ten-year-old was staring out through the curtains as if the sheer force of his concentration could somehow bring the twins strolling around the corner. His back was as stiff and straight as a guard's at Buckingham Palace.

Ryder's heart went out to him. He knew what it felt like when you desperately wanted to help but couldn't, because you were just a kid.

"Hey, Alex," he called out.

Alex started, but didn't turn around. "Yeah?" His voice sounded muffled.

"I was wondering if you could maybe help us figure out where Nicholas and Noelle might have gone." Ryder hated to get Sara's hopes up, but there was at least a chance that Alex might recall something he'd left out of previous interrogations.

Alex finally let the curtain drop, and shuffled over to where the adults were sitting. "Whaddaya mean?" he asked.

Ryder patted the cushion next to him, and Alex drooped onto the sofa. "What did you and Jenny and the twins talk about this morning, after you all got up?"

Alex shrugged. "Nothin'."

"Oh, come on, you can do better than that! Did you talk about school or video games or. . . ?" Ryder drew a blank. He realized he didn't have the faintest idea what kids talked about while they were hanging out together.

Alex lifted one thin shoulder and let it drop. "Just breakfast, I guess. We went into the kitchen and picked out what cereal we were going to eat."

"What did you do after you ate breakfast?"

"Umm...we went into the den and turned on cartoons."

Tess smiled weakly. "Er, you see, 'Sesame Street' isn't on that early."

"*Mo-om!* I'm too *old* for 'Sesame Street,'" Alex said in an aggrieved tone.

Ryder tried to steer the conversation back on track. "But Nicholas and Noelle didn't want to watch television, is that right?"

Alex accompanied his answer with yet another shrug. "They did at first. But after 'Herman the Hermit Crab' was over, they went outside."

Sara's head shot up as if she'd just heard a loud explosion.

Ryder felt a pulse of excitement. "'Herman the Hermit Crab'?"

"Yeah, see, it's about all these fish and crabs and stuff that live in the ocean."

"Ryder..." Sara's voice quavered.

"I know," he said.

"Know what?" Tess asked cautiously.

"The tide pools." Sara leaped to her feet.

"We were at the tide pools yesterday...." Ryder hastily tried to explain to Tess as he chased after Sara.

"The twins were completely intrigued by a couple of hermit crabs Ryder pointed out to them," Sara called back over her shoulder.

Tess stumbled after them. "So you think the kids might have gone back there..."

"Ryder told them how hermit crabs live in other creatures' discarded shells—how sometimes they leave one shell to move into another."

"The twins were disappointed that we couldn't stick around and wait for that to happen, so they could watch." Ryder touched Sara's elbow. "We can go in my car."

"Yes, all right." She followed him down the front steps. Then, at the bottom, she slammed to a halt. She made an abrupt about-face and raced back up the steps.

Tess was still standing in the doorway, chewing her nails. "Sara, what—?"

"It wasn't your fault," Sara said firmly. She'd meant to say it all morning, but she'd been too distracted by fear, too caught up in the desperate urgency of the search.

She gripped Tess's shoulders and looked her best friend straight in the eye. "Whatever happens," she said, swallowing her dread, "it wasn't . . . your . . . fault."

Tears veiled the guilt in Tess's eyes. For the first time in her life, she was speechless.

Sara hugged her. Tess had always been her lifeline in times of trouble, and Sara would never forget that.

Tess pulled back, wiping her eyes. The two women exchanged wobbly smiles. Sara heard Ryder's car roar into life.

"Go find them," Tess whispered.

Sara ran.

"Can't you go any faster?" Sara pushed her foot against the passenger side floorboard in an unconscious effort to step on the gas.

"Not in this fog," Ryder answered, never taking his eyes off the road. Or what he could see of the road through the concealing mists that swamped the shoreline. "We're almost there, though."

"I can't believe Noelle and Nicholas would walk this far by themselves," Sara said, her heart sinking at the possibility that this was all a wild-goose chase. Maybe the twins weren't at the tide pools at all. Maybe she and Ryder were searching in the exact opposite direction from where they should be.

"It's less than a mile from Tess's house to the tide pools. More like half a mile." Ryder spared Sara a wry grimace. "It just seems like a long way because we're so anxious to get there."

Sara's nails dug crescent-shaped dents into her palms. "What if they decide to go swimming? The undertow is awfully tricky along this part of the coast. What if a big wave comes along and—"

"Sara, come on." Ryder removed one hand from the wheel for just a second to pat hers. "They're not going to go for a dip in the ocean on a day like today. It's cold and drizzly."

But Sara noticed he stepped a little harder on the accelerator.

They sped across the deserted beach parking lot as fast as the fog would allow. Before Ryder had even switched off the ignition, Sara was out of the car and running through the sand. Ryder caught up with her near the rocks they would have to climb over to reach the tide pools.

"I'll go first," he said, grasping her wrist to hold her back. "I can make faster progress."

"Go," she said, stepping aside. Both of them were panting hard.

Ryder scrambled up onto the rampart of jagged boulders. Fear-propelled, Sara had no trouble keeping up with him as they made their way across the rocks to the isolated cove where the tide pools were. Freezing spray from the crashing waves drenched them again and again.

Amazing what a difference one day could make in the weather, Ryder thought grimly. Just yesterday, they'd been basking under warm, sunny skies, and a shower of sea spray had seemed as refreshing as darting past a lawn sprinkler on a hot summer afternoon.

But the chill Ryder felt in his bones when he finally crawled into view of the tide pools had nothing to do with the damp, cold weather.

Noelle and Nicholas were there, all right. But what should have been relief quickly turned to horror as Ryder took in the danger of their situation.

Sara came up behind him, grabbing on to his shoulder to peer past him. "Oh, dear God," she choked out.

The tide was coming in. The tide that would eventually recede, leaving behind little pools in the rocky depressions for lots of small marine creatures to thrive in.

Only first it had to rise high enough to cover the cove containing those rocky depressions.

The cove where the twins were now cowering, in the last shrinking spot of unsubmerged land.

"Sara, no!" Ryder clamped his hand around her wrist like a steel manacle to prevent her from clambering farther down the rocks. "The water's too high. We can't possibly swim through those waves to get to them. It's too rough!"

"Ryder, we've got to save them!" Her voice rose to a near hysterical pitch.

"We'll save them, but we'll have to think of another way to get them out of there." The twins were clutching each other, huddled up against a wall of sandstone that rose a good eight feet above their heads. No way could they possibly climb up that sheer cliff.

Sara let out a mournful wail as a particularly large wave rolled in, leaving the twins soaked from head to toe in its churning wake. She yanked against Ryder's grip, and if he hadn't maintained his iron hold on her, she would have flung herself down into the incoming waves.

Both Sara and Ryder had grown up in Hideaway Bay. Both of them were familiar with these tide pools. And both of them knew that this isolated cove would be completely submerged in a good five feet of water by the time high tide reached its peak.

Long before that, though, the waves would have plucked the twins from their precarious island of safety and dragged them out to sea.

"Come on." Ryder made a decision and pulled Sara after him.

"Where are we going?" She resisted, as if she thought he intended to abandon the twins to their terrible fate.

He tugged harder. "We're going to climb up to the top of that cliff above them, and lower down a rope or something to pull them up."

Sara immediately scrambled ahead of him. "You've got rope in your car?" she asked over her shoulder, sounding as if she didn't dare hope for such a miracle.

"No, but I've got jumper cables," Ryder said, panting as he struggled to keep up with her. "They'll have to do."

"You can make faster time than I can," Sara called back. "I'll climb up there and try to keep the twins calm, while you go back for the cables."

Ryder wasn't entirely sure which of them was capable of greater speed at the moment, but he thought it was a good plan. "I'll be back as soon as I can," he told her as they split up. "We'll get them out of there, Sara. I promise."

Maybe it was because this was the first time Ryder had actually promised her anything, but Sara managed to find a small measure of comfort in his words. "Hurry, Ryder," she prayed through chattering teeth. "Please, please hurry..."

The raw, damp breeze whipped her hair about her head, lashing her with tatters of fog as she struggled up the steep ascent to the cliff overlooking the cove. She clawed her way upward over the rocks, heedless of scraped palms, banged ankles and bruised knees. Her breath tore in and out of her lungs, searing her throat with fire.

"Hurry, hurry, hurry," she chanted mindlessly.

The pile of boulders opened out onto a narrow ledge. Sara scuttled on hands and knees to peer down over the side, and didn't know whether to be relieved or terrified when she spotted the twins right below her. The water was swirling around their shins now.

Sara gulped a few mouthfuls of air, trying to douse her own panic before calling out to the twins. Her thudding heartbeat made her voice waver a little on her first try. "Noelle! Nicholas!"

She hadn't wanted to startle them by hollering at the top of her lungs, but the rush of the wind and splash of the waves drowned her voice. She yelled louder.

This time they both looked up at once, and their confused, terrified little faces nearly broke Sara's heart. Their heads tilted this way and that as they searched wildly for the location of her cry.

"Here!" Sara waved her arm in a huge arc.

"Aunt Sara!" they cried out in unison. "Aunt Sara, help us!"

It was all Sara could do not to claw her way down the cliff by her fingernails. Only a few yards separated her from her precious niece and nephew. But until Ryder got here with those cables, it might as well be a few miles. She could never get them out of there on her own.

"Everything's going to be okay now," she called, hoping she sounded a lot more confident than she felt.

"Aunt Sara, the ocean's getting deeper!" Noelle cried.

"I know, sweetheart, I know." She glanced frantically over her shoulder. No sign of Ryder yet. "We're going to get you both out of there soon, I promise. It'll just be another minute or two." *At least I hope so,* she thought. *Ryder, Ryder, where are you?*

Nicholas's face was as pale as sea foam. "We came to look for Herman the Hermit Crab," he cried, his lower lip quivering. "We were watching for him to come out of his shell, but then the water got too high for us to get back to the rocks, and it kept getting higher and higher...."

A vise of anguish clamped around Sara's heart at the thought of how scared the twins must have been when they realized their predicament. How long had they already been trapped in this nightmare?

Another big wave broke near them, sending out a curtain of water that left them both sputtering and rubbing their eyes. "It hurts," Noelle whimpered piteously. "Aunt Sara, the ocean hurts my eyes!"

"An' it's cold!" Nicholas yelled.

Sara was on the verge of going back for those cables herself, when Ryder finally jumped down and landed on the ledge beside her. "Hey, you two," he shouted down to the twins. "We're going to get you out of there now."

"Ryder!" Their thin cries drifted up over the edge of the cliff.

As Sara watched him fumble with clumsy fingers to untangle the jumper cables, she realized Ryder was as frightened as she was. "Damn! Okay, here." He handed Sara one pair of ends, while he struggled to tie a loop with the others.

"What are you—"

"We're going to lower the end with the loop down for them to wrap around their waists, then pull them up one at a time." Taut creases bracketed the tense slash of his mouth.

"Ryder, the cables are too short to reach! It'll never work!" Sara plowed her hands through her hair. There wasn't enough time to get back to the road and flag down additional help....

"It'll work." With one hard jerk, Ryder cinched the knot tight. "If I lower myself partway down to them."

"But there's nothing to hang on to!"

"*You're* going to hang onto *me.*"

Sara nearly went limp with panic. "Ryder, I can't possibly hold your weight and the twins...."

"You won't have to support my full weight. Just hang on to my ankles—*sit* on them, if you have to." He grabbed one shoulder to steady her. "The twins' lives depend on it, Sara." His eyes bored into hers like searchlights. "Think you can do it?"

All at once an icy calm settled over Sara, as if someone had flipped off her panic switch. For the first time, she noticed a trickle of blood near Ryder's temple, where he must have slipped and banged his head on a rock.

"Yes," she said through clenched teeth. "I can do it."

"Good." He gave Sara a quick look that managed to convey encouragement and admiration and a few other elements she didn't have time to analyze. "Let's do it."

He dropped to the ground and leaned over the edge. "Noelle, Nicholas! Listen carefully, now."

Sara couldn't see their response. She was busy searching for a rocky projection, a convenient tree branch, *anything* that might provide something stable to grab onto if necessary.

"Noelle, I'm going to lower this down there, and you put the loop over your head and under your arms. Got that?" Ryder paid out the cables over the edge. "Then, I'll count to three, and you hang on as tight as you can while I pull you up, okay?" He wriggled on his belly until the upper part of his body was over nothing but air. "Then it'll be your turn, Nicholas."

Ryder flicked one last glance over his shoulder, and gave Sara a grim, determined wink. "All set?"

She took a deep breath, deep enough to hold until the twins were safely back on dry land. "Ready."

"Let's do it, then."

Sara crouched down, bracing her feet against the ground and grabbing one of Ryder's ankles under each arm. He scooted forward again, until he could bend over the edge at the waist. Then, the top half of his body disappeared from view over the side.

Time slowed to an excruciating crawl. Ryder lowered the cables carefully, inch by inch, envisioning all kinds of disasters that could occur at this point—like dropping the damn cables. It felt as if his weight were pretty well balanced right now, but hauling up one of the kids would change that drastically.

God, he hoped Sara was physically strong enough to hang on to him!

Then, superimposed over the anxious, upward-gazing faces of the twins, Ryder saw the determined, do-or-die certainty engraved in Sara's eyes when she'd told him she could do it. He thought of how people had been known to lift up cars to rescue their children trapped underneath.

And he felt an almost invincible strength surge through his own body, when he allowed the full force of the truth to strike him right between the eyes.

The brutal truth was that the twins could die. That their lives depended on Ryder's plan working.

And at that moment, dangling over the edge of the cliff, with the damp salt spray stinging his eyes and Sara cutting off the circulation in his feet with her ironclad grip,

Ryder realized just how much those two kids had come to mean to him.

He intended to rescue Nicholas and Noelle, even if it took until his last dying breath.

"That's it, honey! Just like that!" he shouted as Noelle obediently wiggled her head and arms through the loop. "Hang on tight, now! Ready? I'll count to three. One... two... three!"

He felt Sara's grip on his ankles lock even tighter as he slowly lifted Noelle from the water splashing about her legs. His heart plunged as the cables began to twist, twirling Noelle in uncontrolled circles. But, bless her brave little heart, she managed to brace herself against the cliff with her feet and stop the spinning.

"You're doing great, sweetheart!" he yelled. Noelle was rigid, her eyes squinched tightly shut. Slowly, slowly, Ryder raised her upward. His spirits began a parallel ascent. This was going to work! They were going to get them out of there!

After what seemed like hours, he'd dragged Noelle up far enough to get a secure grip on her arm. As if Sara could anticipate his intentions, she hauled back on Ryder's legs at the same moment he finally heaved Noelle up over the side.

Sara grabbed her, cables and all, and hugged her as if she would never let her go.

"Sara, we've got to hurry!" Ryder pried Noelle out of her aunt's embrace so he could remove the loop of cable. "You did great, sunshine. As soon as we get your brother up here, I'm taking you both out for the biggest banana split you ever saw!"

Noelle was quivering like a leaf in a hurricane. Unfortunately, more reassuring hugs would have to wait.

"Sweetie, you stand way back here away from the edge, okay?" Sara quickly resumed her former position as Ryder angled himself over the side of the ledge once more.

He had to force himself to lower the cables slowly, knowing that the potential for disaster still loomed, despite their one success.

Then, below, a wave knocked Nicholas off his feet. A fist of fear slammed into Ryder's gut. He glimpsed Nicholas's red shirt beneath the water, his blond hair swirling on the surface like pale seaweed.

Ryder filled his lungs to scream the little boy's name, just as Nicholas miraculously managed to struggle to his feet again, crying and spitting and blindly reaching upward with his hands.

"Here it comes, Nicholas!" Caution flew by the wayside as Ryder paid out the last length of cable as fast as he could. The breeze carried it to and fro, tantalizingly out of reach, but at last Nicholas managed to grab it.

He had a tougher time getting it properly adjusted than Noelle had—or maybe it just *seemed* much longer to Ryder before the loop was snugly wrapped around Nicholas's chest, beneath his arms.

"Okay, here we go!" Ryder could feel his forearms trembling with exhaustion. His abdominal muscles screamed with pain as he focused every sinew in his body on pulling Nicholas gradually upward. He had to force himself not to wince every time Nicholas banged into the side of the cliff. He was a third of the way up...halfway...three-quarters...almost here now, and—

Something gave way, and Ryder slid a foot toward the edge of the cliff.

"Can't...hold you," Sara moaned through clenched jaws. Sweat trickled down her forehead into her eyes. Her limbs had gone completely numb with the strain of hanging on to Ryder. She could see her hands, clutching his legs like grappling hooks, but she couldn't feel her fingers anymore.

Her feet were losing their purchase against the rock. Its smooth, flat surface offered no irregularities she could use to brace herself against the relentless force of gravity, which seemed determined to drag them all over the edge a few inches at a time.

Friction lost another round, and the three of them jolted forward another half foot toward disaster.

How could she possibly hope to regain any sort of hold at this point? The situation could only get worse. What would happen when Ryder himself was pulled over the edge? He would never let go of Nicholas. But Sara had Noelle to consider. At the critical moment, could she bring herself to let go?

Dear God, how could she make that terrible choice?

Despite a new infusion of desperation into Sara's straining limbs, they all slipped forward another foot.

Suddenly, there were other hands, other voices. The crash of the waves had covered the sounds of the rescuers' approach, and Sara was as stunned to see them as if they'd beamed down from an orbiting spaceship.

People in uniforms seized Ryder's legs, gently but quickly detaching Sara's clawlike grip as they eased her aside.

Ryder couldn't see what the hell was happening, but all of a sudden Sara seemed to have gained superhuman strength and four extra pairs of hands. He felt himself being hauled back onto the ledge, and concentrated on maintaining his grip on the jumper cables and their precious cargo.

The instant his own position was stable, Ryder grabbed Nicholas's thin little arm, worried he might snap the bones like matchsticks, but not about to loosen his grip for anything in the world. With one last burst of exertion, he hauled Nicholas up over the side.

Waiting hands whisked Nicholas back from the edge and helped Ryder to his feet. What the hell—

He gazed around in bewilderment, amazed that so many people could fit onto one narrow ledge. Cops, members of the volunteer fire department—he wondered whether Tess had called out the National Guard, as well.

Some photographer from the local paper was crouched on the rocks above them, snapping pictures as if worried someone was about to snatch his camera away from him. Ryder ignored him, searching for a glimpse of the three faces he desperately needed to see.

Then, the crowd parted, and Ryder staggered forward on unsteady feet through a gauntlet of handshakes and big grins and vigorous slaps on the back.

Sara knelt on the rock, her arms flung around both twins, plastering their cold, wet, trembling little bodies with kisses.

The look she gave Ryder when she finally glanced up at him was a look he would remember all his life. "Thank you," she choked out. "Oh, Ryder, thank you!"

But he didn't want Sara's gratitude. He wanted her love. He wanted to be part of this family. Forever.

As pins and needles began to prickle the numbed blocks his feet had become, Ryder dropped to his knees beside Sara and the children. He slung his arms around the whole bunch of them, sagging with relief.

The four of them stayed huddled there a long time, while waves crashed harmlessly below, and the salt of tears mingled with the salt of the sea.

Chapter Fourteen

Monday morning the phone was still ringing off the hook as word spread about Ryder and Sara's daring rescue of the twins. And, since Ryder hadn't installed a phone at his house, Sara bore the full brunt of the calls. Reporters from newspapers up and down the northern California coast, friends and acquaintances, even complete strangers were eager to hear every last detail of Noelle and Nicholas's narrow escape.

Sara hung up from her conversation with the most recent caller, and seriously considered disconnecting the phone. If she had to relive that awful nightmare one more time, she would go stark raving mad!

She pushed aside the disorganized mess of papers spread out on the kitchen table and got up to pour herself another cup of coffee. Obviously, it was going to be useless trying to get any work done at home today, what with all these interruptions.

This morning, with every protective instinct in her body screaming against it, she'd forced herself to send the twins off to school as if nothing had happened yesterday. For their own psychological well-being, though, it had seemed important not to make too big a deal over their close call—to return to normal, everyday life as soon as possible.

Sara could only cross her fingers and hope that reporters hadn't staked out the second-grade classroom. The four of them were front-page news all of a sudden, and the Hideaway Bay town council was even planning a public celebration this coming Saturday in their honor.

The four of them. Funny how she'd begun to think of them that way. Noelle and Nicholas, Ryder and Sara. A foursome. A team. Perhaps even . . . a family?

No. She wouldn't allow herself to use such a highly charged term, a term booby-trapped with all sorts of emotional pitfalls. She was just feeling especially close to Ryder right now because of the circumstances. Because of the passionate, tender lovemaking they'd recently shared. Because he'd saved the twins' lives.

She knew perfectly well that this family feeling was all an illusion.

But why did it have to feel so real?

The phone jangled suddenly. With a sigh, Sara steeled herself for another round of curious questions about the twins' rescue.

"Ryder Sloan, please."

Sara made a face at the receiver, annoyed by the man's rather rude abruptness. Who did he think she was, Ryder's personal secretary?

She gritted her teeth and answered politely. "I'm sorry, but he doesn't— I mean, he isn't here right now. May I take a message?"

"You know how I can get ahold of him? It's kinda important."

Sara drummed her fingers on the counter, deciding they ought to include charm school as part of journalists' training. "No, I don't know how you can reach him, other than by leaving a message with me." Apparently, the guy wasn't interested in *her* version of the rescue.

"Hmm." For some reason, she pictured him chomping on a cigar. "This is Morley Maxwell calling."

He seemed to expect his name to elicit a delighted squeal of recognition. "Yes . . . ?"

"Ryder's agent."

All at once, Sara's heart dropped like a stone. She quickly set down the cup she'd been in the process of raising to her lips, slopping coffee on the counter.

"Yes?" she repeated, far more cautiously this time.

"See, Ryder left me this number as a place where he could be reached if I needed to get hold of him."

Dimly, Sara recalled Ryder mentioning that to her, making sure it was okay. At the time, she hadn't considered the irony that she might play a crucial link in the chain that would inevitably drag Ryder back to the world of agents and power lunches and movie deals.

"I probably shouldn't reveal too many of the details," Morley Maxwell went on, "since we're still in the preliminary stages of negotiation, but I got a call this morning from a certain film producer whose name I can't mention, but which you would instantly recognize, who wants Ryder to direct his next project."

"I see," Sara said faintly, overwhelmed both by the implications of this offer and by Morley Maxwell's sudden verbal outpouring.

"Now, this certain big-time producer didn't come right out and say so, of course, but believe you me, I could practically *taste* how desperate the guy is to sign Ryder on as director."

"Really," Sara said dully.

"This guy's seen Ryder's work, and is he impressed? Whoo-ee! You bet he's impressed! He's practically drooling over the chance to snatch up Ryder before he commits himself to his next project."

Morley Maxwell paused for breath, or perhaps to suck in another mouthful of smoke before continuing to wave his cigar in the air. "'Course, like I warned this famous producer-who-shall-remain-nameless, an up-and-coming young director like Ryder who does work of that caliber don't come cheap. I mean, it's only a matter of time before some *other* hotshot producer comes along waving big bucks in his face, and then, *zoom!* Ryder's career takes off like a rocket!"

Sara swallowed. Now she had a bitter, smoky taste in her *own* mouth. It came from the ashes of lost hopes and shattered dreams. "I'll have Ryder call you," she managed to croak.

"ASAP, got that, sweetheart? As soon as possible. The quicker I hear from him, the quicker we can get this deal signed."

"I'll tell him." Sara hung up the phone with trembling hands, and lowered herself into the nearest chair before her shaky legs collapsed.

Here it was at last. The tempting bait she'd known would eventually come along to lure Ryder away from Hideaway Bay.

Away from *her.* Forever.

Ryder was whistling as he sauntered up Sara's front walk, toting a bottle of champagne. He'd never dreamed he would ever feel at home in this prim and proper Victorian house, all decked out with its gingerbread woodwork, its sense of tradition, its air of respectability.

But during the last few weeks, Ryder had gradually come to feel as if he actually *belonged* here. Not so much in the house itself, but with the people who lived inside.

Nearly losing Nicholas and Noelle had made everything so clear to Ryder. Now, he realized that what he'd been searching for all his life had been waiting right here in Hideaway Bay for him the whole time.

He thought of how his mother had run off with the first man to offer her an escape, of how his father had sought escape at the bottom of a whiskey bottle. He recalled his own escape ten years ago, and how much it had cost him.

The members of the Sloan family, it seemed, were always running away from something.

Not much of an inheritance to pass on to your kids. But Ryder had learned so much from Sara and the twins about what it meant to be part of a family, he was confident he could overcome his own rocky past and build a stable, lasting future.

For the first time in his life, he knew exactly what he wanted.

A life with Sara and the children. Roots. A place to call home.

And if Sara would have him—if all *three* of them would have him—then Ryder intended to dedicate the rest of his life to his role as husband. As uncle or father figure or friend, whatever the twins needed. Maybe even the role of father to his and Sara's own children someday.

He rapped on Sara's front door. If the upcoming scene played itself out the way Ryder hoped it would, he and Sara would have even more to celebrate tonight than the twins' rescue.

He knew something was wrong the minute Sara opened the door.

"What is it?" he said quickly, stepping inside. "The kids?"

"Hmm?" Sara seemed distracted. Her face was drained of color, except for red rims around her eyes. Her skin was drawn taut over her high cheekbones. "Oh. The twins are fine. They're, um, over at Tess's. I dropped them off there after school."

Ryder's anxiety ebbed a little. But only a little. He peered at her with concern. "Sara, have you been crying?"

She made a weary, dismissive motion with her hand as she turned and walked into the living room. "It's been a rough day," she said, not answering his question. "All these reporters calling...having to go over again and again what happened yesterday..."

Well, maybe that explained why she'd been crying. But something else was puzzling Ryder. "Sara, you, uh, *did* invite me over here tonight for dinner, didn't you?"

She dropped the knickknack she was fiddling with on the mantel and clapped a hand over her mouth. An embarrassed flush restored color to her cheeks. "Ryder, I completely forgot! After that call—I mean, I took the kids to Tess's because I was afraid reporters might pester them here, and I—I completely forgot I'd invited you for dinner." She swallowed and looked miserable. "I'm sorry."

Ryder set down the champagne bottle and took her in his arms. Or tried to, anyway. Something about the way she was angled toward the fireplace, or the way she kept her arms hugged around her middle prevented him from drawing her close. Her body was resistant, unyielding.

Ryder smoothed her hair. "Look, don't worry about dinner. We can call out for something, all right?"

"That reminds me." Sara cleared her throat, avoiding Ryder's eyes. "You got a phone call here today."

"I'm not surprised." His mouth twisted wryly. "When I went downtown to the hardware store this afternoon, I was practically mobbed by people wanting to hear all about the twins' narrow escape." He wished he could figure out why Sara seemed so cold, so distant all of a sudden. "Who tried to reach me here? Some enterprising reporter?"

Sara looked at the floor. "Your agent."

"Morley?" Ryder drew back in surprise. "That's right, I did leave your phone number with him so he could contact me. I'll call him back in the morning."

Sara rubbed her arms as if she were chilled. "He seemed pretty excited about some deal he was working on for you."

Ryder chuckled. "That's Morley. Always excited about some deal." His grin faded. "Sara, talk to me. Tell me what's wrong."

"Nothing." She ran one fingertip along the edge of the mantel, as if inspecting for dust.

"You seem upset about something."

She sighed heavily, but didn't reply.

Ryder was beginning to appreciate how frustrating it was when someone you loved refused to open up with you, to share their problems and let you know what they were thinking or feeling. For the first time, he fully comprehended what Sara had had to put up with during their youth, when Ryder had insisted on keeping his thoughts and emotions all bottled up inside.

"Sara, this isn't like you. One thing you've taught me is how important it is to communicate, to share—"

"Ryder, this isn't working out between us."

He hesitated, certain he must have misunderstood her. "*What* isn't?"

Sara faced him squarely now, having evidently decided the time for evasion was past. "Us. Our relationship. Whatever you want to call it." She took a deep breath. "It's over."

Ryder stared at her. "Sara, what are you talking about? Everything's been going so well—"

"It was over between us a long time ago, Ryder. Ten years ago." She spoke with an almost eerie calm. "It was a mistake to try to start it up again."

"A mistake?" He took a step toward her, but something in Sara's tense posture radiated an invisible force field that kept him at arm's length. "You call what we've shared in the last couple months a *mistake?*"

Sara's face was as pale and smooth as porcelain, her head tilted upward at that regal Monahan angle. "Yes." Her verdict sounded as final, as merciless as a queen sentencing one of her subjects to the dungeon.

Only the storm raging in the depths of her sea green eyes gave her away.

"Why was it a mistake?" Ryder asked, trying to keep his own turbulent emotions under control.

"Because I—I can't forget how you left me once before. How you'll do it again."

"Sara, things have changed—"

"Nothing's changed, Ryder. You and I are still the same people. This is still the same town."

"Yes, but—"

"And I still can't trust you. I tried, but deep down inside, I just can't. I'm sorry."

Ryder felt as helpless as he had yesterday, watching the tide rise higher and higher. "Sara, give me a chance to prove to you that the situation is different now. Believe me, I would never do anything to hurt you—"

"I believed in you once before, and look where it got me." Tears shimmered in her eyes. Or was it only a reflection of her determination? "I'm not going to sit around waiting for the same thing to happen again. I'm calling a halt to this. Now."

Higher and higher, the tide of Ryder's desperation rose. He'd done his best to explain to Sara why he'd left all those years ago. He'd thought she understood, maybe even agreed with his reasons. And he'd thought that during the past weeks he'd managed to chip away at and finally dismantle that barrier of mistrust she'd erected between them.

Obviously, he'd been wrong.

Now, he wanted to make all those promises he hadn't been able to before. Words like *love* and *forever* crowded his tongue, but Ryder bit them back. How could he ask Sara to share a life with him, if she didn't even trust him? Ryder was certainly no authority on relationships, but even *he* knew that trust was one of the fundamental cornerstones on which good ones were built.

Despite all the feelings for each other they'd rediscovered since his return, obviously he still needed more time to prove to Sara that she could trust him not to betray her again.

Only now, it seemed, his time had run out.

"Don't do this, Sara." How could a world that had seemed so full of hope and promise and happiness disintegrate so quickly? Only a few minutes before, he'd been whistling with anticipation about the future they were going to share.

"You and I are right for each other," he continued, mustering the only irrefutable argument he could think of.

Sara could hardly disagree with him. Ryder was the only man she'd ever loved, and seeing the bewildered unhappiness engraved on his face, knowing she'd put it there, was almost more than she could endure.

She could end this agonizing ordeal so quickly, simply by backing off, by agreeing to give him another chance. It would be so easy.

It would be so wrong.

Because one of the many things Sara had learned, during these recent months of instant motherhood, was that it was better to rip the bandage off in one quick jerk, rather than to prolong the pain by peeling it off slowly.

For the twins' sakes as well as her own, Sara had to make a clean break of her relationship with Ryder *now,* before it became even more painful to let him go.

And go he would. Soon. He wouldn't dillydally around here for long, once he learned about the fabulous deal that was destined to bring him fame and fortune.

She *had* to end it between them. Now. Even though it broke her heart.

"Just because we have this...physical chemistry between us doesn't mean we're right for each other," Sara said. Although it didn't *feel* as if she'd said it. It felt as if a stranger had spoken those words.

Ryder's brow darkened. "It's a hell of a lot more than that, and you know it."

"All I know is that, whatever it is, it wasn't strong enough to keep you in Hideaway Bay before. And it won't be *this* time, either."

"What makes you so sure?" Ryder was clenching and unclenching his fists as if he wanted to hit something, reminding Sara of the troubled, sometimes violent youth he'd once been.

"Because I believed in us once before, Ryder. I believed in *you.*" She pushed back her hair with trembling hands. "And you betrayed my trust."

"Sara..."

She backed away as Ryder reached for her, knowing her resolve would crumble if he touched her. Fool that she was, even now the faint, tiny hope still flickered inside her that he might declare his intention to stay, proclaim his love, ask her to be his wife....

Despair dragged down her shoulders. Even if Ryder actually uttered those miraculous words, all of that would change when he spoke to his agent and learned that his career was poised to take off into the stratosphere.

Although Ryder kept his distance, the fiery intensity of his words seared her like a brand. "Can you honestly tell me there's been any other man in your life who mattered? Anyone but me?"

His eyes smoldered like blue flames. Sara shivered under their heat.

"Look at me, Sara. Has there been any other man in your life besides me?"

She ought to tell him yes, there'd been dozens. "No," she said, meeting his gaze head-on.

Satisfaction flickered in his eyes, gentled by a touch of wistfulness. "There's been no one else for me, either," he said quietly. "No one who mattered. No one but you."

Sara gripped the back of the sofa hard enough to put dents in the aged wood. "Then I guess *both* of us are unlucky," she said with a catch in her voice. "Unlucky enough to want the one person we can't have."

"Unlucky?" Ryder sounded hoarse, as if so many personal revelations tumbling out at once had damaged his vocal cords. "Having you in my life was the *luckiest* thing that ever happened to me, Sara."

Her eyes brimmed with tears.

"Every single day, from the first time we met, even during all those years we were apart, I never took for granted what a miracle it was that you would even have anything to do with me."

"Oh, Ryder..." Sara covered her mouth with her fingertips as her throat closed up.

"I've made some mistakes and done some things I regret. But having you in my life could never be one of them." He lifted her high school graduation picture from the mantel and smiled distantly at it, as if fondly recalling the innocent, trusting, idealistic teenager she'd once been.

He set the picture down next to Brad's, and his smile dissolved as he looked back at Sara. "I know I hurt you deeply, and that's what I regret most." Pain shimmered across his bold features, turning them haggard. "I don't blame you for not being able to forgive me for that."

Sara couldn't speak, which was just as well. Better to let him go on thinking she hadn't forgiven him.

"And I can hardly blame you for not trusting me, either." Ryder moved toward her, only this time Sara was too paralyzed by sorrow to move away.

"I thought I had good reasons for leaving you the way I did." He grazed her tear-stained cheek with the back of his finger. "Looking back, I still believe the reasons I left were valid. But the way I did it, without telling you first, without explaining, was unforgivable."

One of Sara's tears spilled onto his hand. As devastating as she'd known this breakup was going to be, the reality was much worse than she'd even imagined.

She didn't know which would be more unbearable—prolonging this scene any further, or hearing the door click shut behind Ryder as he walked out of her life for the very last time.

Her eyes felt swollen, and she knew her face must be puffy and blotched, but Ryder was gazing at her as if she were the most beautiful woman he'd ever laid eyes on.

"We belong together, Sara," he said softly, nudging her chin up with the crook of his finger. "I'll never believe otherwise." The cords in his neck flexed as he swallowed. "But if you want to end this now, I won't fight you. I don't have any right to."

For an instant, the screen he used to shield his deepest emotions from view slipped away, startling Sara with the force of the pain, the guilt, the desperation she saw etched in his soul. She wasn't the only one who would suffer lasting scars from this heart-shattering farewell.

But it couldn't be helped.

"Tell me what you want me to do, Sara, and I'll do it." Ryder grasped her shoulders gently. "It's the least I owe you."

There was only one power on earth that could have kept Sara from hurling herself into Ryder's arms at that moment, and that was her love for the twins. She had a responsibility to do what was best for them, to make any sacrifice to protect them.

Even if it meant giving up the only man she would ever love.

She would have to face this terrible moment eventually. As difficult as it was to believe right now, losing Ryder would become even more agonizing the longer she held on to him.

Clutching that knowledge like a magic talisman, Sara stiffened her spine, drew a deep, ragged breath, and did the hardest thing she'd ever done in her life.

"Go," she whispered.

Ryder flinched as if she'd struck him. His grip on her shoulders tightened in a brief spasm, but then slowly, slowly, he uncurled his fingers.

The look on his face would haunt Sara the rest of her life.

He opened his mouth as if to speak, but didn't. He tilted forward slightly, as if he were about to bestow one final kiss on her mouth, but stopped himself.

Sara saw a replica of her own torment blazoned across his face as he started for the door, walking with the stiff, jerky movements of a robot.

Ryder, Ryder, don't leave me again! How can I find the strength to go on without you?

At the entry hall, he paused and looked back. His eyes appeared dull and hollow, as if something had died inside them. "Even if this is the end of the road for us," he said, as sorrow ricocheted across his beloved, familiar face, "I'll always feel like the luckiest man in the world for having you in my life, Sara."

Tears blurred her final vision of him. She blinked, and he was gone.

Seconds later, she heard the door click shut behind him.

Every muscle in Sara's body was tied in knots, her hands fisted at her sides, her jaw clamped shut. Now, a great, trembling wave racked her limbs, loosening the knots, turning her flesh and bone to water.

She was sinking . . . falling . . . with no place to land.

As her knees gave way, she collapsed onto the sofa.

Gone. Ryder was gone, only this time she'd *sent* him away. Sara's battered brain couldn't make sense of that at first, couldn't quite wrap itself around the idea.

Then, her darting, agitated gaze snagged on the bottle of champagne Ryder had brought. It sat unopened, untasted on the end table where he'd set it down.

All at once, the full impact of the choice she'd made came crashing down around Sara in an avalanche of anguish and despair. So many delicious, meaningful experiences in life she would never taste again, now that Ryder was gone for good.

In a sharp surge of pain and sorrow, she snatched up the champagne bottle, intending to hurl it into the fireplace. But as she drew back her arm, she realized this bottle was the only connection to Ryder she had left now.

She clutched the champagne to her heart instead, and sank back against the sofa cushions, weeping as though she would never stop.

Chapter Fifteen

"Aunt Sara, will Ryder be there?"

Noelle's hopeful question prodded Sara like a finger against a bruise.

"I'm sure he will be," she answered lightly, though her spirits lay heavier than an anchor. "After all, this celebration today is mostly in his honor." She gave Noelle's blond hair a few more strokes with the brush. "I think the mayor's planning on giving him the key to the city for rescuing you and Nicholas last Sunday."

Noelle turned around to regard her aunt with puzzled blue eyes. "But *you* rescued us, too!"

Sara knelt to hug her. "I know, sweetie. But I think people in Hideaway Bay feel kind of bad for the way they used to treat Ryder, and they want to do something special for him."

Noelle tipped her head to one side. "How did they treat him?"

"Well..." Sara stood up and turned Noelle by the shoulders so she could finish brushing her hair. "Sometimes they weren't very nice to him, I'm afraid. Because they didn't understand him."

"But *you* understand him, don't you, Aunt Sara?"

A pang of sorrow shot through her heart. She had to swallow before she could speak. Dear heaven, but she missed Ryder!

"Yes, Noelle." She wove her fingers through her niece's silky hair. "I understand him."

Noelle bobbed her head in emphatic agreement. "I do, too!"

A sad smile touched Sara's mouth, as tears misted her eyes. Explaining to the twins that Ryder would no longer be part of their lives had been nearly as difficult as coping with her own heartbreaking loss.

She'd tried not to make too big a deal of it, telling them that Ryder was awfully busy right now working on his house, and that it wouldn't be long before his job took him someplace far away.

They'd been disappointed, of course, and had asked a lot of questions that had Sara fumbling for answers. But they hadn't seemed particularly shocked or crushed, and Sara had started to hope that maybe losing Ryder's friendship wouldn't be nearly as traumatic for them as she'd feared.

Then, yesterday, Nicholas had asked a question that had knocked the wind out of her, and made her realize that the twins were, indeed, struggling to cope with the fact of his absence.

"Aunt Sara, does Ryder not come see us anymore 'cause we were bad? 'Cause we weren't s'posed to go to the tide pools by ourselves and he had to rescue us?"

"Oh, Nicholas, no!" Sara had dropped the spoon she was using to stir soup for dinner and immediately sat down next to Nicholas at the kitchen table.

She'd smoothed back his hair from his forehead. "Honey, Ryder doesn't think you were bad. He doesn't blame you and Noelle for what happened—he's just happy you're safe, that's all."

Nicholas kicked a sneakered foot against the nearest table leg. "Then he's not mad at us?"

"Absolutely not," Sara said firmly. "He likes you and Noelle a whole bunch, and nothing will ever change that."

"Then how come he doesn't do things with us anymore?" Nicholas asked.

"Honey, like I explained, he's just real busy right now, and..."

With that, Sara had launched into another round of what sounded to her like increasingly lame excuses. It had distressed her deeply to discover the twins might blame themselves for Ryder's sudden absence.

Now, clipping barrettes in Noelle's hair in preparation for the town celebration, Sara was beginning to think she'd completely botched the way she'd handled everything.

She should never have allowed Ryder to get close to the twins in the first place.

Worse, her desperate attempt to salvage the situation was only hurting them further.

Not to mention what shutting Ryder out of their lives was doing to *her*. For the past five days, Sara had felt as if she were dying inside.

In less than half an hour, she would come face-to-face with Ryder again. She would have to smile and be polite and pretend in front of the whole town that nothing had happened.

Only Ryder would know how she was really feeling.

Noelle poked her arm into the sleeve of her coat. "Aunt Sara, if Ryder gets the key to the city, does that mean he can lock it whenever he wants to?"

Sara laughed for the first time in days.

The high school band swung into yet another rendition of the school fight song. They were competing with the excited chatter of the thousand or so people filling the bleachers and rows of folding chairs set up across the floor of the high school gymnasium.

Up on the makeshift platform where graduating seniors would sit in the spring, Ryder scanned the crowd for the three faces he most wanted to see.

The three faces he most dreaded seeing.

He couldn't believe what an enormous void his life had become during the last five days, ever since Sara had informed him it was over between them. Ryder had been a loner ever since childhood, but in the space of a mere few weeks, he'd grown so accustomed to sharing his life with Sara and the twins that his return to an unfettered bachelor's existence seemed bleak and meaningless.

Boy, did he miss them!

But he didn't kid himself that seeing them today would be anything but difficult. Because once the festivities were over, Ryder would be going back to that big, empty, newly restored house of his. Alone.

He craned his neck, and spotted Tess and her family sitting in one of the middle rows of bleachers. Tess waved enthusiastically. Ryder smiled at her, lifting his hand in greeting. At least *Tess* wasn't holding a grudge for the way he'd treated Sara so long ago.

Ryder still couldn't believe that he, Ryder Sloan, former bad boy of Hideaway Bay, was sitting up here next to the mayor, the school superintendent and various other town dignitaries. He hadn't even made it up here for his own graduation ceremony, having been banned from attending because of some infraction of the rules he'd committed.

He ran a finger inside his shirt collar, embarrassed by all this hoopla. Why on earth should people make such a fuss over him, just because he'd helped rescue two kids he loved as if they were his own? Wouldn't anyone else have done the same in his position?

All at once, Ryder detected Sara's presence as clearly as if she'd walked up behind him and laid her hand on his shoulder. Maybe her familiar wildflower fragrance had wafted across his subconscious. Or maybe it was just that special sixth sense he'd always had that told him when she was near.

He rose nervously from his chair and turned around to find Sara and the twins climbing the steps onto the back of the platform. When Sara glanced up, her eyes locked onto Ryder's like a homing beacon. Once again, he felt that same fluttering in his chest, that same quickening of his pulse.

Sara looked absolutely beautiful. Sad, pale, anxious, but beautiful. Her strawberry blond hair danced across the shoulders of her blue silk dress, while the gymnasium lights sparkled off the simple silver chain she wore around her neck. So elegant, so desirable...so completely out of reach.

Ryder would have sold his soul to get her back.

Then the twins caught sight of him. "Ryder!"

"Careful," he called, laughing, amazed by the warm delight that flooded him as they came bolting toward him. "Don't trip over those microphone cables."

Noelle and Nicholas hurled themselves against him. Scattered, spontaneous applause broke out in the audience at the sight of this touching reunion. Ryder hugged one twin with each arm. They both broke into an excited babble, peppering him with a recitation of everything that had happened since the last time they'd seen him.

Ryder didn't have a chance to get a word in edgewise. Just as well, considering that at the moment he was unable to speak past the knot in his throat.

He glanced up to find Sara watching the three of them with a mixture of such pain, such sorrow and regret on her face that he had an overwhelming urge to take her in his arms and comfort her.

But if Sara had her way, Ryder would never have the chance to take her in his arms again.

"Guess we'd all better sit down," he managed to say, indicating the four empty folding chairs. "Might as well get this show on the road."

After some jockeying for position, Noelle wound up sitting next to Ryder, with Nicholas on the other side of her and Sara at the far end. The inner torment Ryder had glimpsed in her face was concealed now behind a composed mask, reflecting that stiff-upper-lip breeding that came with membership in the town's most respected family.

Sara would be mortified if anyone suspected how much she was hurting inside, but Ryder knew better than anyone how much it was costing her to keep her feelings hidden.

He was having the same terrible struggle himself.

The mayor got to her feet, shuffling a stack of papers, and beamed a dazzling politician's smile in Sara's direction. "Everyone all settled? Well, then, I guess it's time to begin, now that Sara and the children have arrived." She stepped up to the microphone.

The next half hour passed in a vague, unpleasant blur for Sara. She was dimly aware of the mayor and a couple of other people giving speeches, of periodic bursts of applause, of the band striking up on several occasions.

Mostly, she was aware of Ryder.

Seeing him again had struck her with the force of a physical blow. She'd been startled and dismayed to see the shadows beneath his eyes, to notice that he'd lost weight in the last few days.

She'd been stunned by the tidal wave of love and desire for him that had nearly knocked her off her feet when she'd stepped onto the platform and met his eyes.

Everything about their situation felt so incredibly wrong to Sara, as if the universe were turned upside down. She and Ryder were meant for each other, yet couldn't be together. The twins were so eager to have him for an uncle, yet Sara couldn't even allow them to have him for a friend.

She twisted her hands in her lap, and bit her lower lip to keep it from trembling. Only a couple of folding chairs and a pair of fidgeting twins physically separated her from the man she loved.

But the distance might as well have been a couple of light-years.

Five days of pain and guilt and remorse had lashed Sara's heart raw. She'd hurt Ryder deeply, and the twins, too, would suffer because of the way she'd made a mess of everything.

She'd risked everyone's happiness on one tiny strand of hope that Ryder might actually settle down for good this time. Risked it all—and lost.

She wondered how many more days it would be before he left.

Then, mercifully, the ceremony came to a close. To the sound of thunderous applause and nudges from the mayor,

Ryder awkwardly stood up, motioning Sara and the twins to join him. The twins hopped up happily, but Sara's cheeks were burning. She'd never felt so self-conscious in her life.

Afterward, as people came up to shake her hand, Sara tried to focus on the reason for this whole elaborate extravaganza. After all, the twins' survival was certainly cause to celebrate, wasn't it?

But although she smiled politely and automatically chitchatted with people, she sure didn't feel much like celebrating.

"How about joining me for a glass of punch?"

Ryder's voice so close to her ear startled Sara, sending bittersweet shivers down her spine.

"Punch?" she asked blankly, too distracted by his compelling blue eyes, by the sensual slant of his mouth to comprehend his question.

He motioned toward the exit of the gymnasium. "There's drinks and food and God knows what else, probably balloons and pony rides, all set up across the street in the park." His lips curved into a halfhearted smile. "What's the matter, weren't you paying attention to the mayor's closing remarks?"

Sara straightened her posture and pulled herself together. It wouldn't do to let Ryder think she was having second thoughts about their breakup. Because then he might try to press his advantage, and right now Sara didn't know if she was strong enough to resist.

Despite the shadows that made the contours of his face look even more rugged, he was still impossibly handsome in his perfectly tailored suit, all freshly barbered and shaved. Somehow, Sara would have felt better if he'd appeared in rumpled clothes and mismatched socks, with his tie hanging askew.

But not a hair was out of place, except for that one rebellious dark lock that always insisted on curling across his forehead.

Sara was searching for a tactful way to decline his invitation, when the twins came bouncing up, having just been cooed over by Miss Elsie, the white-haired town librarian.

Nicholas was rubbing his cheek. "That lady *pinched* me," he said indignantly.

"Me, too," Noelle said, looking puzzled.

"She was just trying to be nice," Sara told them, trying to hide her smile.

"By *pinching* us?" Nicholas looked incredulous.

"She meant it as a gesture of affection, I'm sure."

Noelle plucked at Ryder's sleeve. "How come you're too busy to come see us anymore?" she asked.

Ryder glanced sharply at Sara. "Is that what your aunt told you?"

"She says you don't have time to play with us."

"An' pretty soon you're gonna leave," Nicholas added.

"I see." Ryder's expression was a complicated mixture of sadness, annoyance and regret. He seemed at a loss for how to answer.

Sara immediately felt guilty for putting him on the spot like this. She knew it wasn't fair to place the blame for his absence on Ryder, but how else could she explain it to the twins?

Thankfully, Lorraine Mathis chose that moment to join their little circle. She was a compact, high-energy woman with a no-nonsense manner and lines of exhaustion around her eyes that came from holding down two jobs.

After greeting Sara and the children, she turned to Ryder. "It's high time I thanked you for everything you've done for Shane."

Ryder rubbed the nape of his neck, a sure sign he was feeling uncomfortable. "I'm the one who should be thanking Shane," he told Shane's mother. "He's been a big help to me, fixing up my house."

His house. It was the first time Sara had ever heard him refer to it as anything but his father's.

"Ever since Shane started working for you, well, the change in him has been remarkable." Lorraine positively beamed with gratitude. "It hasn't been easy for me, raising Shane alone since the divorce, especially not having a male role model around."

Ryder scuffed the toe of his shoe against the floor. "Well, I don't know how much of a role model I've been...."

"All I know is that Shane hasn't skipped a day of school in weeks. His grades have improved, he helps me more around the house, and he doesn't spend nearly as much time hanging out with those hoodlums he calls friends." Lorraine rolled her eyes. "I was at my wit's end until you came along. I just want you to know that I will never, ever forget what a good influence you've been on him."

She turned and said, "You're a lucky woman, Sara. I envy you." With that, she stood on tiptoe to plant a kiss on Ryder's cheek. Then she slipped away into the crowd, leaving Sara blushing furiously.

Ryder appeared nearly as embarrassed as Sara felt. "That was, uh, nice of her to say, wasn't it?"

"She obviously meant every word," Sara told him "You've been good for Shane." *And you'd be so good for me. For the twins. If only...*

"Come on, let's go across the street for something to eat," Ryder muttered. "It's getting warm in here." He loosened his tie as if it were choking him.

Sara could hardly refuse, not unless she wanted to drive home with a pair of cranky, disappointed children. But as Ryder escorted the three of them across the street, she felt as if she were plodding deeper and deeper into quicksand every step of the way.

Long tables practically groaning with the weight of food had been set up in the park, beneath shady sycamore trees draped with red-white-and-blue bunting. No pony rides, but the town of Hideaway Bay had definitely done itself proud. Even the weather was cooperating. The afternoon sun had broken through the gray skies that had threatened rain earlier in the day, and now fluffy white clouds scudded across the brilliant blue expanse like ships at sea.

"Where on earth did all this food come from?" Ryder asked Sara out of the corner of his mouth as they stood in line with the twins. "It looks like half the town must have been up all night slaving away in their kitchens."

Just then, someone noticed them waiting, and before Sara knew it, they were all being whisked to the front of the line despite her and Ryder's protests.

Sara accepted a paper cup of punch, but her stomach was roiling too much to eat. Seeing Ryder again, talking to him, just being within a hundred *miles* of him was pure torture. Having to smile and receive congratulations from people as if they were a happy couple made it a thousand times worse.

Ryder himself didn't seem to have much of an appetite, judging by the amount of food remaining on the paper plate he was balancing in one hand. Of course, how could he eat when people kept coming up to shake his hand or slap him on the back?

He'd just managed a hasty forkful of potato salad when a tiny, white-haired woman tottered up to him and peered at him through the lower part of her bifocals.

"Ryder Sloan, is that you?" she demanded in a creaky, impatient voice.

Ryder gulped his food down. "Yes, ma'am."

"They tell me you're some kind of fancy Hollywood director now."

Despite this painful reminder that Ryder would soon be leaving to start work on a new film, Sara had to repress a smile. She wondered how long it would take Ryder to recognize his old high school English teacher.

He threw Sara a helpless, silent plea for assistance, but she only widened her eyes innocently.

"Er, well, I don't make the Hollywood type of movies, ma'am. So far I've only directed documentaries."

"Educational films?" she snapped out.

"A fair portion of them."

She gave a curt, satisfied bob of her head, like the swat of a ruler against knuckles. "Good."

Ryder blinked, then warily studied her closer. "Mrs. Jenkins?"

"Who'd you think I was, the Queen of Portugal?" She cackled with glee as Ryder actually turned pale. "Don't worry, I'm not about to send you to the principal's office again. I'm retired now."

"Oh. Well, I'm, uh, glad to hear it. I mean, you've certainly earned it."

"Forty-three years I taught school, and one thing I learned during all that time was how to recognize talent when I saw it." She poked Ryder in the chest with one bony finger. "And *you,* young man, had talent."

Ryder's features shifted to convey amazement. "I did?"

"Of course you did! Plain as the nose on your face." Her mouth twitched disapprovingly. "Whenever you bothered to turn in your assignments, that is."

Ryder yanked on his already loosened tie. "Not exactly a model student, was I?"

"Only because you didn't apply yourself." Mrs. Jenkins adjusted her spectacles and sniffed. "But I'm pleased to see you've turned into such a fine young man, after all."

Then she patted his arm. "I'd best be off, now. I heard Ida Wiggins brought some of her yummy rice pudding, and I want to get some before it's all gone."

She chucked Sara under the chin as if she were three years old. "Nice to see you again, too, Eleanor."

Ryder cocked an eyebrow as Mrs. Jenkins bustled off. "Eleanor?"

Sara shrugged and gave him a sheepish smile. "She has a habit of confusing me with my mother."

"I see." Ryder scratched his head. "Never thought I'd see the day when old Mrs. Jenkins would have anything nice to say about me."

He glanced down at all the food still on his plate and sighed. "Guess I'm not going to have much room left for Ida Wiggins's rice pudding."

He was interrupted again before he had a chance to scoop up more than a mouthful or two.

"Hello, Sara." Bob Fellows, the chief of the small Hideaway Bay police force, greeted her with a peck on the cheek. Sara had never seen him out of uniform, and today was no exception.

He hitched up his belt, nudged his hat in the direction of his receding hairline, and turned to Ryder. "Don't know whether or not you remember me..." he began somewhat awkwardly.

"Not *remember* you?" Ryder guffawed. "After all the times our paths crossed? How could I ever forget the first cop who threw me in jail?"

Fellows flashed a crooked grin. "By golly, you sure were an expert on gettin' yourself into trouble." He hooked his thumbs through his belt loops. "That was back before I even made sergeant."

"Heck, with all the practice you had hauling me in, it's no wonder you kept getting promoted." Ryder shook his head as if he couldn't quite believe he was standing here reminiscing with his old nemesis.

The chief rubbed his jaw. "Guess we've both come a long way since then, huh?"

"You can say that again."

Fellows cleared his throat. "Anyway, I just wanted to say that was a mighty brave thing you did, both of you, saving those kids." He nodded toward the playground, where Noelle and Nicholas were soaring back and forth on the swings with some of their school friends.

Ryder shifted his feet. Sara could practically feel the discomfort vibrating through him. "We just did what had to be done, that's all," he told the chief.

Bob Fellows squinted at him. "I always figured you'd come to no good," he said, brandishing a beefy finger under Ryder's nose. "Now, I'm happy to admit I was wrong."

He tipped his hat at Sara before moving off in the direction of the food tables.

Ryder stared after him as if the man had just performed a double back flip in midair. "Well, I'll be..." He swallowed. "Never thought I'd ever live to hear him say *that*."

Sara hesitated, then touched Ryder's arm. "I'm glad, but not surprised, that he's changed his opinion of you."

Ryder tried to ignore the jolt of electricity that arced through him at Sara's touch. She'd said it was over, that she still didn't trust him. And unless he could somehow, someday win her trust back, there was no point in tormenting himself with desires that had to remain unfulfilled.

"I just can't get over how people in this town have changed," he said, still marveling over the fact that the citizens of Hideaway Bay had gone to such trouble to honor someone they'd once looked down their noses at.

Sara squeezed his arm. "Maybe *you're* the one who's changed," she said softly. "You don't have such a chip on your shoulder anymore."

Ryder gazed into her wistful green eyes, those eyes that had always been his touchstones for everything decent and honest in the world. "I always thought I was cursed," he said. "Cursed by my past. That I was destined to live under the shadows cast by my parents."

Sara's brows feathered together in sympathy. "You make your own destiny, Ryder. We all do."

"Do we?" He wondered about that. He'd been convinced, once, that Sara was his destiny. But now, it seemed as if mistakes from the past had risen up to throw roadblocks in the way of the future he so desperately wanted.

"I figured I could never have a family of my own," Ryder said thoughtfully, "because I didn't know what a real family was. Because my father was a drunk, and my mother abandoned me."

"Oh, Ryder." Sara's eyes shimmered with compassion. "You broke free of your past long ago. Look at what you've become! A successful film director, a role model for troubled kids, a respected member of the community..."

But she didn't mention the one achievement that would have meant more to Ryder than any of the others. Becoming part of a family. Sara's family. *Their* family.

He had to find some way to make her forgive him for the way he'd hurt her. The whole town had apparently forgiven him for his past. Why couldn't she?

"Sara..."

"All right, you two. Time to record this event for posterity!" Mike McCoy, photographer for the *Hideaway Bay Gazette,* herded the twins over. "Let's get the four of you standing together here.... Kids, you get in front, that's it. Someone take that plate of food from Ryder. Sara, Ryder, move closer together. Come on, Sara, he won't bite!"

"Are we gonna get our pictures in the paper?" Nicholas twisted around to peer up at his aunt.

"It certainly looks that way," Sara murmured, wishing the ground would open up and swallow her. She felt like the world's biggest fraud, smiling for the camera as if posing for a family portrait, while inside her heart was breaking.

"Come *on,* Sara, scoot closer to Ryder!" Mike motioned impatiently. "That's better. Ryder, put your arm around her, will you? Kids? All set?"

Sara would have felt more comfortable snuggled up to a complete stranger. She was acutely aware of the warm weight of Ryder's arm around her shoulders, of the scent of his after-shave, of the familiar, hard length of his body pressed against hers.

It felt like heaven.

It felt like torture.

"Okay, on three, all right?" Mike positioned his camera. "One...two...say cheese, everybody!"

"Cheese!" the twins chorused.

Sara did her best to smile, though it felt as if her face were about to crack into a million pieces.

"Three!" Mike snapped the picture. "That was great, guys. Let's get a few more shots, okay?"

After what seemed an agonizing eternity, Sara was finally able to make her escape. Leaving the twins in Ryder's competent care, she fled to the far side of the park, which was blessedly deserted at the moment.

She sank onto a wooden bench partially hidden behind the huge, gnarled trunk of an ancient oak tree, and buried her face in her hands.

But the tears wouldn't come. She'd used them all up during the past few days, it seemed.

She let her head drop onto the back of the bench, closed her eyes, and focused on the soothing trills and chirps of the birds in the branches overhead.

After a few minutes, another sound intruded on the fringes of her consciousness. The *tap, tap, tap* of someone approaching along the path.

Hastily, Sara straightened up, combed back her hair with her fingers and smoothed the wrinkles from her dress. Maybe whoever it was would pass right by and leave her some measure of peace. She didn't think she could face another round of chitchat at the moment.

The tapping stopped. "Eleanor? Is that you?"

Sara muffled a sigh. "Hello, Mrs. Jenkins." She didn't bother to correct her.

Mrs. Jenkins wobbled over and sat down beside her. "My, what a nice spot you've found for yourself. So restful." She poked Sara in the ribs. "Had to get away from all that commotion for a while, did you?"

"It *was* rather..." Sara scanned her vocabulary for an appropriate word "...overwhelming."

"I'm on my way home now to wait for my phone call. My daughter in Chicago always calls me about this time on Saturday."

"That's nice." Sara had always been fond of Mrs. Jenkins, once she'd gotten over being intimidated by her. But right now, she wished the retired English teacher would just leave her alone.

"Your young man's certainly made something of himself," Mrs. Jenkins continued, adjusting her position as if she intended to settle on the bench for a good long while. "First a movie director, and now a college professor."

Sara's brows knit together uncertainly. "College professor?"

"Why, over at the school in Eureka, of course! They're lucky to get someone of his experience to head their new film department."

Now Sara knew how Alice must have felt when she first tumbled through the looking glass. "Mrs. Jenkins, I-I'm not sure I understand."

The elderly woman's lips crimped into an impatient seam. "The *college,* Eleanor. I had lunch with a group of my retired teacher friends in Eureka yesterday, and heard the news that your young man has accepted a position as head of the new film department."

"Ryder?" Sara asked, unable to make any sense of this. "Are we talking about Ryder Sloan?"

"Really, Eleanor! Haven't you been paying attention?"

Sara brought a shaky hand to her temple. Could any of this be true? Or was Mrs. Jenkins simply confused?

How could Ryder have accepted a teaching position at the college? He was leaving town soon . . . wasn't he?

Maybe he'd accepted the job before his agent had called to offer him that fabulous deal. But then, why hadn't he ever mentioned anything about the college to her?

The heaviness that had dragged at Sara's spirits for days suddenly lifted, like a fog blown away by a stiff ocean breeze. The faintest wisp of hope stirred inside her, but it was enough to set her heart racing.

Mrs. Jenkins might have her facts all wrong. Or maybe only *some* of them were wrong. But one thing Sara knew for sure.

She had to talk to Ryder. Now.

She sprang to her feet and bent over to kiss the surprised woman on her wrinkled cheek. "Thank you," she said breathlessly.

"Thank you? Whatever for?" Mrs. Jenkins's eyebrows rose over the tops of her bifocals.

But Sara was already gone.

Chapter Sixteen

"What happened to Sara?" Tess licked her fingers and dropped the chicken drumstick she'd been munching on into the nearest trash can. "All this revelry get to be a bit much for her?"

Ryder gave Noelle a push. She squealed as the swing rose through the air. "I guess so," he said to Tess. "One minute she was here, and the next minute...*poof!* She was gone."

"Probably sneaked off to find some peace and quiet, the big coward." Tess dusted her hands together, and was uncharacteristically silent for a moment. Ryder got a kick out of watching the struggle raging across her face.

Naturally, curiosity won out over politeness. "So," she said, probing her cheek with her tongue, "I get the impression that things are a bit rocky between you and Sara at the moment."

Ryder blew a stream of air through his lips. "You can say that again." He gave Noelle another push.

"What seems to be the problem?"

You had to admire Tess's nerve, if not her tact.

Ryder shrugged. "She doesn't trust me. She can't forgive me for the way I ran out on her ten years ago."

Tess chewed on a fingernail and frowned. "That doesn't sound like Sara. I've never known her to hold a grudge."

"Maybe no one ever gave her this big a reason before."

Tess gave Ryder a playful shove. "Come on, you're not such a bad guy."

His mouth quirked into a grim line. "Tell that to Sara."

"Okay, I will. Here she comes right now."

Ryder gave Noelle one final push before he wheeled around. Sara was indeed hurrying toward them, her reddish gold hair flying back over her shoulders like a pair of wings. When she got to the edge of the sandy rectangle where the playground was located, she paused long enough to remove her shoes.

Then she marched across the sand on nylon-clad feet.

"You look as determined as Carrie Nation, on her way to bash up a saloon," Tess teased her.

Sara greeted her friend with an absent smile. But her expression became downright serious when she turned to Ryder. "I need to talk to you," she said.

"Whoops! Guess I'll be going now...." Tess began to tiptoe backward through the sand.

"Keep an eye on the twins, will you?" Sara asked her, halting Tess in her tracks. "We need to go someplace private."

Her gaze drilled into Ryder's, as hard and dazzling and impossible to resist as diamonds. What on earth could have gotten her so riled up all of a sudden? It was the first time she'd looked him straight in the eye all day.

Whatever it was, Ryder felt relieved to see that old sparkle in her eyes, that imperious uptilt of her chin. Relieved . . . and somewhat apprehensive.

He exchanged glances with Tess, then followed Sara through the sand, steadying her by the elbow when she paused to slip her shoes back on. "Mind telling me what this is all about?" he asked. He had to step lively to keep up with her.

"As soon as we get someplace where we won't be interrupted."

Ryder doubted they were going to find anyplace in this crowded park to hold a private conversation. But Sara veered off the path and made a beeline past an enormous oak tree that must have been a hundred years old. She kept going until they reached a grove of concealing pines a fair distance from the path.

Then she braked to a stop and whirled around, cheeks flushed, eyes glittering feverishly.

Ryder waited, but Sara suddenly seemed reluctant to speak, like a diver perched on the edge of the high board, who all at once realizes that the water is a long, long way down.

Uneasiness began to gather in the pit of Ryder's stomach. Whatever Sara intended to say, he had a feeling he wasn't going to like it much.

Finally, she blurted it out. "Is there any truth to the rumor that you're going to be teaching at the college in Eureka?" She squared her shoulders as if bracing herself for a blow.

Confusion lifted Ryder's brow. He wasn't sure what he'd been expecting Sara to say, but it sure hadn't been *that*.

"Well . . . yes," he said, surprised by the almost violent reaction that flashed across her face. "The college contacted me earlier this week to offer me a job as head of their new film department, and I accepted."

"This *week?*" Sara seemed stunned by the information.

Ryder gave her a rueful smile. "Guess I caught their attention, after all the publicity in the papers about the twins' rescue."

"But—but—" Sara pressed her fingertips to her temples as if summoning a psychic vision. "But what about your agent? What about the wonderful deal he offered you?"

"Morley?" Ryder frowned. "When did you— Oh, that's right, he tried to get hold of me at your number."

"He told me this offer was going to be your big break." For some reason, Sara acted as tightly drawn as a bowstring.

"Well . . . I guess he was right. It could have been." Ryder was mystified about why she kept harping on Morley's phone call.

"Then—why didn't you take it?" Lines of tension bracketed Sara's mouth.

Ryder struggled to make sense of her question, of her entire demeanor. "Because I—wanted to stay here in Hideaway Bay with you. With Noelle and Nicholas."

Sara's face turned white, as if he'd slapped her.

"I know you told me it was all over between us," Ryder said quickly. "But I just can't accept that, Sara. It's not going to be so easy to get rid of me." He took the risk of touching her hair. "No matter how long it takes, I intend to prove that you can trust me this time."

"But what about your career?" Sara's eyes darted back and forth across his, as if frantically seeking sight of something. "You can't just give up making documentaries—not with your talent, not after all the success you've had."

"I'm not planning to quit directing entirely." Ryder rubbed his jaw. "But from now on, I'll just have to work filmmaking around my teaching schedule and any other. . . er, obligations I might have."

Sara stared at him. Then she closed her eyes and swallowed. "I thought you were leaving," she said in a faint voice.

All at once, certain things began to make sense to Ryder. "Let me get this straight," he said slowly. "You heard about this fantastic new project Morley was lining up for me, and you assumed I'd take it? That I was going to pick up and leave town, leave you and the twins behind?"

Sara's lashes fluttered open. Her eyes were filled with doubt and confusion. "I didn't believe we could keep you," she said softly. "I thought it was only a matter of time before you'd leave, the way you left before. And when your agent called, I—I assumed that time had come."

Then the truth dawned on Ryder in a blaze of illumination. "So you broke it off with me right away, rather than wait for me to end it by leaving."

Sara nodded miserably. "I knew that the longer you were part of our lives, the harder it would be when you were gone." She twisted her hands together. "For the twins' sakes, as well as my own, I decided that the sooner we made a clean break, the better."

"Oh, Sara." Ryder bundled her into his arms as an enormous wave of hope and relief broke over him. "Sweetheart, you should have talked to me about this. We could have cleared things up, and spared ourselves a lot of unhappiness."

"I know." Sara's voice was muffled against the lapel of his suit. "But I was afraid, Ryder—I was so afraid!"

He drew back so he could study the beautiful face that had haunted his dreams for so long. The face he wanted to wake up to every morning for the rest of his life.

"Sara, we can't be afraid to talk to each other, to share what we're thinking and feeling."

She bowed her head. "I was so sure you were going to take that offer and leave. I didn't dare let myself believe there was a chance you'd stay."

Ryder tipped up her chin with his knuckle. "Do you believe it now?" he asked seriously. "Do you believe in *us?*"

Sara gazed deep into his eyes, searching for her answer. But when she finally found it, the answer was in her heart, where it had been all along.

"Yes," she whispered, as soul-deep certainty rose up to fill all the empty, aching places inside her. "I do believe in us, Ryder."

"Sara." His eyes lit up with joy as he lowered his mouth to hers.

Sara flung her arms around his neck and kissed him until she could barely breathe. The love she'd tried so hard to repress erupted inside her, warming her with its passionate radiance, dizzying her with its depth.

When their lips parted at last, Sara's knees were trembling. Ryder sifted his fingers through her hair as if he couldn't believe she was real. "I love you, Sara Monahan," he said solemnly. "It feels like I've loved you practically my whole life."

"I love you, too, Ryder." Sara blinked back tears. "I guess I never really *stopped* loving you, even all those years we were apart."

A shadow briefly crossed his handsome face. But Sara no longer regretted those years. After all, they were part and parcel of the long, roundabout journey that had led them both to this blissful moment.

Ryder took both her hands in his. "I want us to be a family, Sara. You and I. Nicholas and Noelle. All four of us."

Sara's breath caught in her throat.

"Marry me, Sara. Please." The rest of the world seemed to dissolve, so that all she could see was Ryder's face, all she could hear was the sound of his voice. "I want to spend the rest of my life with you," he said.

Sara's heart soared. "I've never wanted anything else," she replied as soon as she could speak.

Ryder gripped her hands. "Then you'll—"

"Marry you?" All at once, Sara felt like singing with joy. She donned a doubtful expression instead. "Well... that depends."

All the color drained from Ryder's face. "Depends... on what?"

Instantly, Sara regretted her teasing. "Why, on the twins, of course!" She pursed her lips. "I could hardly marry you unless Noelle and Nicholas approved."

Ryder worked at his tie as if it were strangling him. "Do you, uh, think they will?"

"Do I think they'll approve of having you for an uncle?" Laughter bubbled up inside Sara's throat. "Good heavens, they'd never speak to me again if I turned you down."

"Then..."

She kissed him lightly on the lips, as if to seal a promise. "Of course I'll marry you, Ryder. We belong together, remember?"

She'd never before seen such an expression of pure, uncomplicated happiness light up his face. "Oh, Sara..." He seized her in his arms and hugged her until she thought her ribs might crack.

She didn't complain, though. Not one little peep.

"We'd better go back," Ryder said after a while. "The kids will be wondering what happened to us."

"I can't wait to tell them our news."

"You're sure they'll be happy about having me for an uncle?" Ryder finally removed his tie completely and stuffed it into his pocket.

"Ask me that question in about five minutes," Sara replied, "after you've seen the looks on their faces when we tell them."

Her lips were kiss-swollen, her hair was a mess, her eyes were sparkling like fireworks. As soon as they rejoined the festivities on the other side of the park, the whole town would immediately know what she and Ryder had been up to.

And Sara didn't mind a bit.

"Come on, let's hurry," she said, linking her arm through Ryder's. "All of a sudden, I feel like celebrating."

* * * * *